I0682439

Nikita Beach

Kirsten Sutton

Nikita Beach

Written by Kirsten Sutton
Copyright © 2017
ISBN: 978-0-6482290-6-3

The rights of Kirsten Sutton to be identified as author of this work has been asserted by them in accordance with the copyright, Designs and Patents Act 1988

All rights reserved. No part of this publication may be reproduced, stored in or introduced into a retrieval system, or transmitted, in any form or by any means (electronic, mechanical, photocopying, recording or otherwise), without prior written permission of the writers. Any person who does any unauthorized act in relation to this publication may be liable to criminal prosecution and civil claims for damages.

Published with the assistance of: www.loveofbooks.com.au

Dedicated to all the amazing surfers
and lifeguards out there, around
the world

Part 1
Growing up with Issues

Nikita Beach

Chapter 1

Zack:

Zack was so unhappy. He didn't want to be here, but he didn't want to be anywhere else either. He didn't know what he wanted; only that he should feel less alone.

"Who cares?" Zack told himself. "I don't know what I want." He took one last drag of his cigarette, and dropped it on to the gravel road of the Nikita Beach parking lot. He then stomped it out with his foot.

He had been on a staple diet of Bananas, frozen pizzas and cigarettes, for a couple of weeks now. It seemed to be working out for him, although he was never hungry.

Zack looked out across the beach, one more time. He picked up his cigarette butt. Walked across the grass, and flicked it into the nearby bin. The beach was so beautiful. He didn't want to ruin it for everyone else. Besides which, he detested cigarettes. He was going to stop smoking them tomorrow. Just not today. Today was the infamous, Saturday morning, expression session.

Out on the ocean, the sets could be seen coming from the horizon. There was a surprisingly steady stream of waves, but the wind was on-shore and it was ruining the line up. It was choppy to say the least, and because it was the weekend, there were too many people out. Of course, none of this was helped by the fact that it was low tide.

Zack checked his watch. It was actually right in between low and high, but Zack would have preferred to come out, right on high tide. In fact, he would have preferred not to have come at all. Just like when he had not bothered to go to school the last few days. Instead of coming here, he could have been at home; hauled up on his couch; reading a book about vampires.

He came today for his friends' sake. His friends were becoming weary of him, or maybe they were just worried about him. He didn't deserve their concern. He wasn't a very good friend.

"I have to get out there." Zack prompted himself. Surfing had once been his biggest joy, but now it was never enough to fill the void. It was also never big enough.

He opened the hatch to his green, beat up Honda civic. His board was threaded diagonally through the front seats. He tugged at the end of it, and pulled it out. A colored white and red board, 6'2, thin rails, and slightly concave through the middle.

It was a good board. Something his dad had bought him for his fourteenth birthday. When times had been better. When he was still, at least, receptive. Times were not so good now.

Zack headed down the sandy wooden steps, down to the beach. He bumped into someone as he got down to the last step.

"Hey Zack" a voice called out.

Zack looked up suddenly, as he neared the water. He hadn't noticed anyone, around him, so far.

A world war could have been going on, around him, and he wouldn't have noticed.

The person that had said hello to him, was one to the younger kids from Zack's school. Zack couldn't remember his name. "How are you going?"

"Alright" the kid mumbled.

"What's it like out there?" Zack asked. He nearly fell over as he did up his leg rope.

The boy answered honestly. "Crowded" He shrugged "cold."

Zack nodded his head. "Great."

He took a run off, jumped over the shore break, and paddled quickly through the rip. Once he was out the back, he made his way across the line up, to find Damien.

Damien Grisham was Zack's best friend. He was also the best surfer in the water right now. He was the best surfer at school, and probably in the whole town. Except for maybe Zack himself. Everyone knew it.

It was already winter. They were out in their steamer wetsuits, in freezing cold water. Despite the conditions it was big today. Secretly Zack knew that. It was what had drawn him out. He woke about six AM, every morning, and waited in the dark, until the surf report came on the radio at seven.

"I didn't think you'd show up." Damien said. He was sitting on his surfboard, looking vaguely annoyed.

"Why wouldn't I?"

Damien shook his head "because you're a flake."

Zack couldn't think of a come back. "Leave me alone. I'm too cold for this."

"Fine" Damien said. He watched the approaching wave, and took off on it.

He had only caught three waves, and had been in the water for about half an hour, when he was realized that his friend was talking to him again.

"What are you talking about Damien?" Zack asked finally, watching his friend's mouth move up and down. He hadn't caught a single word, but he could hear the noise.

"I was talking about you." Damien said indignantly. "I want to know what the hell your problem is."

"Problems" Zack corrected him "as in plural."

"Can't you be serious for just one second?"

"No." Zack thought about it for a moment. "I don't think so."

"Gee, suddenly your funny now?"

Zack leaned over, and swung his legs around, on top of his board. He was lying down, waiting for the next wave. "I'm catching the next wave in."

He swung the board around to face the beach, and then looked back. He quietly waited for the next wave to loom up behind him.

"When was the last time you even had a girl?" Damien called out; turning everyone's attention to their conversation.

3

Zack could feel the weight of a hundred stares. "What?" He didn't understand the question. "What has that got to do with anything?"

"More than you think."

"I went out with Stefany last week." He said agitated. He waited for the wave to pass. Then lifted his body up on the crest, so he could sit up on his board again.

"You've had one date in a year." Damien argued. "And you had a fight with her in the cinema. Everyone knows about it Zack."

"So?"

"What was the fight about?"

"I bought her own popcorn. She finished it five minutes into the movie, and tried to eat mine. What would you have done?"

"I don't know. Let her?"

"I'm not supporting her eating habit."

"Maybe she just likes popcorn." Damien said simply.

"Maybe she just likes eating." Zack sighed. "All she kept talking about was being on that stupid netball team. I couldn't take it."

"You talk about surfing. She can talk about netball."

Zack vigorously shook his head. "Netball's not a sport. You can't even bounce the ball for crying out loud. I don't even know why I asked her out. Oh, wait a minute. Yes I do... You told me to."

"I thought she was nice." Damien tried to explain.

"She's not." Zack looked at him. "You thought she was popular, and easy."

"Well, she said she wouldn't do you, if you were Brad Pitt's brother, so you've burned that bridge."

"I burn all my bridges." Zack glared at his friend. "It's not even about that."

"It's always about that."

"Yeah in a one-track mind like yours, but I want a girl who." Zack stopped in mid-sentence. "I just don't care alright."

"Do you want people to think you're gay?"

Even Zack had to laugh at that. Then he finally shook his head. "I don't care what people think"

"You should."

"Why should I?"

"Because their worried about you." Damien's voice got softer, and he looked down at the nose of his board. "Joel is worried about you, and so am I."

Damien had a strange way of showing his feelings. He had just changed the subject sixteen times before he came out and said what he was thinking.

Zack was just as worried; about himself.

"I care what Joel thinks. I care what you think, but I don't answer to anyone else. And I'm not going to go out with some superficial bitch, just because everyone at school thinks I'm gay."

"Then go out with someone who isn't superficial."

Zack looked around the lineup. No one had caught a wave since they had started their fight; they were all listening. He put his head down and stroked the blue water with his hand. "I just don't care."

"You've already said that, but that's the problem, and I'm not…"

"Why do you care so much about who I go out with?" Zack asked honestly. "Why do you care so much if it means more girls for you?"

"Usually I wouldn't argue with that logic, but Joel's worried about you, and I think you need to get laid. "

"Really?" Zack laughed. "In that case why don't you get off my back and worry about Joel? He's the Virgin." Zack remembered that everyone was listening in and immediately regretted the remark. It didn't matter; most people at school were virgins. Zack had started early.

Zack shrugged his shoulders. He swung his board to the south, and started paddling to the other end of the beach.

"My point was - you don't care about anything any more." Damien said, paddling beside him. Refusing to let him leave.

"I'm here aren't I? I care about surfing."

"Your head's not in the game." Damien paused. "Not even here."

"What? I'm not a surfer anymore because I haven't got laid in a year?" Zack yelled. "I know every girl in town, and I'm not interested in any of them."

"You don't know every girl in town. These days you probably wouldn't know the name of every girl in your class."

"Which class?"

"There are some really beautiful girls out there, and just because you're mother left you. That doesn't mean your girlfriend is going to as well." Damien immediately put his hand to his mouth, as if he had said something wrong. He shook his head at himself. Then he looked up at the sky. He started to speak, but Zack stopped him.

Zack's eyes squinted narrowly. "Comparing my girlfriends to my mother isn't going to help me."

"Wait, I didn't mean that the way it sounded."

"No I get it." Zack nodded. "You just don't want to have a nut case as a best friend." He said, quickly trying to lighten the mood. "Thanks for the pep talk."

"Look Cummings." Damien said calling him by his last name. "I accepted your mental problems a long time ago. This is about your girl problems.

Zack laughed easily. "Yeah right" he looked back assessing the swell lines. He decided he would take the third wave of the set. "I'm going."

"Are you coming to school tomorrow?" Damien asked carefully.

"Of course, why wouldn't I?"

"Because, you only came two days last week."

"I was sick."

"Yeah well that's funny; I thought you were just trying to avoid the rumors about the cinema." Damien tried to diplomatic. "You know the gossip from before has all but gone. It's not going to be rehashed by some stupid fight you had with Stefany, at the drive in."

"It wasn't the drive in, it was the cinema." Zack said bobbing over the second wave. He only had a moment.

"Are you coming on Monday?"

Zack smiled at his friend's persistence. "Yeah I'm coming. You should worry about your own damn schooling. I get better grades than you do."

"Yeah, throw that in my face." Damien mumbled.

Zack heard the comment, but he was already paddling for the wave. He had to concentrate on the late take off. He didn't see the girl till the last moment.

She had already got to her feet and he should have pulled back, but he didn't. He was already committed. He couldn't seem to stop the motion of jumping to his feet.

The girl was just a kid, and he had never seen her before. She was a tall and slim kid, in a black and purple steamer. He hadn't been paying attention, but even so, she seemed to come out of nowhere.

She was shaky on her board. She wasn't very good from what he could tell in that split second, but he reacted quickly. He did a quick bottom turn, and carved up the face, so she could slide straight past him, as he did a reentry off the lip.

He couldn't see her behind him, but by some miracle the trick worked. He went up the face, got a moment of air, and came straight back down, in a 180-degree flip.

The girl came out in front of him. She rode the wave fairly straight, after she ducked past, and Zack tried to stall on it; crisscrossing it diagonally, from behind her.

It was when the wave began to close out, that they both came down.

It was her fault, or at least she was the one that lost if first. She must have forgotten he was there, and tried to climb the face for one last maneuver. She was trying to do a forehand grab; but instead, she fell back when the board flung out from beneath her. The walls just wouldn't hold up anymore.

Zack was coming in right behind her. As she fell, she must have smashed her foot on *his* board, as she plunged into the water. Zack immediately tried to get out of her way, by diving in to the wave, but the chain of events instantaneously causing their leg ropes to get tangled.

It was cold and dark. The wipe out lasted for ages. It tumbled them around like they were in a washing machine. Zack tried to grab hold of the girl as they flew into more shallow water, but another wave came in right behind them. She jolted forward in his hands.

One of the boards smashed him in the head as he reached out. That's when the leg rope must have snapped.

It must have been some impact for her. He wasn't sure if she was still conscious. His own lungs were screaming out for air, as the wave finally subsided. Finally, he could try to get to his feet.

Zack was groggy for a moment; his legs were unstable, trying to hold him up. His head injury was emitting a sharp pain, as he tried to focus his eyes.

The girl was still there in the water. Her body was limp, and bobbing around in the shore break. He lunged forward for her, turning her over. Her face was pale. Her lips a slight shade of blue.

Zack quickly unhooked her leg rope, and scooped her up in his arms. She was just a girl; a beautiful girl, that hardly weighed anything, as he picked her up. She had long dark hair that fell down carelessly. It blew about in the wind, but it was already all messed up from the wipe out.

She had a pretty face that was kind of small and sweet. She had braces on her teeth, and maybe just a few pimples. She was so skinny though. He could feel her bony body dangle so freely in his arms as he carried her up the beach, and dropped her on the sand.

It was 9:30. The lifeguards didn't come on duty until ten, and if he wanted to save her, he would have to do it himself. He rolled the girl on her side, and checked her air way. It seemed to be clear. He checked her pulse, but it was very faint.

The bronze medallion Zack had earned for first aid seemed like it had been a million years ago. He had learned all this stuff at school, but he was scared now, and his fingers were clumsy. He quickly leaned down and gave her mouth-to-mouth, blocking her nose with his fingers. He gave her two long and slow breaths, while watching her chest rise and fall.

He checked her pulse again.

It was slightly stronger but still very slow. Yet again he quickly rolled her on her side; he undid the Velcro on her wetsuit behind her neck, and then pulled down the zipper. He again, rolled her on her back and then climbed over the top of her. His knees on both sides of her thighs, he reached down and pulled down the wetsuit.

If he had to do compressions, he wanted to see exactly what he was doing. He couldn't help but look down at her body. A purple bikini top, golden brown skin, a flat stomach, small breasts, and he couldn't tell her age; only that she was younger. She could have been as young as twelve. Her face was so pretty. Even while unconscious, she looked so sweet.

He got off her, and leaned down to resume resuscitation.

He was watching her chest, rise and fall, with every gasp of air, he pumped into her.

He was going in for another breath when she responded. She started coughing, and wheezing, helplessly.

He closed his eyes for a second. She was alive. He took a huge sigh of relief, then he rolled her on her side again.

It was agonizing to watch her, as she vomited up sand and water.

Zack looked around bewildered. No one had seen it happen. It had all happened so quickly. Anyone walking past must have just thought that he was making out with her. It had probably been less than three minutes since he dropped her on the sand. It felt like an hour.

Zack looked at her again; he couldn't escape the feeling that the young girl looked familiar. She lay down on her back coughing for a few moments before she fell silent. She was peering up at him with small brown eyes. Eyes that sparkled in the sunlight.

"I'm sorry." It was the only thing he could say. Her gaze paralyzed him. He was sitting down next to her, leaning on one arm, watching her every movement.

The girl didn't say anything for a long time, but then she spoke quietly. "You're bleeding."

"What?"

"Your head" she told him. "It's bleeding."

Zack's head did feel strange; he had a headache that was getting worse by the minute. Now that he could fully concentrate on it, it was reaching the point of agonizing pain. He couldn't worry about it right now though. He couldn't worry about anything but her. She was the one that nearly died.

He sat back on the sand and ran his fingers over the left side of his head. The sensation was wet and gluggy. His scalp was bleeding freely, and it was running down the side of his head. He pulled his hand away and saw that his fingers were completely stained with blood.

What was worse was that, now; he was feeling strangely light headed and sick. His vision kept getting blurry. Still, the girl was his concern now.

She was still there beside him, weak and still coughing occasionally. He was worried that she could have a concussion, and fall unconscious again.

"But are you ok?" He asked, desperately, trying to keep his voice even.

She was looking at him fondling his head wound, and she looked confused. "Are you?"

Zack nodded his head, slightly disorientated. "It's just a scratch." He looked her up and down, and then looked away. "What's your name?"

"Kali"

Zack gasped. His eyes opened wide, and he could feel beads of sweat run over his forehead. He suddenly felt afraid "Kali what?"

"Kali Lockhart."

Zack looked around bewildered again. He was so tiered, he wanted to sleep. The girl was someone he suddenly didn't want to be around. He could do worse things to Kali than simply drop in on her. He could really hurt this girl, he already had.

Something in the foreground caught Zack's attention. It was Damien running up the beach trying to balance three surfboards under his arms.

"Kali Lockhart." He repeated before turning away, and throwing up, on the sand beside him.

"Zack! What the hell happened? Are you alright?" Damien threw down all the boards and ran up to his best friend. "Is she alright?" He said pointing to the girl. "What happened?"

"I'm fine." Zack said exasperated. He was holding himself up, and trying not to close his eyes. "She drowned." He tried to explain. "And look at her ankle, I think it's broken."

"What happened?" Damien pleaded again.

"We had a wipe out."

"And then what? You went head first, into a sharp rock?"

"Just shut up and help her." Zack barked at him, annoyed.

"Are you ok?" Damien asked the girl.

Kali slowly sat up. "I'm fine." She whispered shyly. She looked across at Zack, saw the blood, and then fell down again, fainting.

Zack watched her. His mouth dropping open. "Go find a phone, and call an ambulance." He screamed, using a nearby beach towel, to put pressure on his head.

"Who is she?"

Zack closed his eyes. He couldn't think clearly. He shook his head as if he couldn't understand what was going on. Then he opened them, and caught Damien's gaze. "That's Kali Lockhart."

A drop of blood fell from his chin, and fell on the ground. It made the golden sand turn red. Zack sighed to himself, "That's Ryan's sister!"

"Are you serious?" Damien asked, going over to attend to her, but his attention strayed towards his friend. "Damn Zack. You look green."

"Go get help!" Zack felt another dizzy spell come on. He couldn't lift his head anymore. He fell down beside Kali and the world turned black.

Chapter 2

Kali:

K ali Lockhart lay back against the end of the bathtub and closed her eyes. It seemed to be her favorite place these days. Outside it was cold and the world was harsh, but inside the bath tub, the water was hot and steaming. It soaked into her body, and her skin, and her hair.

Everything that happened on the weekend, had been so strange. Strange people, popular people, Zachary Cummings, Damien Grisham, the lifeguards, the doctors, all looking down at her as she laid on her back; falling in and out of consciousness.

It had been all her fault too; she knew Zack was going to go for that wave. She knew it, and she snaked him, at the last second.

It was scary out there. The waves had been bigger than they looked from the shore. Kali had been out for twenty minutes without catching a single wave.

She got pummeled when she tried, unsuccessfully, to duck dive a wave from one of the bigger sets. As she had gotten dragged into shore, the current must have pulled her towards the rip. When she paddled out again, she was nowhere near where she had started off.

She ended up paddling out, right where Zachary Cummings was sitting. He was having a fight with his best friend Damien Grisham.

Kali had just wanted to get out of there, but apparently so did Zack.

Then, of course, they had a wipe out.

Zack had practically split his head open, while trying to save her. Everything that had happened had been her fault. His blood had even spilt in her hair, while he was giving her CPR and he didn't even notice.

And now he thought it was his fault.

There was a raiser at the end of the tub. Kali didn't know what it was doing there. She picked it up and looked at it for a moment before pressed it against her wrist, and then pushed down.

Sometimes she hurt herself. She punished herself for not being good enough.

Kali took the blade away and looked at her wrist. There was just a thin red scar, and maybe a drop of blood. It was nothing bad, like the others, and she could cover it up with her watch band.

It was a crazy thing to do, but she was officially the youth of a nation, so it came with the territory. Kali sighed to herself and bent her knees, sliding down to immerse her body in the hot water. She reemerged quickly and lathered her hair up with Herbal Essences conditioner.

Her life was so emotionally exhausting. Since her mother left, her brother stepped in. He raised her in a different world. He had showed her a life she could never possibly be part of. And now he was dead.

Ryan Lockhart the most popular guy in school, and his sister Kali; the most unpopular. Ryan had been three years older than her. He was only seventeen when he died.

Kali wrung out her hair and hopped out of the bath tub. She dried herself and then threw on a bath robe. She looked in the mirror, but she never knew if the girl staring back at her was pretty or not.

It was a perfectly crisp, and cold winter morning. Kali walked outside on to the deck and stared out, across the valley, at the sea.

She lived in a seaside town. It was a beautiful town and she loved it, but it was an 'elite' place to be. She never, exactly, fit in, but she couldn't imagine living anywhere else. Kali felt like her dysfunctional family belonged here, and almost everyone else, were the outsiders.

Kali was too much of a daydreamer anyway.

She walked, slowly, to the edge of the deck and put her hands on the railing. It was cold outside but not as cold as it had been lately. The sun was shining in the sky and there were no clouds around. It was about eight in the morning.

She would have to start getting ready to go to school in a moment, but that's if she went at all. She didn't want to go, and no one was going to make her. Her dad was at work, and her sister had probably spent the night at her boyfriend's house. Kali just stood there freezing in her blue bathrobe. Her hair was wet, and dripping down her back.

She looked up suddenly. The peaceful silence had been interrupted by something inside. The phone was ringing. Kali ran in the house and stared at the phone in horror. She decided if she was going to answer it or not.

"Hello?"

"Hi is that Kali?"

Kali smiled nervously. "Yes."

"It's Zack."

"Zack who? Zachary Cummings?"

"How many Zack's do you know?"

Kali was caught off guard by the question. "I don't really know any, but I remember you." She shook her head. "I mean from what happened on Saturday. I know it was you."

There was a pause on the other end of the phone line. "Yeah, I'm really sorry about that Kali."

"It's ok." She jumped in.

"I don't usually do that. I mean I never drop in on people. I'm usually a nice guy. It's just I didn't even see you, and I was distracted."

Kali was alerted by the tone in his voice, and how fast he was speaking. His manner was desperate. He was almost afraid.

"It's not your fault." She tried again to persuade him.

"You nearly died."

"But I didn't... and you don't have to worry about it." She sighed. "It really wasn't your fault." She stopped short before telling him that it was really her fault.

14

"You don't have to say that Kali." He seemed to readjust the phone in his hand. "I can't believe I didn't notice you out there."

"Why should you?"

"You were the only girl out." He cried. "I should have been making sure you got your own waves, instead of being the arse hole to drop in on you."

"You're not an… It was an accident." She pleaded. "Really I'm fine."

"Are you?"

"Yes."

Zack exhaled. "I just rang you up to make sure you're ok."

Zachary Cummings had picked up from where her brother left off as being the most popular guy in school. He was also the best surfer. Ironically Zack seemed just as nonchalant and indifferent about his popularity as her brother was. Like they only gave it to you, if you didn't want it.

"I was worried about *you*." She told him.

This time it was Zack's turn to be caught off guard. "You don't have to do that."

"I don't know what happened. I think I fainted."

"Yeah, you did."

"When I saw the blood." She added softly.

Zack went quiet for a moment, and then spoke hastily. "It was just a few stitches, nothing to worry about." He paused. "I wanted to ring you up to say I'm sorry."

Kali's number wasn't listed in the phone book. She wondered briefly how he got it.

She also wondered about his personality. He seemed to be so sincere and caring, and not the guy he was rumored to be.

From everything she had heard, Zack was supposed to be nonchalant and sarcastic. He didn't have any patience for anyone, and didn't care about anything. Apparently, he even started an argument with some girl in a packed movie theater, while the movie was showing.

Kali realized she was hesitating too long. "You said that on Saturday."

"And I meant it."

"It wasn't your fault."

"Do you know you were unconscious? I had to give you mouth-to-mouth resuscitation. It could have been a lot more serious Kali."

He sounded mad at her, for not being more upset.

Kali closed her eyes. "Thank you for ringing, but I'm fine. And thank you for the apology, but you didn't really…" She stopped in mid-sentence. "It was really nice of you to call me."

"What about your ankle?"

Kali looked down at her feet. She knew something had been bothering her about the way that she was walking. The tiles and floorboards were so cold, she had forgotten that her ankle had been hurt. "It's just a sprain."

"It looked really swollen. I thought it might be broken."

Kali smiled. "It's not. What about your stitches, are they really noticeable?"

"No, you can't even see them under my hair."

He spoke to her as if they were already friends from before, but Kali had never met him before. She found it strange to speak to him. It was as if they were picking up this conversation from the middle, and not the beginning. It felt like he was talking to an old friend.

"I wish I was a better surfer, so this wouldn't have happened."

"You looked pretty good to me"

She smiled again, because he was lying. "Thanks."

Zack started so say something, but then stopped. He went silent again for a moment. "Are you going to go to school today?"

Kali had been leaning towards not going, but if Zack told her to go, then she would go. "Yeah I guess."

"Maybe I'll see you there then."

It was doubtful. He probably wouldn't even remember what she looked like, when he got back to school. "Yeah maybe" she said casually, trying to sound aloof.

"Ok I'll see you later." Zack hung up the phone, and Kali carefully put down the receiver.

She had to hurry if she was going to make the bus, but she didn't know if she really wanted to see him again. It would be too awkward.

Zack was friends with everyone at school. He also had two best friends; Damien Grisham and Joel Geller. He didn't really need to be her friend. He didn't need to pretend to care about her.

Chapter 3

Kali:

"Amber is out of control." Brenda moaned.

Kali was sitting at her high school hang out at lunch time. She snapped back to reality when she heard the blunt statement.

"I know she's got problems, but she doesn't have to sulk about it. I'm sick of listening to her whinge about how unfair everything is" Sharon started off. "I mean she gets everything from her parents. It's never good enough. My parents never give me anything, and I don't complain."

Sharon was supposed to be Amber's best friend.

"I think she should see a psychiatrist, that's all I can say." Brenda said matter-of-factly. Then on the contrary she started talking again. "Did you see what she was wearing today?"

Gillian adjusted her sunglasses on her nose. "Yeah I know! We all dress grunge anyway and here we are on mufti day at school. She looks like she is some surfer-girl who is sponsored by Billabong." She shook her head. "You can tell Amber just does not fit in."

Kali bit her bottom lip, and looked down at what she was wearing: A pair of blue denim shorts, and a Rip Curl sweater. She was also wearing sneakers, and socks again, because she had no talent for buying shoes. The other girls had sandals and long skirts on. They looked like hippies.

What Gillian was getting at, was a thinly veiled insult, that was indirectly, directed, straight at Kali.

She was the weakest link and they humiliated her for it. She was awkward and shy and the other girls had no patience for it.

Kali's friends had big powerful personalities, and Kali's personality was like a wall flower. She would shrink in their presence every day. She always wanted to talk to them, but she never knew how, and it always made her feel so inferior.

Her friends had the world at their feet. They played netball, and went to dancing lessons, and took shopping trips with their mom. It seemed like they were always so confident, and Kali was never sure how to communicate with them.

Kali in fact, had become so despondent lately, she had become the perfect target for bitching, backstabbing *and* gossiping, but the truth was, they didn't include her because they didn't expect her to fit in. It never mattered what she wore, or what she did. She was always the outsider, and they had nothing in common.

It's not like her friends wanted to know that that it was four feet, and glassy, at Crystal Beach on the weekend.

Kali looked down and frowned.

She had told Zack she would come to school today, but now she was doubting weather it was worth it. She had the perfect excuse not to come. She was still coughing up sea water, and her ankle *was* sore. It was Monday at lunchtime and she had the whole, excruciating, school week to get through.

Her friends were talking pretty loudly. Kali zoned out again. She wondered again, what it would have been like, if she were actually awake, when Zack had his mouth on hers; giving her resuscitation.

Today she felt even more isolated than usual. Today there was lots of people milling about her hang out. Many of them were chatting rampantly and eagerly about something exciting that happened on the weekend.

Kali could have sworn that she heard Zack's name a few times. They were talking about how Zack almost killed some girl, at the beach, on the weekend.

Kali felt removed from that conversation too, even though she was the primary player in it.

The events of the weekend were still too raw and personal. She was still reliving them. She didn't want to let them out for public discussion.

Kali looked around. In front of her hangout, the English block loomed in the distance, and the science block was to her right. On the left, was the school quadrangle. Clover high was a pretty big place. There were lots of students at this school.

Kali's wondered if she would *ever* make it out of here.

"I can't believe it's this hot, in *winter*." Celeste said as she was watching the boys play handball on the quad.

Kali snapped back in again and looked at each of her friends.

Brenda was soaking up the sun in a skimpy singlet top that was so tight it was cutting into her chest. Even though it *was* winter, she was wearing a skirt so short that when the breeze blew past, you could see her under ware.

"So what do you think of Daniel. He's been rallying that ball for an hour" Susan said. She was short with blonde hair, and blue eyes. She was the prettiest of all of them, but she knew it, and she was licking her lips, looking at Daniel Prewitt, playing hand ball on the quad.

"He's no Zachary Cummings." Brenda said grinning. She shrugged her shoulders and nodded. As if she had any kind of chance with Zachary Cummings.

"But he'll do." Susan continued.

Susan and Brenda had a crush on Zack. In fact, Kali thought they all did. Zack was the most popular guy in school, so it was only natural.

"Daniel's all talk." Celeste sighed. She was beautiful, with grey eyes and long, light dirty blonde hair. She was stuck up, and somehow looked sad about it.

Kali wondered what Celeste meant by that. Celeste was nicer to Kali when Ryan was alive. She had the biggest crush on her brother.

Kali turned her head and watched the guys playing hand ball.

No sooner did she turn her head, she saw someone she recognized in the crowd.

Zachary Cummings was in the distance. He was walking down the pathway. He was walking towards her hangout, and he was with his best friend, Damien Grisham.

Damien had been with Kali in the ambulance, and the hospital. He was specifically there for Zack, but he looked in on Kali quite a few times. He was very kind and attentive.

Kali watched Zack. He hadn't seen her yet. He continued down the path, in her direction. He looked deep in conversation with Damien.

Kali felt sure that they were heading straight towards her.

She didn't want this confrontation. She didn't want to be singled out. She didn't want people to know that *she* was the reason that Zack had stiches on his head.

Somehow Zack knew how to find her.

He walked closer. As he looked up, he surveyed the area until their eyes met, and then he waved at her.

Kali froze.

Zack's screwed his face up. He waved again, as if he was scared that he got the wrong person.

Kali tried to make her muscles move. She briefly waved back. Then she sat there, exposed. Brenda was looking up, trying to see what the distraction was.

She didn't want this meeting, but it was too late. Susan and the other girls had already seen Zack and Damien.

There was a moment of confusion.

"Hello Kali" Zack called out, as he came down the path and moved nearer to her.

Everything stopped.

Everyone stopped talking, moving, even breathing.

Everyone looked equally horrified. The hottest guy in school couldn't possibly be talking to Kali 'looser' Lockhart. The crowd turned, and stared blatantly as Zack.

Kali watched him. She felt like she was going to faint. "Hello."

The two boys walked closer and stopped short, about a meter in front of her. "Hi Kali." Damien said.

21

Kali smiled. "Hi Damien." She said softly.

All eyes were bouncing between the three people in the conversation. Kali didn't know what to say.

"I just came to see for myself: That you were ok." Zack said.

"I told you on the phone I was fine."

"I didn't know if you were coming today." Zack said.

"I said I would."

"Yeah, but you were pretty banged up last time I saw you. I didn't mean that you should come if you weren't ready" He looked pretty distressed, looking down at her bandaged ankle. None of her friends had asked her about it. Zack looked at her foot as if he was about to start crying.

Kali nodded. "I feel fine." She smiled. "You can hardly see your stiches underneath your hair." She lied.

"Yeah, my hair's pretty thick." Zack said awkwardly.

"Did you have a concussion?"

"I'm over it now." He said, not exactly answering the question. "My focus was on you."

"I'm sorry." Kali said quickly.

"Don't apologize." Zack said, exasperated.

"Yeah but I was the one who…."

"Yeah Kali." Damien jumped in. "Look at this guy. He's the tosser that dropped in on you." he lightly smacked Zack in the ribs. "I mean who does that? What a tool" He smiled at her. Then, just as quickly, he lost his smile. "Seriously, you gave us quite a scare on the weekend."

Zack was dismayed by the earlier comment. He lightly punched Damien in the shoulder. "I said I didn't see her."

"Yeah, well." Damien countered. "I don't think that's good enough! I nearly lost fucking both of you."

Damien looked like he was suffering post-traumatic stress disorder.

Kali nodded awkwardly. "Yeah, Ryan told me that the two of you went surfing, Saturday mornings, at Nikita."

Zack looked up startled. He looked at Damien and they exchanged facial expressions. People often had a physical response to Kali saying her brother's name.

"Ryan probably told you to stay clear of us." Zack said sadly.

That's exactly what he said.

Kali looked longingly back into Zack's eyes "No." She said adamantly. "He was just telling me, who was at the top of the pecking order."

Zack stared at her for a long time. "So you *do* blame me."

"No." Kali said quickly. "You saved my life."

Zack stared at her, as they stood at an impasse.

She noted that the two boys actually looked kind of out of it. They were emotionally drained from the weekend. They were wrapped up in something that resembled anxiety. They were standing there in their school uniform, even though it was out of school uniform day.

"We *do* usually surf Saturday morning." Zack said blankly. "Maybe you should come with us sometime."

Damien nodded. "That's a great idea."

Kali gulped down a lump in her throat. They were asking, either, because of guilt, or because they felt sorry for her. Either way, Kali wasn't sure how to respond.

"OK." She said finally.

"Great." Damien said. "And feel free to come up to our hangout, at lunch time. You could come hang out with us. Any time you want."

Zack gave Damien a funny look.

Kali kept nodding her head. "Ok."

Damien was so excited that she was still alive.

He would have said anything to appease her. Zack, on the other hand, had an unrelenting look on his face. It was as if he was desperately trying to tell her something more than what he was saying.

"Ok then." Kali said.

She quickly turned to gauge the people around her. She was getting death stares from her friends. "I will tell you when I'm free." She assured him.

"Ok." Damien said. He nodded at her and she nodded back.

Then she nodded at Zack. His green eyes contained so much passion. "I'm glad you're ok." He told her earnestly.

Then it was over.

Damien and Zack turned around and walked away. Apparently, no goodbye was necessary. Her friends in the hangout were whispering about her, while she was standing right in front of them.

They didn't look impressed. No one would be happy about what just happened.

Chapter 4

Joel:

Joel Geller knew there was something wrong when he walked in to the kitchen for breakfast. His father was standing over the dining table.

He was standing, rather than sitting, with a cup of black coffee in one hand, and a thin folder in another.

The folder was open to the back page.

His father seemed to be reading and re-reading the remarks section at the bottom of his work. Joel recognized it immediately; his legal studies assignment.

Joel took a step back; his father did not look impressed. Joel suddenly did not feel hungry. He turned to leave, but he was not quick enough. His father looked up suddenly and caught a glimpse of him standing in the doorway.

"Wait."

Joel stood still. He watched his father put down the coffee. There were various shadows playing across the old man's face.

Joel waiting for the yelling to begin, but it didn't immediately start. He looked up, just in time to see his father's hand hurtling towards him.

He saw it coming, out of nowhere, but wasn't quick enough to block it.

When it hit him, he was forced to feel the sting. His father slapped him across the face, and just as quickly, pushed him against the wall.

"What is the son of a lawyer doing getting a B on a legal studies paper?"

Joel's shoulder hurt. He had knocked it against the wooden cabinet as he was pushed back.

"I don't know…. It was a B plus…. It was on family law, and I've always studied litigation. Like you. I should have done better."

Joel's father grabbed him by the collar. He pulled him forward. Their faces were just an inch away from each other. Joel could see the bulging vein in his father's forehead. It was a vein he had become eerily familiar with.

"But it is the law isn't it? You do have a good grasp on the law, don't you?"

Joel spoke carefully. "I thought that was a good assignment. I don't know why I got a B." he tried to explain.

"I don't know why you don't just ask those deadbeat friends of yours about family law? I'm sure Damien and the other one… what's his name?" Joel father asked, clicking his fingers. "Oh yeah Zack" He mocked. "I'm sure they can bring you up to speed."

Joel gasped. "Zack's parents didn't get divorced! They were perfectly happy until his mother died, and I'm sure he like to thank you for the support."

His father looked at him like he was an idiot. "I know about that kid, and don't think I'm going to represent him when he gets in trouble."

"Zack's not in trouble."

"I don't know why you hang out with them." His father badgered him. "Just look at you; always loitering around at the beach with those two clowns. You're putting popularity over schoolwork and wasting your life away. You're like the three stooges."

"And what's wrong with that? We have fun."

"Well what about your grades? And your girlfriend?" His father asked incredulously. "Justine's parents wonder what you're up to half the time, and there are better friends to be had. Matthew Jenkins is in most of your classes and you don't even talk to him."

"Just because he's the son of a partner in your firm doesn't mean I'm going to be best friends with him." Joel tried to explain, "He's a dick head anyway; he does drugs."

"That's outrageous, Bill's boy doesn't do drugs. I'm not so sure about you though."

Joel shook his head. "Thanks for the vote of confidence."

"Who knows what you get up to these days? You're always out."

"Yeah at the library studying." Joel said under his breath. "It's better than being here with you!"

"That's enough of that. Maybe we can put an end to you leaving the house all together. Except to go to school."

Joel smirked, feeling a sudden wave of adrenalin. "Try and stop me."

Joel realized instantly that that was a mistake. He was actually afraid of his father.

"Enough with the lip. Show me some respect. I am your father" The man demanded. "Maybe I should take away that surfboard of yours, or should I say the five of them, that clog up the garage."

Joel held his breath for a moment. "No dad, you can't."

Joel's dad had always been fairly indifferent about him surfing, but he definitely didn't like it, or take it seriously.

"I'll do better next time." Joel tried to assure him.

"You better." His father shook his head, annoyed. "Hurry up and get to school."

It was so refreshing to be yelled at in the morning. Usually his father could wait until the end of the school day before starting in on him, but today Joel couldn't even get out of bed without getting into trouble.

Nothing was ever good enough.

The pressure his father put on him sometimes made him feel like he couldn't breathe. The worst part was everyone at school thought that his life was perfect.

Joel was popular, smart and rich all at the same time. None of it felt real to him. He was smart because he studied all the time. Most people thought it came naturally, but in reality, he had to work hard for his grades.

He was admired because he was best friends with Damien and Zack. They were the real thing. Joel just tagged along.

And he was rich because he was rich. His father was an attorney, and the family had money before that as well.

Joel didn't ask for much. He worked summers doing research at his father's firm. When he could, he preferred to pay his own way, which was most of the time.

Surfing was his sanctuary, and it was actually his mother who bought him his first surfboard.

He was always a good swimmer, and he did well in his cross-country running meets. She recognized that he was a good athlete, and he was creative. So she gave him an outlet for all that energy.

His mom probably never expected that he would become so good at the sport, or that he would devote so much time and energy to it. Her gift had been thoughtful. As if she sensed how domineering her husband would become. She gave Joel the perfect escape.

He felt like surfing was never his destiny, but he conquered it anyway, because he could.

Damien and Zack were surfers. They were the best in the whole town. The friendship had started there, but it had lasted a long time. Joel was awkward sometimes, but Damien and Zack were good friends, and they definitely had his back.

At school, Zachary and Damien were the equivalents to being James dean. True rebels without a cause, but Joel was a nerd. He was driven and dedicated, and he had a crazy class load. Just like his dad wanted.

At the moment, Joel was the only one who had a girlfriend. He had been going out with her forever. She was what his father would call 'in his league'. Her name was Justine. The two of them had been growing apart for a while now, but they were still together. They were still virgins.

Joel wasn't particularly attracted to Justine, but he kept the charade going because he didn't know what else to do.

Justine liked to ride the wave of Joel's popularity. Zack and Damien didn't like her much. They avoided her where ever possible.

Joel didn't talk to anyone the first three periods, today. The fight with his father was bothering him more than it usually did. He also had a headache today.

He found himself wondering to the library at lunch time. It was quiet in the library.

He slowly walked to the tables and put his folder and his pencil case down.

His fingers strayed through the subjects in his folder. He looked to see which assignment he would get a head start on first.

There was a girl there, on the opposite side of him, at the table. She was a quaint little thing, sitting alone. She was quietly reading a passage from a thick text book on the table. Her eyes were straying from the text book to her work book. She wrote something down with a pencil that had bite marks on the end of it.

There was something about her. He couldn't look away. The girl had golden brown hair that was thick and long. It hung around her small and innocent face. She had braces on her teeth. She was thin, and timid. She was a pretty little thing.

Joel jerked his head suddenly, after he realized something.

This was the girl that Zack had been talking about all week.

Joel leaned back on his chair, watching her. She had a frown on her face. She didn't seem to understand the work. She kept shaking her head as if she was discouraged.

"Hey."

The girl looked up, smiling slightly. Her hair was a little frizzy around the edges. Her small brown eyes looked gentle.

Neither Zack nor Joel had ever seen her before the day at the beach, but Joel had noticed her around. She wasn't the prettiest girl he had ever seen, but she was one of the sweetest. She always looked kind of sad, which was understandable, since what happened to her brother.

She nodded her head embarrassed. "Hi."

"I'm Joel."

Yeah I know." She nodded again. "I'm Kali."

Joel smiled back at her. "I know."

She was looking in his eyes. She had a stare that was engaging to say the least.

"So, you're the one."

Kali looked shocked. "Pardon."

"You're the one that Zack ran over with his surfboard."

Her face seemed to freeze. She looked at him with almost a defensive glare. She went to say something, but no words came out. Then she forced herself to speak. "My surfboard was involved too."

"When it first happened, everyone thought it was Kali Eastwick."

"She doesn't surf."

"It doesn't seem to matter." He gave her a warm smile. "You never spoke up."

"I didn't say anything because I didn't want Zack feel worse than he already does. It was just an accident." Kali said desperately. "He feels so bad about it."

Joel quickly rubbed at his eyes, they were sore today, and it was in conjunction with his headache.

"The fact that he saved you, has brought back the first signs of life I have seen in Zack in a long time." Joel closed his eyes again. "If he feels bad, it's not because of you."

Kali wasn't sure what to make of that. She stared at him for a long time "Why weren't you there?" She asked finally.

"Where?"

"I thought the three of you went surfing every Saturday morning."

"How did you know that?"

"My brother told me." Kali told him.

Joel thought about Kali's brother: Ryan Lockhart was such a puzzle, both before and after his death.

"I was sick." Joel told her.

Kali looked at him obtrusively, as if she was looking right through him.

Joel felt suddenly exposed. He felt like he was letting his emotions show, about what had happened with his father that morning. Whatever she was seeing. She knew there was something on his mind.

"Are you still sick?"

"My school work is making me feel a little burnt out at the moment."

"So you came up here to do more of it?"

Joel laughed softly. "I came up here to get away from everyone."

"Sounds familiar." She said softly.

"What?"

"Nothing." She sighed. "I'm glad you sat at my table. Thanks for sitting with me."

"I didn't recognize you before I sat down, but I wanted to meet you."

Kali nodded. "I'm glad to meet you too."

"What year are you in."

"Year 9."

"You look younger than that." Joel opened his notebook and picked up a pen to start writing, but his shoulder started to hurt. The girl seemed to notice his discomfort, and watched him again intently.

"You must be pretty smart."

"I do alright." He smiled. "Why? You look like you need some help over there."

Kali giggled. "I'm usually good at math."

Joel got up for a second and leaned across the table. The girl had an equally tumultuous life as Zack. He didn't want to upset her.

"A problem involving triangles?" He said looking at her work book.

Kali nodded shyly.

Joel looked around the room. The library seemed fairly quiet and empty.

Joel immediately got up and walked around to the other side of the table. He pulled out a chair and sat next to her. "I can do triangles."

He felt a tingle go down his spine as he sat down. She had a strange effect on him.

She was shy, but it was like she was judging him. Reading his body language or something. As she looked at him; she looked empathetic to what he was going through.

How did she know he was going through anything?

"How's your ankle." Joel asked her, changing the subject, from the subject that was in his head.

The girl looked shocked for a moment. "It's much better, I can hardly even feel it." She smiled. "Thanks for asking."

"You're welcome."

"What about you? Did you hurt your shoulder?" She asked, staring at him blankly.

"It's fine. I just jarred it this morning…. Getting out of the car" He lied, stunned at her insight.

"Oh, ok." She nodded, but she continued to stare at him.

Joel shook his head. It felt like she was subtly provoking him.

Suddenly he had an overwhelming urge to break down, and tell her his life story, but at the same time she had a calming effect on him.

His intuition was screaming that this girl was different, and she was going to change everything.

"Let me explain these triangles." He said, trying to shake it off.

Chapter 5

Zack:

Zachary Cummings briefly opened his eyes and looked out his bedroom window. There was a tapping noise that was disturbing his slumber. Something was tapping on his window pane. He looked up through the blinds and the glare temporarily blinded him.

He quickly rolled over and looked at his alarm clock; it was 10:14. The day had already begun with out him.

Zack usually woke up early at 5AM. He laid there restlessly in bed, waiting for the surf report, or for the phone to ring, or for the morning crew on the radio station to stop yapping and play a decent song for once. He waited for anything positive to make the day more bearable.

Today it was cloudy and windy. The light outside was not of direct sunlight, but of a sun that was trying to shine through gray cloud. The sky was made up of a silvery, ultra violet glare.

The wind was strong and making a whistling sound as it blew through the trees. It rustled the foliage, and occasionally made a creaking sound. The tree branches swayed back and forth in the wind.

All these noises he recognized immediately, but they were not that sound that fascinated him from outside

Zack jumped as the taping sound started again. He quickly turned around to see that it was a bird tapping on his window pain. The bird was black and gray with a splash or red through its feathers. It was a medium sized bird and it was determined to wake him up.

The inside of the house was dead quiet. The tapping noise was strangely disturbing like the bird was mocking him. Zack lay on his back looking at his wristwatch. He made sure the time was correct, and it was; it was now 10:17.

From where he lay he could see the clouds hanging low in the sky. There was also a lot of fog around. A fog that could rationally represented the last days of winter, but could irrationally represent a dark time in history. It could sit over the town like a witch's curse.

Zack sat up on his bed and rubbed his eyes. He jumped out of bed and threw on a t-shirt. He grabbed a black jacket and a blue pair of jeans. Recently the weather had been unnaturally warm, but today was cold, and there was a wind chill factor.

He was not going to school today, but he already knew that. The awful feeing in his stomach had been growing stronger for a week. Now the day was here.

Zack knew exactly what day it was; it was the first anniversary of Ryan Lockhart's death. Exactly one year ago today, Zack had been lying on the black tar road, at one-o-clock in the morning, looking at the yellow flames of his friend's car.

He looked outside again, but the bird was gone. The only thing he could see now was the girl's face in his mind's eye: Kali.

The girl would not be at school today either. It was the one-day of the year that she would almost certainly falter. Zack knew exactly where to find her.

Zack put some boots on his feet, and walked out to his car. He would go to Nikita beach. It was his favorite beach. Ryan's favorite beach, Kali's favorite beach.

It would be so hard to come face to face with Ryan's sister now. After everything that had happened. She would be so upset and there was nothing he could say to make it better, only worse.

Zack's car struggled to make it through the wind. He pulled into the parking lot and saw her immediately. The Beach was basically empty. She was cowering, by herself. Sitting on the surf club steps. The loneliness was portrayed all over her face. Her expression wasn't hard to read.

The wind was blowing up a storm, but she ignored it. She sat still, on the concrete steps. Her body was still, her eyes vacant. She was sitting like a statue, as she looked out at the ocean.

34

It was very cold. The sky and the clouds were dark, but Kali only wore a thin white lacey jumper over the top of her school uniform. On her feet were big black roc boots, with yellow stitching, that came half way up her ankles. She had goose bumps on her legs, and when he looked closer, she was slightly shivering.

She didn't appear to notice the wind. It was howling now. Picking up sand and blowing it all over the beach. Zack could hardly stand still from the wind gusts that were pushing him forward and back. The air was moist. It was surly going to rain soon.

If it did rain, she probably wouldn't move.

Zack stood watching her, for a long time. She didn't know that he was there. She was not crying, but her eyes were red.

"I knew I would find you here."

Kali seemed to jump, and then quickly turned her head to look at him. "Zack? Pardon?"

"I thought I might find you here." He said again.

Kali shrugged her shoulders. "Why did you think that?"

"Because Ryan died a year ago today" He said flatly. "And this is where you spread his ashes."

"How did you know?" She asked curiously.

"I made it my business to know."

Kali looked confused. "It was Ryan's favorite beach." She shrugged. "Mine too."

"I know." Zack smiled at her. "Mine too."

"I haven't been here for a while." She said helplessly.

Zack took two steps forward. He was close enough to touch her, but he didn't dare. "I know."

"It's been so cold." She tried to explain. "And it's so wild today"

He looked out at the ocean. The ferocious gray waves were thrashing the bay. The waves were breaking in every direction, and pounding against the rocks, on both sides of the beach. The spray flew meters into the air. The waves were huge, but closed out.

"It's crazy." Zack agreed.

"Why did *you* come here today?" She asked curiously.

Zack felt like if he was standing outside of his own body. All of his actions, since he got up, felt like they were on autopilot.

"I was looking for you."

Kali shrugged her shoulders, playing with a lock of her own hair. She was twirling it around her index finger. "Why."

"I was worried about you."

"Why." She asked, unmoved. "I'm just a girl you met on the beach. It's been two months. If you still feel guilty, it should have worn off by now. You don't have to worry about me."

"Most of my friends are just people that I met on the beach."

"Yeah but you're popular." She spoke softly "and older."

"Well I'm older." Zack didn't know if he was popular or not. Such things had mattered to him when he was a kid. Now he didn't know, or care less. "I came here to pay my respects to Ryan, as well."

"Were you friends with him?"

"Not really." Zack lied. He looked away at the looming clouds.

"So you're just being polite."

"No. I came here to be with you…because I knew you'd be upset."

Kali looked at him surprised. "Most wouldn't remember this date, or have moved on with their life."

"Ryan was a legend around here. He was the best surfer in Clover. He deserves some respect."

"Yeah he does… in some way." Kali looked at him strangely. "Did you know that he was drunk when he died?"

"I don't know the details." Zack lied again.

"I thought I had a brother who was smarter than to drink drive."

"Your brother was smart." Zack breathed in deeply, inhaling the salty air.

"How do you know?"

"I *did* know him a little."

"A little?"

"I saw him around the beach. We travelled in the same circles." Zack said briefly.

"But you weren't really good friends?" she enquired, curiously.

"Not really." Zack lied for a third time. Then something made him continue. "Ryan did a lot of stupid things. But he was a good guy. He was a smart guy."

Kali looked at him and shrugged her shoulders.

"He practically raised me." She said softly.

Zack closed his eyes. "I know. It was so unfair."

"You seem to know a lot"

"I looked up to your brother." Zack pleaded with her. "I idolized him."

"I'm glad he was such a role model… to both of us." She sobbed. "Look how that turned out."

"Don't be so hard on Ryan, Kali. He made a mistake. We all make mistakes."

"Drink driving isn't a mistake. It's stupidity."

"Yeah I know." He reached forward and touched her on the shoulder. He waited till she looked up, and then caught her eye. "But you have to forgive him anyway."

"Why should I?"

Because it should have been me that day.

"Forgiving is the first step to healing." Zack said finally, ignoring the rasping confession that was stuck in his throat.

"You sound like a psychiatrist." She said softly.

"I thought it sounded like wisdom." He told her.

"Maybe it did." Kali said reflectively.

Zack looked around. The wind was picking up, even more than it already was. They were both, practically being blown over, but Kali seemed content to just sit and dwell on her sad thoughts.

"Did your brother teach you to surf?" He said quickly trying to change the subject.

"He was teaching me." She paused. "I am not that good."

Zack looked at her. "It's not about being good."

"Tell that to my brother."

"I did." Zack shook his head.

Kali let go of her knees and spread her legs down the stairs. "Did Ryan tell you about me? When I met you. It felt like you already knew me" She enquired curiously.

Zack breathed in deeply. "He talked about you all the time."

You were his pride and joy. Even a stranger could see that. It was all talk though. I never met you. I never saw you. He wouldn't let me, or anyone else, near his little sister. I didn't ever see you until he was gone. Not until that day at the beach... when I dropped in on you... and almost killed you

Zack exhaled. He realized he had been holding his breath. "Or at least, that's what I hear. I mean... that's what his friends say."

Kali nodded. She didn't know what to make of him, or his words.

"It's kind of nice that you came." She smiled at him wistfully.

"I wanted to come."

Kali was sitting on one of the middle steps leading up to the surf club. She was huddled with her legs up to her chest. Her arms were clasped around them tightly. Her legs were far enough apart so that Zack could tell she was wearing blue underwear. It seemed the cold was starting to get to her now.

Zack breathed in deeply. He sat down next to her, on the step. "I just know a little something about losing someone close to you. That's why I came here."

Kali rubbed at her eyes, looking at him curiously again. "Who did you lose?"

Zack didn't say anything. He was stunned, and completely caught off guard. She was the only person in school that didn't know that his mum died.

"It doesn't matter." He said offhandedly. "I don't want to talk about me."

"I don't want to talk about me either... or him."

Zack pulled off his jacket and rested it over Kali's shoulders. It was currently spitting, and the rain was going to break any second.

"You didn't have to do that. I don't mind the cold" She said, sheepishly.

"I wanted to."

"But *you'll* freeze." She persisted.

"I have another jacket in my car."

"Then go get it." She shook her head. "You should just go. I am not the best company today."

Zack sighed. He reached over and rubbed at her arms, creating heat friction. "I don't want to go, and you are good company."

Kali looked up, and nodded. "You remind me of him."

"Of Ryan."

"He was the coolest." Kali said softly.

Zack smiled, but suddenly it started to rain. The rain poured down with torrential force. Out of nowhere, it hit them like a monsoon.

Zack jumped up quickly. He took Kali's hand. He looked in her eye for a moment and then forcibly pulled her up. Then he led her to his car. She followed him, hesitantly.

Zack never locked his car. Anyone that wanted to steal his car was probably doing him a favor. He ran to the passenger side door and opened if for her. Hastily she jumped in.

He went around to the driver's side, and dove in the front seat.

For a moment he just sat there, staring out the fogged up window. They sat listening to the rain pelting on the car roof. Zack put the key in the ignition and turned the heater on.

"It's pouring." Kali said.

"Yeah." Zack agreed. "We haven't had rain in ages. I think the drought has broken"

Kali smiled "It's just what we need; a down pore."

Zack nodded. He looked back out towards the sea. "It feels like we are the only two people left on earth."

"Maybe we are." She smiled at him.

"Do you ever feel lonely even when you're around a crowd of people?" Zack asked suddenly. Surprising even himself with the question.

"Sometimes." Kali said slowly. "I think Ryan liked being lonely. It gave him an edge." She commented. "I'm surprised you guys weren't better friends."

Zack closed his eyes and took a deep breath "Ryan wasn't lonely, I was jealous of him, because he had you."

"You were jealous of him?"

Zack breathed in deeply. He kept saying more than he should. "A lot of people were jealous of Ryan Lockhart." He said quickly.

Kali gave him a funny look. "He would have liked you."

The remark stung Zack. There was so much history there. "At least someone could. I'm not that likable these days."

"What?" Kali said incredulously. "Not counting your million friends at school, and you're beautiful girlfriend"

"My girlfriend? Caroline thinks I'm a hopeless." He said referring to his new girlfriend. "You think she is beautiful?"

"Didn't she sign up with a modeling agency?" Kali asked ironically.

"Did she? I don't know. Damien told me to ask her out. He gave me a lecture about not having a girlfriend"

"I remember. I was there."

"So was all of Clover."

Kali giggled.

He nudged her. "Do *you* want to go out with Caroline? You can have her if you want."

"No thanks."

"You're no fun." He smiled at her and nudged her again. "I don't feel lonely around you."

Kali rested her head back against the car seat. "Me neither."

Zack shrugged. "We should hang out." He nodded at her. "You should come up to my hangout at lunchtime. Like Damien said."

"Really?"

"Really Kali. We should be friends. I'll protect you."

"Protect me from what?"

"From whatever's out there." Zack looked at her.

Kali looked back at him. She looked confused and puzzled. She had no idea how much he meant it.

Chapter 6

Kali:

As Zack dropped Kali off at her house, he handed her an invitation to Damien Grisham's party, which seemed like the weirdest thing ever. Yet he really seemed like he wanted her to go.

As she got inside the house, she stood in the door of the lounge room, and watched over her sister Belinda for a moment.

Belinda looked distressed. She ran her fingers through her hair and gritted her teeth as she read the last few sentences of her work in her workbook. She was studying for her Higher School Certificate exams.

Kali watched her sister curiously and wondered how the two of them could be so different. Belinda was mature, confident and grown up. She was outgoing and had healthy relationships, and she was far prettier than Kali.

Finally, Belinda looked up and saw Kali standing there in the door way.

"I thought you were at school." She said curiously.

Kali didn't move. She rested her body against the sliding door and looked into Belinda's eyes "Not today."

"Does that mean the school is going to call again?"

Kali gave her a bored look. "Maybe, but I'd let the machine pick it up."

"I always do." Belinda took a deep breath in. "We have to talk." She sighed sorrowfully, but then her expression changed. "Where have you been?"

"Outside."

"Outside is a pretty big place."

"Outside in Clover."

I know you've been to the beach, I can see the sand in your hair." Belinda sighed. "You do know it's raining, don't you Kali?"

"Yes."

The rain was actually pouring on the roof so hard, Belinda had to practically yell so Kali could hear her. "I'm not your mother Kali." Belinda started carefully. "I can't make you go to school, but you're never going to learn anything, if you don't."

"You think I would go to school on this day?"

"On this day" Belinda repeated.

"Do you even know…?"

"A day we don't need to be reminded of." Belinda snapped back.

"He was your brother." Kali screamed. "He was your twin brother."

"I know." She said sadly.

"You should have been at the beach today too! That's where we scattered the ashes."

"I know. I was there. I remember."

"You never even got him." Kali sobbed.

"I loved Ryan, Kali." Belinda said frustrated. "Could you please stop insinuating that I didn't? We were very different twins, but he was my brother." She demanded. "He meant a lot to me. He still does."

Kali looked at the floor. "We never talk about him. If we stop talking about him, I might forget him."

"We'll never forget our big brother." She said softly.

Ryan had been about 18 minutes older than Belinda.

Kali looked down, sadness engulfing her whole body, and the tears started to fall. "It just hurts."

"It hurts a lot. It wasn't fair." Belinda said, irritated. "Just because I don't let you see me cry, doesn't mean I don't."

"I know."

Belinda looked at her sadly. "I know that he was everything to you."

"Yeah, he raised me." Kali mumbled.

Belinda blinked. She looked at Kali. Then something caught her attention, but she looked away. "Ryan was complicated. He had his secrets."

Kali wasn't sure what to make of that.

"You know Kali" Belinda began leadingly. "It's not just *Ryan* we don't talk about: It's *you*." She informed her. "I don't know what you're interested in? Who your friends are? What subject is your favorite? I don't know anything about you."

Kali nodded "Because you're never home." She said hopelessly.

Belinda nodded. "Ok, maybe I go out a lot, but we should make time, and we have to talk."

Kali shook her head. "Talk about what."

Belinda chewed on her lip for a moment. "Maybe about the fact that I had to hear it off the grape vine: What happened between you and Zachary Cummings."

"What happened between me and Zachary Cummings?" Kali asked incredulously.

"The accident you had." Belinda said exasperated. "You said it was a surfing accident Kali. You didn't tell me that Zack almost took you out, with his surfboard."

Kali huffed. "No *I* almost took *him* out with *my* surfboard. It was my fault!"

"Come on Kali." Belinda raised her voice. "I know you've been hanging out with him, and *Damien Grisham*. What's going on?"

"Nothing's been going on! Kali scolded her. "Really Belinda?" She mocked. "That's what interests you? That I talked to them a couple of times in my entire life?" Kali shook her head. "We just see each other around school! It nothing more." She tried to explain.

"Whose jacket is that?" Belinda snapped suddenly.

Kali's facial muscles tightened. She put her hands in to the pocket of the jacket. "It's was Ryan's."

"Where, exactly, were you just now?"

"The beach."

"Who was there?"

"It was freezing today. The beach was empty."

"We gave all Ryan's stuff to charity."

"I kept this." Kali mumbled. She wanted to crawl inside the jacket, so she could avoid this conversation.

Kali looked out the window. The wind was still intensifying. It was lashing the house and making the windows rattle. It was cold and dark, and the only light was the dim orange glow from the light bulb.

"You're a bad liar."

"It's Zack's jacket." Kali finally admitted.

"What are you doing with him?"

"Nothing you have to be worried about."

"Let me decide what I should be worried about."

"Nothing happened, he gave me a lift home. I didn't understand why he..." Kali stopped in mid-sentence. "He knew what day it was today. He knew about Ryan."

"Of course, he did."

"What does that mean?"

"It means; of course, he knew what day it was"

"Why would he know?"

Belinda didn't answer her. "Did anything happen between you and him?"

"No, nothing happened." Kali declared.

Belinda looked out the window. "I don't think you should be hanging out with him."

"Why?"

"You're just a kid." She whispered. "There are things about him." She began, carefully. "There used to be rumors, and they weren't very nice."

"Don't treat me like I'm nine years old." Kali demanded.

"I don't remember exactly." Belinda sighed. "You know he used to be best friends with Ryan?"

"Best friends? That's not true."

"You were only in primary school. It was when mum left. You wouldn't really remember." Belinda informed her. "Ryan wouldn't let you see him like that. Every time Ryan disappeared; that's who he was with: Zack."

Kali shook her head. "No, Zack just said they saw each other around the beach sometimes." she argued.

"He's lying." Belinda shook her head. "I don't know what happened between Ryan and Zack, but the friendship ended, and I mean abruptly."

"Why would Zack lie about that?"

"Exactly" Belinda emphasized. "I don't think you're ready for the kind of friendship he has to give. He's older than you."

"He's not a bad guy. He's nice to me."

"I'm sure he is." Belinda smirked. "I just don't think it's a good idea." She paused. "I was with his friend Damien, and they're only interested in one thing. Zack's already got a girlfriend."

"You were with Damien?"

"I went out with him a few times." Belinda said quickly.

"Really."

"It was a while ago."

"But Zack doesn't want me for his girlfriend Belinda." Kali reasoned. "You don't even know him."

Belinda closed her eyes, and rubbed her temples. "I can't dictate your friends." She sighed, and then changed tack. "I guess it was inevitable that you met him sometime."

"Why inevitable."

"Because you're a surfer." She paused for a long time. "And he's lonely."

Kali nodded, it was a curious thing to say. "So am I." she whispered.

Belinda suddenly got up. She walked towards Kali but then detoured. She picked up a letter from the corner of the table, and showed it to Kali. "I got this today."

"What is it?"

"It's an early acceptance letter from the University of Sydney."

"You got in?"

"Yes."

Kali gasped. "Congratulations." She said excitedly, and leaned over to give her sister a hug.

"I don't know if I should go." Belinda said hesitantly.

"Why."

"I'll be leaving you all alone."

"But this is what you wanted. It's what you've always wanted."

"That was before Ryan died."

"Early acceptance is a big deal." Kali said excitedly. "Ryan would want this for you."

"He would want me to be there for *you*."

"He would want *you* to live your dreams"

"But what happens if you get in over your head? Or you get hurt again?"

"I'll be fine." Kali tried to assure her.

"You're my sister, I don't want to lose you as well."

"You won't lose me." Kali said. "This is your dream. You have to go." She repeated.

Belinda stared at the letter. "I know."

Chapter 7

Kali:

Zack had invited Kali to Damien's party tonight.

He seemed really enthusiastic at the time, but a week had gone by. Kali walked the twenty-minute distance to Damien's house. Just out of pure curiosity. She had nothing better to do tonight.

She thought she would only stay ten minutes, but she was still nervous about coming.

She had an awful time getting dressed. In the end she decided on a red dress, with a leather jacket which she borrowed from her sister's closet, and her signature roc boots.

Damien's house was two-stories. The front door was colored by shards of green and red glass. There was not much lawn on the front yard. There was just a pathway up to the door. There were a few garden beds, with bushes of daisy flowers, and a few roses.

As Kali walked in, she inhaled the aroma of popcorn, marijuana smoke, and the pungent smell of alcohol.

She began walking slowly around the house, not really knowing what to do with herself. First she looked around the first floor. There was a den that had a few people talking, and listening to music. There were also people in the bedrooms getting stoned.

Slowly she wondered up the stairs. She glanced in each of the bedrooms. She bumped into a few people on the upstairs dance floor, and there were also a few people on the lounge, watching a movie. The kitchen had lots of snacks and drinks piled around.

It was all kind of exciting, but she was eager to find the boys. She figured she might say a meager hello. Maybe a quick conversation, and keep moving, back to her house.

Then suddenly, as if by instinct she stumbled onto the veranda.

She found Damien and Joel sitting round on deck chairs. Damien had a guitar in his hand. She didn't see him at first, but Zack was there too. He had a cigarette in his hand and he was smoking it.

Kali instantly froze. She didn't know what to do. Turn around and walk away, or stand there like an idiot. She didn't fully trust them yet.

All of them, on different occasions, had been so nice to her. That didn't mean, however, that she had the right to talk to them at a senior's party.

"Kali!" Damien yelled suddenly. He yelled so loudly, it caught her completely off guard.

He put his guitar down. He jumped out of his seat, and came to give her a big hug. He gave her a kiss on the cheek, and she could smell the alcohol on his breath.

"Hi." Kali smiled, still surprised.

"How are you going girl?" he asked her.

"I'm good. I'm really good."

"Fantastic. Look who it is Zack! It's Kali!"

Zack was standing on the furthest edge of the veranda.

He was standing at the opposite end of the Veranda, away from the Damien and Joel. He was standing there defiantly, alone. Kali didn't see Caroline anywhere at the party.

Zack looked good. He was wearing a dark red sweater, and a pair of blue jeans. He turned and nodded at Kali.

He gave her a condescending smile. Then he waved his cigarette hand around, for a second. As if it was a feeble attempt at waving to her. Then he looked back over the edge of the balcony.

Damien gleamed. "Joel this is Kali." He said, trying to kindly introduce them.

Joel laughed. He got up, and looked into Kali's eyes. He was obviously drunk as well. "What do you mean this is Kali? I know Kali. We hang out at the library on Wednesday. Don't we Kal?"

Joel walked over to Kali and also gave her a big, drunken, hug. She smiled nervously.

Zack spun around. "What?" He grunted. Suddenly coming to attention. "You hang out with her where?"

"At the library." Joel said, shrugging.

Zack stared blatantly at Joel. He stared at him suspiciously for a length of time.

Joel tried to shake him off. "So, how are you enjoying the party?"

"It's really good." Kali said awkwardly.

Realistically, she had been here all of ten minutes, and hadn't spoken to anyone else. "I'm really enjoying myself."

"Good, it's about time you let your hair down." Damien said putting his hand on her shoulders. "You have to tear it up tonight."

"Don't stand there spouting clichés at her Damien." Zack said irritably.

"What the fuck is wrong with you." Damien yelled at Zack. "Don't worry Kali. He's just in one of his moods." He pawed her shoulder. "I'll give you a tour around my house."

Kali was still completely taken aback. "That would be great."

"No" Joel yelled. "She my little helper. I'll show her around." he slurred his words.

Zack had lost interest. He had turned away and looked back into the abyss, off the balcony.

Kali looked at Joel and Damien. "Give me a minute." She smiled, but let herself out of Damien's grasp.

She walked over to Zack. She was confused by his antisocial behavior, but still drawn to him anyway.

"I didn't know you smoked."

Zack was startled; he didn't see her come over. He eventually just shrugged his shoulders. "I guess some people can surprise you."

"You always surprise me."

He seemed different, amused by something. "You should go inside. It's getting cold out here."

"I'm not cold."

Zack caught her eye. "Suit yourself."

Kali lied she was cold. "Are you having fun tonight?"

"Fun?" Zack seemed disconnected from the word. "Do you ever have fun Kali?"

Kali nervously wiped the hair away from her face. "Not very often."

"Why not?" He asked, condescendingly again. "You're more fun than you think you are."

Kali stared at him.

He had completely put a wall up against her. "Thanks." She said, sarcastically, but then started to step back. If he was going to be antagonistic, she didn't have to stick around

He took a drag of his cigarette. "We should have fun tonight. We have to learn to get on with our lives." He said reflecting on something far more than this party

He often referred to something that was just below the surface. Kali didn't know what it was.

It was probably safer that he didn't lower his guard. There was always so much that he held back. One crack in the dam, and he could lose it completely. Kali wasn't' sure what she should say. She watched him closely. "That's what my sister keeps telling me."

Zack flinched. "We're so young. It shouldn't be like this."

Kali nodded and stood for a moment quietly. "Parties are supposed to be fun right? So we shouldn't have to try so hard."

Zack laughed. "I guess there is something really wrong with us if we can't have fun at a party."

"There is probably something really wrong with us anyway." Kali giggled. "But I'm glad you guys are here."

Zack turned to her. He ran his fingers through her hair, over her left temple. "I wanted *you* to come."

Kali nodded, she closed her eyes. His touch gave her goose bumps. He took his hand away and focused on the cigarette. "I didn't think you'd come."

Kali looked in Zack's green eyes. He looked back into her brown ones. She blushed. "I guess some people can surprise you."

Zack laughed. He leaned forward and kissed her on the cheek.

Kali *couldn't* smell alcohol on his breath. He was sober, but the kiss had been very tender.

"Are you sure you don't want to go inside. It really is cold out here." He said again looking away.

"No, I'm fine." She slowly turned and made her way back to Damien and Joel. They were watching her and Zack.

Damien tried to lighten the mood. He grabbed a beer from the esky and gave it to her. "Come sit with us Kali." He patted the empty deck chair, and beckoned her.

The beer was an incredibly cold bottle. It was almost hurting her hand as she held it. She had never drunk alcohol before tonight.

"What are you guys doing?" Zack yelled.

He came up quickly, out of nowhere, and hoisted the beer out of her hand. He did it so fast her head spun. He held the beer, and looked at it. "She's too young!"

"So are we." Damien replied. "We're all under age here Zack."

Zack shook his head angrily and Kali had never seen him angry before. "Not her."

Kali watched him puzzled. She didn't know what to say. He wanted her to have fun, but he felt threatened if she tried to.

"Just relax." Damien ordered him.

Zack stared him down. "She's not drinking. Look at her. She's tiny. Two drinks and we'd have to get her stomach pumped."

"She could probably hold her liquor better than you." Damien persisted. "She's not her brother, Zack, and she's not you."

Kali looked at Zack confused. Zack knew exactly what he was talking about. He withdrew slightly. "Please don't give her that. She's just a kid."

Joel looked between the two of them. He changed tack, and tried to ward off the mounting tension. "Ok fine."

Damien shrugged his shoulders and looked directly into Zack's eyes. "Whatever you say" he held his hands out, as if he was submitting to an issue that was far deeper.

He looked at Kali. "The kitchen is in there. I'll go get you a soft drink."

"You don't have to." Kali said quickly.

Damien took Kali's hand and led her to the kitchen. There people sitting at the dining table, in the next room, playing a card game. They were mumbling amongst themselves.

"Hey Damien." One of the girls called out as they approached. Damien acknowledged her with a flick of the hand, giving a fiendish smile.

"Coke or Fanta?"

"Fanta" Kali answered.

"Who's that?" One of the card players yelled out motioning to Kali.

"She's none of your business Paul."

"Oh, I know you. You're Ry…" He stopped suddenly. "Belinda's sister." He said finally.

Kali nodded, reluctantly.

"How are you going rug rat?"

Damien handed Kali her drink.

"So, what's up Damo? You're going after the younger sister now as well? Wasn't the older one enough for you?" Paul hesitated, and belched loudly. "I heard Zack had you covered with the rug rat."

Kali looked at Damien who was positively red. "Classy Paul" he yelled at him. "She's just our friend, you fucking spastic."

Damien looked back at Kali, trying to gage her reaction.

Kali felt very confused.

There were so many things that Kali didn't understand. There were so many things that people referred to, that people whispered about. Belinda herself, had said something about being with Damien.

Damien grabbed Kali's hand. He led her downstairs.

Joel and Zack followed them down here; but dispersed in different directions. They were talking to two totally different groups of people. Zack was sitting on the sofa with a few kids who looked stoned.

Joel was off in a different corner of the room. He was in deep conversation with what looked like the smart kids.

"I wonder what he's talking about." Kali whispered, motioning to Joel.

"Super strain chaos theory" Damien joked. "I'm going to the bathroom."

Kali stood against the wall sipping her drink. A song called 'cosmic girl' came on the stereo and a few people got out of their seats to start dancing. Kali put her drink down on the window ledge so that she could go join them

She felt exposed dancing in her outfit. She never filled out her clothes the way she wanted to. They always seemed to hang off her, which made her look too skinny and featureless. She never denied herself food but sometimes she didn't eat because she wasn't hungry.

She was really getting into the song, when the atmosphere changed again for the worse.

"What the hell." A boy said suddenly. "How did Kali Lockhart get in here?"

Kali looked up. People her own age, from her own year, were at the party.

Mark Landon and Dean Kent walked by. Dean was sometimes nice to her, but Mark was a Jackass. He always teased her.

"Get lost guys." She told them softly.

"What's going on Kali?" Dean asked her sarcastically.

"Hey Kali." Mark said. "No friends in your own year. So now you have to crash the seniors party?"

Kali looked away and went to leave.

Suddenly Damien was moving towards her.

"What did you say punk?" Damien asked Mark.

Mark gulped thickly, and shifted his weight from one foot to the other.

"Nothing." He mumbled.

"Yes, you did." Damien stepped forward and pushed him against the wall. "You've got two seconds to apologize."

Everyone had stopped dancing, everyone had stopped talking. The music was still loud, but the clarity in the room was epic. Everyone was standing around watching.

Kali felt terribly embarrassed.

The two seconds came and went. Mark was still making up his mind. His friend Dean, had backed away quickly.

Kali found herself with Joel and Zack on either side of her. Zack looking particularly distressed at the situation.

"Damien is a black belt in Tai Kwon Do. He did it when he was a kid." Joel whispered in Kali's ear.

It seemed like everyone was standing in a horseshoe around Damien and Mark. Kali was in the middle. She thought Mark was right. She was a looser. There was no need for this.

No one seemed to be worried about Damien's stark reaction.

If he truly was a black belt, he could really do some damage to this kid. "Don't worry about it Damien." Kali called out. She began to step forward, but Zack cut her off. He held his arm out across her body, so that she couldn't move.

Damien looked back at her and shook his head. "They are not going to talk to you like that kali." He yelled at her. "Especially not in my house! Apologize." He screamed at mark.

Mark opened his mouth up and down, but apparently didn't make the time limit. Damien swung his fist back and planted it in Mark's stomach.

"No." Kali called out desperately.

"They are going to apologize." Damien yelled back at her. He grabbed Mark by the shoulder and swung him around in to the middle of the floor.

Kali looked on horrified, Mark couldn't defend himself. He was young and stupid. He was clearly all talk. He tried to throw a punch, but Damien blocked it easily. He gave him a black eye in return.

"Do something." Kali yelled at Zack, who was in just as much in shock as she was.

Zack looked at Kali, looked at Damien, and then looked at Kali again.

"Damien." Joel finally jumped in. He ran forward to put himself in between his friend, and his friend's assailant. "He's not worth it."

Zack tuned to Mark and pushed him towards the stairs. "Get the hell out of here." He watched Mark fumble for the exit. "You're lucky." He growled. "I wouldn't have stopped him so soon."

Damien looked disorientated for a moment. He shook his head, to shake himself out of it. He looked at Kali apologetically. Then he sprinted.

He headed quickly for the back yard. Joel and Zack instinctively ran after him. Kali followed them shortly behind.

She caught up to them, as they were sitting on a concrete bench in the furthest corner of the yard. It was only Damien that was sitting; the other two were standing around him. Kali walked up and stood with them.

"Why did you do that?" Kali asked, confused.

Damien looked up at her. "I don't know."

"He deserved it." Zack piped in.

"I'm not going to let anyone take advantage of you."

"He wasn't trying to take advantage of me."

Damien looked up at Zack. He started speaking, but it seemed like a private conversation. "I couldn't do anything about Rochelle, but I could do something about this."

Zack nodded as if he understood perfectly what Damien was trying to say.

"What?" Kali asked as if she had missed something, she took a step back. "They make fun of me sometimes. You shouldn't worry about it."

"Don't *ever* take any notice of what they have to say." Damien said sternly.

"What do you expect anyway?" Joel joined in. "They're body boarders."

"I don't listen to them." Kali said.

Damien nodded. "Good."

Kali grimaced. "You defended me."

Damien did something that completely surprised her. He got to his feet, came towards her, and put his arms around her. He gave her a warm hug. He held her so close for so long. "You're special."

She hugged him back, but yet again, she felt like she didn't understand what was going on.

Damien pulled away and smiled at her. He looked at Zack. "Did I hurt him badly?"

Zack was standing four steps away. He was facing away from them. His expression had changed, he looked bored. He had a cigarette in his mouth, and a lighter in his hand, ready to light it. He took a drag and then exhaled, turning to look in Kali's eyes. "He's got a few bruises."

"Do you think he's going to tell anyone?" Joel asked seriously.

"Just his mommy" Damien sniggered. "I don't care who he tells. The whole school is going to know about this by tomorrow."

"I just hope my father doesn't find out I was involved, or he'll kick my arse." Joel said pensively.

"So what" Zack muttered indignantly. "We got into a fight."

"Over a girl" Damien reached out and touched Kali on the cheek.

"What, and you're the expert?" Joel yelled at Zack.

"You weren't even involved Joel. You tried to break it up." Zack continued to enjoy his cigarette "Even though he deserved it."

"What are you doing over there? I thought you quit." Damien yelled.

Zack huffed. "I did." He stopped smoking and glanced over at the three of them. "What made you snap?"

Damien shook his head. "I don't know... "I wanted to protect her. "That day at the beach. I was so scared."

They were talking about Kali right in front of her. She felt strange.

"Use the force Damien." Joel snickered.

"Would you stop with the Star Wars references?" Zack said.

Damien scratched his head. "It's a great movie."

"It's six movies." Joel argued. "Everyone is going to know about this." He repeated.

"Defending the same girl that Zack tried to kill." Damien smirked. "Of course, they will."

"Shut up Damien." Zack yelled at him

"No one will care." Kali tried to reassure them.

Zack dropped his cigarette on the ground, and stepped on it. "Something bad always happens at parties."

Kali only just heard it, but no one else was listening.

"How do I get all these people out of my house?" Damien asked, suddenly exhausted.

"We'll just wait it out."

Kali felt like her head was spinning. "I should go." She found herself saying, as she started moving away. "I'm sorry that I ruined your party."

She felt the overwhelming need to go, and not ruin anything more.

She found herself stumbling through the back yard towards the gate.

"It's ok Kali. Come back. You didn't ruin anything." Zack called out to her.

Kali felt so embarrassed she had to go. She just caused so much drama. She had to get home where it was safe. She ran home and hardly stopped running till she got there.

Chapter 8

Zack:

Zack was lost in thought, but he wasn't thinking about anything in particular. It was so peaceful. He was sitting on his recliner in the dark, listening to the rain on the roof.

The knock at the door was so soft that he could barely hear it.

It was Kali. She had texted him earlier saying said that she might stop by. She was bringing his jacket back.

He was eagerly awaiting her visit. It was lonelier than usual tonight. No one was with him. It was just a regular Thursday night. His dad was at work. His mom was gone. The house was familiarly empty, and cold, like a ghost town. The rain was just part of the eerie atmosphere.

Zack had just put a frozen pizza in the oven. He was waiting for the buzzer to go off, when he finally went to answer the door.

The girl awkwardly stood in the doorway. The night was black around her. A rush of cold air blew in. The rain had been pouring down for about three days now. Kali looked up at him for a moment. Her eyes were translucent. It was hard to look away from them.

She was still wearing her school uniform. She had a navy blue jumper and a blue skirt on. She was wearing her black Roc boot shoes. She wore them everywhere she went.

Her long brown hair was slightly wet as if she had been in the rain, but she had an umbrella with her. It was red, and folded up. Hanging by a string around her left wrist.

In her right hand she was holding a black jacket. It's was Zack's black jacket; the one he had given to her at the beach. It seemed like a long time ago now. In reality it was just three weeks ago.

"Come in, Kali it's freezing out here."

Kali nodded and walked past him.

"How are you?" He took her umbrella.

Kali nodded earnestly. "I'm ok." She walked into the lounge room. "I'm sorry I ran off at the party, the other day."

"It's ok. We understood, as long as you understand; you didn't ruin anything." Zack told her. "That kid did."

Kali looked away. "He was making fun of me. Kind of embarrassing."

Zack shook his head. "Don't you ever listen to them." He demanded, and touched her arm. "You're my friend now. I'll protect you."

"You can't" Kali shook her head. "I'm shy, and I'm an easy target." She shrugged. "I make myself an easy target."

"No, you don't, and besides; they'll see how easy it is when I flush their head in the urinals."

Kali shook her head. "You're funny." She glanced at the pictures on the wall. "Do people still do that?"

Zack laughed to himself. "No." He admitted. He watched Kali. She looked around his house humbly, as if she saw great beauty in it.

"I wanted to bring this back to you." She said holding up his jacket.

"You should put it on. You look cold."

"That would defeat the purpose of bringing it back." She shrugged. "Don't worry. I'm not cold."

He did worry her. It was freezing tonight and all he ever wanted to do was warm her up. Ever since the first day he had met her, when she was cold and not breathing.

"Do you want to sit down?"

Kali ignored him. "Are you watching 'Home and Away'?"

"No."

"It's playing." She motioned to the television.

"I wasn't watching it."

Zack quickly grabbed the remote. He flicked the channel to another station. He moved forward and quickly took the jacket from her. He threw it on the chair where he was just sitting.

Kali nodded. She walked over and stood next to him.

"So, you're here by yourself?" She asked curiously.

"Yeah, my dad's out."

Kali thought about that for a moment. "Oh, ok." She smiled awkwardly. "Caroline is not here?"

Zack smiled too. "No, she's not here." He shook his head. "She's at home." He marveled. "She's having dinner, at the dinner table, with her family."

Kali giggled. "I didn't know people still ate at the dinner table anymore."

"Yeah, people still do it. Joel's family does as well. It like something out of 'Pleasantville."

"I liked that movie." Kali said quietly.

"Sometimes I go over to Caroline's house. Her family is very pleasant." He told her.

Kali nodded. "Really, that must be intimidating." She shook her head. "I mean interesting."

"It is." He confessed. "It's very contrite. The parents talk to the kids about how their day went. Then they ask *me* how *my* day went." He admitted. "I never know what to say when they ask. It feels like a lot of pressure answering that one question."

"Yeah, I hope you come up with something good." Kali smiled at him.

"I always do." Zack shook his head. "So, what else is the matter Kali?" he asked bluntly.

"What do you mean?"

"You have that look on your face." He said, watching her facial expressions closely.

"What happened at the party?" Kali asked suddenly.

Zack exhaled slowly. "Nothing happened."

"But Damien was so mad."

"Damien was just letting off steam."

"No. There is more to it than that."

"No. There is not." Zack sighed. He looked at her. She did not look convinced. "Ok." He gave in. "What do you want to know?"

"Who is Rochelle?"

Zack bit his lip. He thought about the question for a long time. "Rochelle is Damien's sister. She lives in Sydney with her dad. From what Damien has told me, I think she's a drug addict."

Kali looked shocked. She wasn't expecting that.

"That's why he was so upset?"

"Yeah." Zack answered somberly. "He wanted to save you, because he couldn't save his sister."

"Wow." Kali said softly. "That must be really hard on him."

"It is." Zack explained. "Rochelle was a nice girl. She was thoughtful when I knew her, but she was naïve, and she didn't handle the divorce well."

"And what about Joel?"

"What about him?"

Kali looked apprehensive and pensive. "Joel didn't stop the fight early enough. I saw the look on his face. He was gunning for that kid. He wanted to see him get hurt."

Zack was surprised by her observation, and the fact that she would voice it. "Joel's angry at the world because his dad hits him."

Kali gasped in surprise. Then she nodded meekly as if she somehow already knew that. "Really."

"Yeah."

"Did he tell you that?"

"No."

"Then how do you know?"

"I'm not an idiot Kali."

Zack put his head back against the couch. He listened again to the rain on the roof.

"Joel's not like us, he's smart and he's selfless, but he's kind of a mess. You should see him on manic Mondays after his father

61

is in his face all weekend. Joel freaks out. He always tries way too hard." He looked Kali in the eye. "He's not just on the library on Wednesdays Kali, he's always there."

Zack could hear spite in his own voice. It surprised him.

"I guess you and Joel have been getting acquainted." He said curiously.

"He helps me with my homework." Kali whispered. "Why did you just tell me all that?"

"Because you asked."

"But I didn't expect you to tell me everything. You don't even know me."

"Yes I do." Zack ran his fingers through his hair. "Kali you have to understand. We all have our issues. What happened at the party had very little to do with you."

"Yeah I guessed that." She raised her eyebrows again. "What's your issue?"

Zack smiled to himself. She was pushy. "Too many to count."

She slowly sat down on the couch and he sat down beside her.

"I'm glad you're here." He said softly. "You can share my frozen pizza."

"I like frozen pizza" she told him softly.

Zack was interrupted: the pizza timer went off. Zack heard the noise and jumped up. "I'll be back in a second."

The pizza was slightly undercooked; just the way Zack liked it. He cut it up evenly, and put it on to 2 plates. He filled up two glasses of Fanta and took the meal out to Kali. She accepted it humbly.

He watched her eat. She was so delicate. She nibbled her food, and sipped her drink.

Zack found it fascinating to just watch her. He finished his meal long before her.

"Did you like it?"

Kali giggled again. "Of course, it's pizza."

"When you texted me earlier. I bought Fanta. I noticed you liked it at the party."

"Really. You remember that."

"You always seem surprised...that I care." He said earnestly.

"I'm surprised that anyone cares." Kali said softly. Her voice was shaky.

"Is that why you're upset tonight?" Zack asked again.

Kali held out, but then shrugged. "I found out my sister is leaving to go the University of Sydney."

Zack nodded. "And you don't want her to go."

"I don't know." Kali shrugged her shoulders. "I don't want her to leave me all alone."

"Yeah I don't blame you. I hate being all alone." Zack grimaced. "Ryan always told me that Belinda would get a doctorate, and become some high-flying lawyer, or stock broker. I'm not surprised she's leaving."

Kali gave him a funny look. "He said that? In one of the casual conversations he had with you?"

There was an edge to her question. Zack wished he could keep his mouth shut sometimes. "Yeah." He said quickly.

"You're right about my sister's future, but she has a different story to tell about you and Ryan."

"Like what." He said softly. He could feel his stomach churning; tying itself in knots.

"My sister said that you and Ryan were best friends once."

"What exactly did Belinda tell you?"

"Nothing. She didn't know anything. She said that your friendship ended suddenly."

Zack shook his head. He exhaled again. He suddenly felt exhausted. He felt like crying. "That story's for another day, Kali. Please."

Kali nodded. She looked him in the eye. "Ok." She said reluctantly.

"Wait" Zack cried. He moved closer to her. He put his hand on her leg. "It's a long story..."

"Who do we have here?"

Zack jumped a mile high. He instantly moved away from Kali. He took his hand off her leg. His dad had just walked in the room. "Hi Dad"

"Hi Mr. Cummings" Kali said shyly. She watched Zack's father circle the room and stand in front of them. She cowered under his glance. "I'm Kali. Kali Lockhart."

Zack held his breath.

"Kali Lockhart?" His father looked at Zack. "That's Ryan's sister?"

"Yeah Dad" Zack nodded. "She's a friend of mine."

Kali looked at him, then she looked at his dad.

"I didn't know Ryan had a younger sister." He glared at Zack disapprovingly. "Just how young is she."

"I'm fifteen." Kali said hesitantly.

"Fifteen? You shouldn't be hanging around with my son." He said that in a sarcastic tone, but it wasn't clear whether he was joking.

Zack looked down at the floor. She gave a nervous smile. "He's a good friend to me."

"Let us all hope so."

"There is some leftover chicken in the fridge dad." Zack interrupted.

His father looked straight in Zack's eyes "Alright." He nodded at Kali. "Good night young lady. It was nice to meet you. I'll see you tomorrow Zack."

Zack jumped up and followed his father into the kitchen. "Are you going straight to bed tonight?"

"I'm pretty tired son." His dad started biting into the chicken leg. "She looks very innocent that girl. Make sure it stays that way."

"We're just friends dad. I swear."

"I'm taking the key to the liquor cabinet." He huffed. "I don't want history to repeat itself."

Zack tried to keep his voice down. "Don't you trust me by now?"

"What happened to Caroline?"

"Caroline is my girlfriend. Kali is my friend. She just came over to talk."

"Talk to you?"

"This is important dad. Just be nice to her."

"That goes double for you." His dad finished his meal and went to his room. Zack watched him walk away.

"I'm sorry about that." Zack said softly, as he rejoined Kali, on the couch.

Kali looked up innocently and yawned as if she didn't just hear the entire conversation. "Maybe I should be getting home."

"No don't leave 'Chicago Fire' is on next."

"I like that show" Kali smiled. "It's my favorite."

Zack slowly reached over. He brushed the hair away from her eyes. "It's mine too."

He kept looking over at her, as they watched the show. Her body was just an inch away from his. She was so young, and she was innocent. She was like a doll on his couch.

He didn't realize that 'Chicago Fire' was a double episode. They started the show enthusiastically enough, but she barely hung on till the end. When he looked over, as the ending credits rolled, she was fast asleep.

He watched her for a while; breathing in and out, in the dark. The television was turned off. The lights were off. The night was silent, except for the rain on the roof.

Zack finally picked her up and took her to his bedroom. She felt like a little kid in his arms. She weighed almost nothing.

His dumped her in his bed. Then straightened the covers on top of her. She still had all her school clothes on. "Good night Kali." He told her. She had stayed perfectly still, even while he moved her.

He tucked her in, as best he could. Then leaned down to kiss her on the cheek.

The girl had so much of Ryan in her, but she was so much her own person as well. It surprised him that she was fifteen now. The last time he talked to her she had been fourteen. Her birthday must have come and gone, without him knowing.

Zack smiled at her company. He rolled out his sleeping bag, and went to sleep on his bedroom floor.

Chapter 9

Zack:

It was still dark when Zack woke up in his room. He found himself on the floor. Sleeping fairly uncomfortably, in between the covers of his sleeping bag. His looked briefly at his watch, which said it was 6:20AM.

It had been harsh on the floor last night. His back was a little sore from the block of wax he had been sleeping on all night, and it was a little cold. Never the less, he had a strange feeling. He didn't feel tired. He was excited. Exhilarated even. He was eager to embrace the day, and he hadn't felt like that in ages.

Zack turned his head upward on his pillow, and stared at the ceiling.

That's when he remembered there was a girl in his bed.

A girl named Kali Lockhart.

Zack looked over to see the sleeping girl. She was wrapped up so tightly in the blankets. He must have tucked her in so well last night.

Zack picked himself up off the floor and took a jacket out of his closet. He quickly wrapped it around his body, to warm himself up.

Just like Kali, Zack had slept in his clothes last night. He was also wearing his school uniform; long gray pants, he took his blouse off, but he had slept in his navy woolen jumper.

He got up and sat at his chair by the desk.

He looked down at the innocent girl. Zack wandered what she was dreaming about.

Her expression was so innocent. It was killing him. He just sat there and stared at her for the longest time.

He could have done anything he wanted. He could have leaned down to kiss her. Kiss her face. Kiss her neck. Pick her up with one hand. Lay her down on the floor with him. She would not resist, she would not understand.

Yet he would never do that. He would never taint the one thing that could save him.

Zack moved close to her.

"Kali wake up." He said softly.

Kali's nose twitched.

She moved her head. Then her eyes started to flutter. She woke up. She was a little hazy. She stared looking around her. Then she became confused when she saw him. "Zack?" She asked curiously.

"Good morning." He smiled at her.

"Where am I?"

"You fell asleep on the lounge last night." Zack explained to her.

"And you let me sleep here?" She asked disorientated. She sat up against the pillows. "In your bed? Where did you sleep?"

"In my sleeping bag. On the floor" he ventured.

"But it's freezing."

"I didn't feel it." Zack lied. "You should get up, and get ready. We're going for a surf."

"Huh?" Kali rubbed at her eyes. Still trying to wake up.

"I said we are going to go for a surf."

Kali looked at him confused. She glanced at the alarm clock on the bedside table. "It's not even seven yet."

"I know."

"But it's winter." She complained. "Who gets up, to dawn patrol, on a cold day like this? And besides, it's a week day."

"Haven't you ever gone surfing before school before?"

"No."

"Your brother used to." Zack bit his tongue.

Kali caught his eye. She froze for a second. Then she looked around curiously.

"Isn't it still raining?"

Zack looked out the window. He saw outside what he knew he was going to see: Not a cloud in the sky.

The sun was finally coming up, and there was a reddish hue in the sky. It was going to be a beautiful day. "Look outside." He told her, beaming. "The rain's gone!"

Kali glared at him. She turned her head, and looked around the dimensions of his bedroom. At everything in it, then she took a deep breath in. "Nikita?"

Zack reached forward to touch her shoulder "Nikita."

"I don't have a surfboard...or a wetsuit." Kali said suddenly, sitting up in bed.

"That's ok. We can fix that." He picked up his mobile phone on the desk and started dialing the numbers. "I have to ring Damien and Joel."

They all met up in the parking lot. There was a bit of fog around, but the sun was quickly heating up the cold air. Zack and Kali were waiting by Zack's car.

Damien and Joel drove in to the parking lot in Joel's jeep. They had their surfboards strewn in the back, and they were already suited up in their wetsuits.

Kali had to sneak inside her own house, to grab her board and steamer. Zack had dropped her off on the curb. She had run into her house like a secret agent. She got in and out, in about a minute and a half.

She had already used the public change rooms to change into her wetsuit.

Damien got out of Joel's car and walked over to them. "What do you call this?" he asked sarcastically.

"It's called morning" Zack looked at him amused.

Damien grimaced. "It's not like *you* to be up for the early anymore."

"What can I say? I was inspired this morning."

Damien glanced at Kali. "I'm surprised to see you here Kali. You're up early." He queried her.

Kali shrugged her shoulders. "It's a beautiful day today."

Damien's eyes were burning with confusion and curiosity.

"You could have told us that you were going to bring a beautiful girl with you this morning." Damien winked at Kali.

Kali blushed.

Damien turned to Zack. His eyes were burning into the back of Zack's skull. "I had no idea you two would be up together; this early in the morning."

"I woke Kali up. I knew she'd want to come with us." Zack said belligerently.

"You woke her up." Damien repeated. "With a phone call, or a flick of the wrist?"

Zack grinned. "Wouldn't you like to know?"

Kali shook her head. She blushed again. The tone in her voice was embarrassed. "I went over to Zack's last night to return a jacket that he lent me. I fell asleep on the couch watching 'Chicago Fire'. He let me stay in his bed. He slept on the floor."

Kali explained it clearly. She was embarrassed. Joel was standing behind Damien. They were both listening very attentively.

Damien thought about it for a moment. He looked at Zack one last time, and just shrugged. He wasn't completely satisfied with the answer, but he would deal. "How good was Chicago Fire last night?" he said finally.

"Yeah I know." Zack agreed.

"So." Damien said. He raised his eyebrows and walked along the golden sand beach. "Happy Birthday for yesterday Kali."

Zack did a double take. "What?" He looked at Kali. She blushed for a third time.

"Thank you." She responded nervously to Damien.

"Did you have a nice day?"

Kali nodded and grinned. "Yeah, it was really good."

Damien patted her on the back. "Good, I'm glad."

"Yeah Kali. Happy birthday for yesterday." Joel came up and gave her a quick kiss on the cheek.

"Thanks Joel." She said smiling at him warmly.

She looked down at the ground. Her smiled turned to embarrassment again. "I have to go wax up." She informed them. She headed towards her surfboard, further down on the beach.

"There is a wax comb on my beach towel, Kali, if you need one." Zack called out. She nodded, and quickly kept walking away.

Damien stared at Zack. He was shaking his head obnoxiously. "Thank God you only have a single bed."

Zack smiled mischievously at the remark. Then he shook his head, resolutely. "No, it's not like that. I swear Damien. I would never touch her."

"Well, good, because I don't have to remind you that she's barely fifteen, and there is so much history there. It could bring us all down."

"Alright Damien, I know."

"As long as you know."

Zack nodded.

"So, anyway, how the hell did you know that it was Kali's birthday yesterday?"

"Didn't you know?"

"No."

Damien shrugged. "Belinda told me."

"Belinda? Do you still talk to her?"

"Well, I was *with* her, wasn't I?"

"You hooked up at a party. You were both drunk. You were both upset about her brother. I didn't know it was a relationship."

"Well I am a mature adult Zack. I can cordially keep in touch with the girls that I have been with. I don't just throw them away like you do." Damien shook his head. "Like you did."

Zack scratched his head and looked down. "Ouch."

"Yeah, I know. I'm sorry." Damien sighed and shrugged his shoulders. "Yes, Belinda still talks to me. We get along, or we did. At the moment, she has plenty to say about you. She told me, to tell you, to stay away from her sister."

"Oh, seriously. I knew she had it in for me. She hated me even when I was friends with Ryan."

"Well you weren't exactly at your most promising when you were friends with Ryan."

Zack nodded doubtfully.

"I tried to explain to her that you were just friends with Kali."

"We are just friends."

"Well, Belinda's not exactly convinced." Damien slapped Zack on the back. "But don't worry. I'll make her see the light."

"She's fiery that girl."

"Yeah I know" Damien marveled. "I told you. I slept with her."

Zack nodded. He looked around at the gorgeous beach.

Joel and Kali were already out the back. The beach was bright. The water was glassy. There was only a slight breeze. The waves were about three to four foot, and they were clean.

He knew it would be like this, as soon as he got up this morning. He knew it would be the perfect conditions today, and it was.

God was smiling on him. Zack thought to himself.

Zack had not initially been a Christian, but Joel's Christianity was starting to rub off on him. He appreciated it when good things happened. Like those good things were fate; to make up for all the bad things.

He glanced back at the ocean to see Kali, on her surfboard.

She was sitting out the back, talking to Joel. He couldn't help but feel proud of her. Or jealous of Joel. He felt like he was looking at *his* girl.

Damien picked up his board and ran down the beach. "Last one in is a rotten egg." He called out. It was something they used to say when they were kids.

Zack grabbed his stick and waded into the water. It was high tide, so he quickly lost his footing. He dived under the wave. The cold sensation hit him like he had just dived into a bucket of ice.

It may have been a beautiful day, but the water was still freezing. He started paddling. There was not much resistance. He followed the rip out the back to where Joel was sitting.

Joel was watching him. He was breathing in slowly and he stretched his arms back out behind him.

"I'm glad for the wakeup call this morning. Joel mumbled.

"I'm glad you finally keep your mobile phone turned on. Every time I ring your house, your dad never puts you on the phone."

"That's because he hates you." Joel said frankly. "He hates all my friends, but I woke up with a headache this morning. Now it's gone. I'm glad you called. *I'm glad Kali inspired you.*"

"She's just my friend Joel!" Zack told him, adamantly.

"Good." Joel said graciously "This is my wave." He said enthusiastically. He turned around, paddled, and then he was gone.

"What are you waiting for guys?" Damien called over. He was just a few feet away. He took the third wave of the set, and then he was gone too, momentarily.

Zack looked at Kali "Why didn't you tell me it was your birthday yesterday?"

She shrugged. "I didn't want to make it a big deal."

"You were right there, at my house, and I didn't even know." Zack sighed.

Kali shook her head, embarrassed, then looked out at the ocean. She didn't say anything, she was just scanning the water for ripples and sets on the horizon.

Zack watched her and smiled. "You have the same hunger for surfing that Ryan did." He said softly, not really sure if he meant to say that out loud.

Kali smiled sadly. "Except he was actually good at it."

"We can make you good." Zack nodded. "By the time we're done with you. You'll be ready to surf Hawaii."

Kali giggled. "I don't know about that."

Zack smiled again, then turned to see a wave looming up in the distance. It was in just the right place. It would break at just the right spot. Kali would only have to paddle straight forward to catch it. "This one's yours Kali. Go!"

Kali smiled, and swung her board around. She paddled fast, and got it perfectly.

"Happy birthday for yesterday Kali." He called out, as she rode the wave away.

Zack grinned. He took the next wave in the set, and caught up to Kali in the shore break.

Kali shook her head and laughed. "That was amazing."

Zack looked at the euphoric expression on her face. She was so happy.

Suddenly an idea sprang to his head. A seed was being planted in his imagination.

"Maybe Hawaii's not too out of reach, after all." He suggested, looking off, into the great expanse of ocean. "We'll see."

Chapter 10

Damien:

School was going to be ending in a couple of weeks. Damien Grisham only had one year left, and he didn't know whether he was happy or sad about that.

He knew he was going to have to get himself on the qualifying circuit if he was going to make it on to the glamorous world of surfing. The only world he wanted to be a part of. Yet, the road to getting him there was going to be lonely, and expensive, especially if he didn't win.

He suspected that he was good. Everyone told him as much, but he wasn't the best. Zachary Cummings was the best surfer in this town.

Zack and Damien often battled it out for first place in the junior contests, but Zack usually won in those days when he actually competed, or cared less.

If Damien's own friends were better than he was - what was the rest of the surfing stage look like?Damien and Zack were very different surfers. They could both ride big waves, but their approach to surfing was poles apart. Damien was driven. He surfed using skill. He did it for the passion. Zack just surfed like there was no tomorrow. He surfed to fill the void in his life. He was always right there on the edge, just an inch from falling off it.

Zack couldn't keep it up, but Damien hoped his skill would get him through.

As Damien got home, the front door to his house was unlocked. His mom was usually at work. He figured she had just come home early, but it wasn't the case.

Instead it was his sister Rochelle who was home. She was sitting on the couch.

"Great the circus is back in town." Damien mumbled under his breath. She looked a little *off color* for someone who was only nineteen years old.

"Hi Rochelle."

She looked up startled. "Hi little Brother."

"Nice tattoo." He raised his eyebrows, spying the unicorn tattoo on the back of her shoulder.

"I thought you hated tattoos." She said suspiciously.

Damien sighed. He didn't really know how to talk to his sister anymore. It was getting more difficult every time he saw her. "I don't... but I like that one." He lied.

"You sound so convincing." She mused.

"The tattoo goes well with the nose piercing." He replied.

"Well I thought so too. That's why I got both of them done." She said sarcastically.

"So... how's dad." He queried.

"He's busy with his new wife and daughter. Dad's a tool. If you want to know about dad, then you should ask dad. He's never going to ask about you, or me, and I live with him."

"Not very often you don't."

"Well I hate listening to the baby cry." She said annoyed.

"The last thing dad said to me, when I saw him, was: I better go talk some sense into my sister, because he thinks you're on drugs."

"And then you did."

"And you told me to get lost... In so many words."

"You should have minded your own business."

"Well I tried, but here you are again. So, to what do we owe the pleasure for this time?"

"I have some news."

"Is it that you've graduated crystal meth, and headed straight for the needle?"

"I don't use drugs Damien, not regularly." She moaned.

"Then what are those track marks on your arms?"

"Experimentation."

"Did you really just say that? Can't you just lie, and say you've contracted diabetes or something?"

"There's nothing to worry about little brother."

"Because you can control it?"

"Don't think for a second that you know what my life is like." She said irritated. "Besides, what happened to 'how are you going?"

"How are you going?" He asked dryly.

"I mean… say it again in an upbeat tone." She complained.

"Well, like I said: The last time I saw you, it didn't exactly end on a pleasant note." He commented.

"That's because you were being unreasonable." She protested.

"I was worried about my sister the druggo."

Rochelle suddenly got a faraway look in her eye. "I'm not a druggo, and I'm fine. Thanks for asking."

"Ok then, Rochelle, what have you been up to?"

"Stuff." She said happily. "I want to tell you, but let's talk about *you* first." She gestured. "What have you been up to? Are you still winning those surfing competitions?"

"What do you care about surfing?"

"I don't." She said honestly. "But I do care about you. You used to win those things all the time."

Damien nodded apologetically. "Yeah I'm sorry. I have won a few competitions lately. I'm doing ok."

"That's good." She smiled at him. "And what about your social life. Who's your latest girl?"

Damien shook his head. "I'm not dating anyone at the moment."

"Wow, really? I never thought I'd see the day."

"I broke up with someone a few weeks ago. I'm just concentrating on my studies." He confided in her.

"Well, you really only ever play the field anyway."

"I think it's more than that." Damien said quietly. "But, come on Rochelle, what's your big news.

"Maybe I should wait till mom comes home, and tell you both together."

"No. Why don't you tell me now?" He insisted. "That way I can calm mom down, when you do tell her."

"What is that supposed to mean?"

"Well, I don't know what you're going to say, but is that alcohol on your breath?" He asked blankly. The smell had been distracting him since he sat down.

Rochelle shook her head. "I had one beer."

"Well it smells more like about ten."

"Damien have you ever thought about loosening up for once in your uptight life" She said incredulously. "I mean, do your friends know that you're such a control freak?"

"Don't talk about my friends." He told her sternly. "And, no. Only you and mum know that about me."

"Well it's really annoying, so you might want to work on that."

"I'm just trying to protect my mother." Damien yelled. "She works really hard, and she has nothing, but she sends you money every month, and from the look of it, it goes straight up your arm."

Rochelle suddenly, out of nowhere, slapped him across the face.

He looked out the window and took a deep breath in.

"I'm sorry." She said, disorientated.

Damien's face was stinging. "I don't want to fight with you Rochelle."

He looked at his sister. She was so upset. She sobbed softly to herself. It was hurtful because it was true. He knew that.

"Tell me your news Rochelle. I'll be happy for you, I promise."

Rochelle dried her eyes slowly, and then jumped up. She sat on the edge of the couch next to him. She held out her hand, and flicked her bony fingers. "I'm getting married!" she told him excitedly. She held her hand out further, so Damien could get a better look at the tiny diamond chip in her engagement ring.

Damien had to dig deep to force a smile on his face. "But you're just a teenager, you're only nineteen."

"I'm twenty next month, or did you forget?"

"I didn't forget… Who is this guy?"

"His name is John."

"John?" Damien repeated dryly.

"Damien." She cried. "You said you'd be happy, you could at least show a little bit of excitement." Rochelle made a face.

"No I am. I'm just surprised" he said, nervously. "I didn't know you were seeing anyone serious."

"We've been going out for six months, and he popped the question already." She grinned. "He loves me so much."

"So soon?" Damien asked softly.

"What is your problem?"

"Well, don't you think you should straighten yourself out, before you get married?"

"Straighten out what exactly?"

"I don't know, your life. Your family. Your finances." Damien paused, "your sobriety."

"What does sobriety mean?"

Damien grimaced. "It means... well it means sober."

"Far out Damien what is your problem? Mum will be happy for me."

"Mum doesn't know what you're doing to yourself Rochelle."

"Please don't screw this up for me Damien?"

"I just don't think this will last."

"You don't even know him!" She screamed.

"I don't need to know him, I know you."

"What is your problem?" She asked him for a third time.

"You don't even have a job, and now you're committing to this, for the rest of your life."

"I'm getting married Damien. I'm not joining a cult."

"You can't do this. I mean what is he? Your dealer?"

Rochelle's face went bright red. "What would you know? You go through more girlfriends than Hugh Hefner." She shrugged her shoulders. "You are so out of line right now. You have no idea what goes on in my life."

"Well your right about that." He looked her squarely in the face. "Why don't you tell me?"

Rochelle looked away. "Everyone else in the world gets excited about weddings, except for you. Seriously, you have issues Damien."

"Oh, *I* have issues?" He said irritated.

Then something made him stop. He toned his voice down, and looked around.

"I'm sorry." He said slowly. "I am happy for you. That is exciting news."

Damien looked at the floor, in front of him. He felt his chest go tight, and his palms start to sweat. He felt anxious again.

He never told anyone about it, but sometimes anxiety troubled him. Like when he was worried about his sister, or his mother, or money. Or when he came off his shift at the surf shop, and had a bunch of school assignments to do.

Damien really needed to get on track. He needed to go somewhere where he could test his limits, and push his boundaries, and make his life his own. His sister scared him, and so did his future.

He needed to secure a future away from all this. He just had to figure out how to do that.

Damien sighed. "So, tell me about your fiancé...." He said hopefully

Chapter 11

Damien:

"I want to take her to Hawaii."

Joel looked at Damien. "Caroline?" he asked, shocked.

Damien had a good look at Zack's face. He had seen the glint in Zack's eyes for a couple of weeks now. Zack had been planning this for two weeks and, he hadn't said anything about it. Not to Damien, who was thinking exactly the same thing – except without the girl.

"He's not talking about Caroline." Damien told Joel, bluntly.

"Then who?"

Zack didn't answer.

"Kali" Damien said, incredulously.

"What."

Zack nodded. "I'm serious. I want to take the girl to the islands."

"Why?" Damien asked, curiously.

"Why not." Zack deflected.

"Because it's insane."

"No, it's not, and you know it's not." Zack looked Damien in the eye. "It's time."

Damien caught Zack's eye. "I know, but you can't take her."

"What the hell are you guys talking about?" Joel said, unsure of what was going on.

Damien ignored Joel. "When?"

"At the end of the next school year. After we finish our HSC exams."

Damien shook his head. "You can't take her to Hawaii, Zack."

"I have to."

81

"No, you don't." he said emphatically.

"Yeah, I really do Damien. You don't understand."

"What's to understand? She's a fifteen-year-old girl Zack. Are you out of your fucking mind?"

"No, I'm not." Zack said exasperated. "I know exactly what I'm doing. We have to get her away from all this.

"Away from all what." Damien asked incredulously.

"She's drowning. She hangs out with those bitches she calls friends. Her sister is leaving for Sydney. Her dad ignores her. Trust me, if I ask her to come, she'll come."

"It's not about asking her. It's about being responsible for her."

"I know what I'm responsible for." Zack said reflectively.

"This is the first time you have ever talked about going Hawaii. It kind of bothers me that she's the one that inspired it"

Zack looked away and grimaced. "Who cares who inspired it? We are talking about Hawaii."

"I know." Damien breathed it in. "I know what it means." He said again.

Damien looked around the school yard from the vantage point of his school bench. It was nearly the end of lunch time. The bell would ring soon.

Zack had probably, deliberately, started this conversation at the end of lunch, so they wouldn't have time to argue with him.

Damien wished terribly that he had the whole story. He was playing some sort of game with Kali, and no one else was in on it.

"Look Zack" Damien said, trying to speak realistically. "She's obviously not ready for Hawaii. I'm not even sure *we* are ready for Hawaii."

"We can train."

"You can't train someone, in a few months, to surf the North Shore of Oahu."

"Well it's a year." Zack articulated. "And Kali can surf Waikiki. I'll take her there myself. She can just hang out. I don't expect her to surf the North Shore."

"What if she decides *she* wants to? You'll get her killed Zack."

"I'll protect her."

"You can't protect anyone on Hawaii. You know that."

"Well I can trust her. She's shy. She won't get into any trouble. She'll make it."

"What you're proposing is so dangerous. Instead of going over there to have fun, and get girls, you would be taking one, and would have to look after her."

"She can look after herself." Zack said irritated "She deserves a chance at happiness."

Damien glanced at Joel. "Far out Zack, what is your interest in this girl?" He shook his head. "What do you really want with her?"

Zack whimpered. "Nothing."

"No, there's something. We all know how far this goes back."

Damien glanced at Joel.

Joel didn't know all the details about what had transpired back in the day. He only knew what happened at the beach, when Kali got hurt. He was just sitting there cautiously watching them fight it out. He was curious and perplexed, but he didn't say anything.

"It's what her brother wanted." Zack mumbled finally.

Damien was taken aback for a moment. "What do you mean by that?"

"Ryan was going to take her to Hawaii. After graduation he wanted to live there for a while. He wanted to take Kali with him."

"You're not her brother Zack."

Zack turned away. "I know." He chewed on his bottom lip for a moment. "Her brother's dead."

"Well you're not responsible for that. You don't have to fill his shoes." Damien said desperately.

"You don't get it Damien." Zack told him, sorrowfully.

Damien didn't get it. For some reason Zack had an enormous guilt complex about Ryan Lockhart's death.

It was strange, because Damien was sure their friendship had ended, long before that fateful day. They were barely acquaintances when Ryan got killed.

Zack closed his eyes, and spoke hastily. "Just let me talk to her." He said flatly. "She can make up her own mind."

Damien nodded. He didn't quite understand yet, but apparently; this was the way it had to be.

Zack was right. Kali was part of this equation whether they liked it or not.

He would just have to go with it: If this was the only way it was going to happen. He wasn't going to fight it. He wasn't going to interfere. He would have to swallow his doubts.

This was what Zack wanted, and Zack wouldn't be talked out of anything. Wild horses couldn't drag him off this particular cliff.

Besides, this was going to happen anyway. She would come. They would face the danger, together, head on.

Zack didn't put it up for debate. He would not tolerate any argument.

Damien watched him closely. Zack breathed in deeply and grabbed his back pack. He got up, and shook his head.

"Damien, get on board or get out of my way. I'm taking Kali to Hawaii next winter. If you don't agree, I will have no trouble going without you." Zack turned his head, and looked at Joel. "Joel, the same goes for you."

Zack walked off, and Damien watched him go.

Joel looked at Damien incredulously. "What the hell was that about? Next winter?"

Damien nodded. "The Hawaiian winter." He sighed. "Just think about Joel."

"I can't believe it." Joel said shrugging.

Damien shook his head. "No, you can. You just don't know it yet."

Joel nodded, confused.

Damien got up and started walking to class. Then the bell rang.

Chapter 12

Zack:

Maybe it was all happening too fast, but for Zack, it felt like it was out of his hands. The decision had been made, and it didn't even feel like he made it.

It felt like, some force of nature, had made it. They had to go to Hawaii. It was in the stars, and it was destiny.

Having something to look forward to, meant the world to Zack. Without it, he might relapse into his melancholic state of mind. He didn't want to feel that way, and he didn't want to be back there again.

Now that he knew about this plan, he woke up excited every morning. His life had purpose.

The only problem was: the pieces weren't all on the board yet.

He was staring at one of the pieces right now.

"What did you really ask me here for?" Kali asked curiously. "So, we could play on your swings?"

Zack smiled at her. He had asked Kali to come over to his house. He was desperate to talk to her.

He waited outside the house and when she turned up, he took out to the backyard. His swing set from years ago was still operating, along with his trampoline.

"No I just wanted to talk to you." He said quietly.

"Talk about what?" Kali asked curiously.

"I don't know, just stuff."

Kali shrugged nervously. "Well, you start first."

Zack laughed. "Well, don't put me on the spot like that."

"I'm always put on the spot." Kali said suddenly. "They want to know what happens between you and me, and Damien and Joel and I tell them nothing, but because I'm so quiet, they think I'm hiding something. They don't believe me. They keep talking about me behind my back and asking me weird questions."

"Who's them?"

"I don't know. The girls."

"The mean girls." Zack said stoutly.

"They're not all mean, but I'm always shy around them."

"Don't worry about them." Zack said dismissively.

"Don't worry about them?" She asked indignantly. "The girls that I hang out with every day?"

"Zack put his hand under her chin and forced her to look up. "You're a beautiful articulate girl. You are just as good as they are."

Kali looked away. "Yeah right." She shook her head. "And I'm not."

"Don't doubt yourself." He told her, but as he stared her, she looked so hurt and unsure. "You talk to me easily enough." He exclaimed.

"It's easy around you."

"For me too." Zack climbed up on to the trampoline, and beckoned to Kali to join him. "Come sit up here with me."

Kali looked around slowly and then started to climb up on the trampoline. She sat quaintly next to Zack, but not too close. She was wearing a yellow skirt and a red t shirt.

The hotter than expected spring sun was beating down on them.

Kali shook her head. "It's a nice breeze."

Zack stared at her. "Kali, I have to ask you something." He began. "But I have to tell you something first." He continued slowly. "You'll never forgive me, but... It's just... I have to get you to agree to what I have to ask you... But it will be hard when you hate me."

Kali moved closer to Zack. She put her hand on his shoulder. "Zack, you're not making any sense." She smiled at him. "But whatever it is, it's ok."

"No it's not." He shook his head. "I have to explain."

"What." Kali asked softly.

"I never really talk about it." Zack mumbled. He looked at a patch of grass, on the ground, in the distance. "But I have to tell you something now."

"What is it?" She asked again curiously.

"It's going to hurt Kali."

"Tell me."

Zack closed his eyes and took a deep breath.

When he opened them, Kali had shuffled closer to him. Zack looked at her. She was sitting with her legs crossed.

Without even knowing it, His hand was on her leg. He let it fall under her skirt, onto the inside of her thigh.

"I was in trouble before." He admitted. "I was angry at the world, and I made this friend. He was older than me, really popular. He was always at the beach as well." He hesitated. "His mum left, so he was going through the same thing I was."

"My brother." Kali said softly

Zack nodded.

Kali closed her eyes. He continued stroking her inner thigh, with his fingers.

"He could have had any girl he wanted and…" Zack looked away "Once we got cocky. We met this girl. She was kind of naive. Kind into both of us. We were all so high on something. So Ryan laid her down at the surf club and then he took her, and then I…"

Kali eyelids fluttered, incredulously. Zack's was moving his hand even further up her thigh.

Zack didn't mean to do it. He was distracting her. He was re-creating the mood so she could see, how it could so easily, happen.

She closed her mouth and nodded. His fingers were tantalizing her. There was a euphoric look on her face.

"But of course the girl got pregnant. She didn't know who the father was, so she had an abortion, and we both felt awful. That's when our friendship ended."

Kali stared at him breathlessly. She looked like she was about to melt.

Zack continued to stroke her, as he watched her, watching him.

She looked him in the eyes. Then he finally said it out loud. "That's *why* our friendship ended." He told her.

His kept staring at her, as his hand steadily rose up. His finger moving in a circle over her soft skin. Up and up, then finally his fingers were brushing up against her underwear. Kali froze like a statue. She moaned involuntarily. Zack took his hand away.

He looked in Kali's eyes. "I'm sorry kali."

Kali looked at him for a long time, breathing in deeply. "No, I get it." She whispered, still breathing heavily. She looked so hot and bothered, it looked to be hurting her. "I figured he wasn't a saint."

Zack shook his head and buried his face in his hands. He was actually starting to cry, he could feel tears in his eyes. "Kali it was a different time." He moaned, trying to explain.

"Yeah. I've seen 'puberty blues' Zack I get it."

"We were going through a lot. We were just letting off some steam, but we didn't think of the consequences"

Zack was trying desperately to make her understand. It's just that she wasn't as upset as he thought she'd be.

"Kali looked down somberly at the same patch of grass Zack had been staring at.

"Kali I want you to have something." Zack reached in his pocket and pulled out a jewelry box. "It's for your birthday, that I missed." He opened the small box and showed it to her.

"It's a necklace." Kali said, stating the obvious.

"It's for you…if you like it. I saw it in the window of the jewelry store and it made me think of you." Zack carefully took hold of the thin gold necklace with the turtle charm.

"It's pretty." Kali said, confused.

"You're pretty." He slipped it around her neck and fasted the clasp. "Would you forgive me for something, if I asked you to?"

"For what." She asked, slightly disorientated.

Zack took a huge breath in. "I was in the car."

"What?"

"We were drunk. We were out at this party. I was talking to your brother. I hadn't seen him in ages. We got into an argument over who the best surfer was. Then, we went to check beach conditions at one-o-clock in the morning. That's when he had the accident. That's when the car spun out, and we lost control. I was thrown clear. I was in the car when your brother died. He was driving, but I didn't stop him. I was just as drunk as he was."

Kali put her hands across her mouth. "What?"

Zack started crying and couldn't control it. He was practically convulsing.

"You brother was with me when he died." He said, burying his face in his hands again. "We were both drunk. We were both there when the car crashed, but I got myself clear." He shook his head "I'm sorry Kali. I'm so sorry." He sobbed helplessly.

"I didn't know?"

"Nobody knows. Nobody knows anything about it, except me. I rang the cops from a pay phone, but he died instantly. That's what the coroner said. It was too late."

Kali looked stunned. She didn't seem to know what to say. Zack was crying so hard he couldn't control himself.

"I'm so sorry Kali." Zack reached out and and cried on her shoulder. He held her body so tightly, and close, that he could have been hurting her. He just couldn't let her go.

Kali rearranged herself, so that she was holding him back.

His hands were against her bare skin underneath her t-shirt. He pulled her even closer.

He could see she was crying too. There were many tears streaming down her face.

He kissed her neck. "I'm so sorry Kali." He kissed her cheek. "I'm so sorry." Then it happened. He started kissing her lips. Hard and deep. For a long time.

He pushed her back on the trampoline. He was practically on top of her.

They rolled to the side, and she gave as good as she got. She was pushing back into him, and kissing him passionately.

The kissing was feverish, almost violent. Zack ripped off her shirt. Then he took off his shirt so he could be closer to her. He felt his skin touch hers.

Kali was wearing a bikini top for some reason. His kisses moved across her face, and her chin, and then back on her mouth. He put his hands all over her body, and kissed her mouth so hard; he was practically sucking the air out of her lungs.

Finally a warning bell sounded in Zack's brain. He had to stop. He literally had to separate himself, because they were so intertwined.

Kali was just a girl. An innocent girl. But she didn't know her own strength. He actually had to *pry* her away, because she was holding on so tightly.

As Zack unraveled himself, away from her. He accidentally pushed her.

She flew forward. She flew so far forward that she fell off the trampoline. He hadn't meant to push her so hard, but he had to separate himself.

For crying out loud, he had to stop this madness. He pushed her, and heard her moan, when she hit the ground.

"Are you alright?" Zack sprung forward. He jumped down to the ground, next to her.

"I'm fine." Kali got up obviously hurt, and humiliated.

"We can't do this Kali."

She stared at him "I know."

"I didn't mean to hurt you. Not again."

"I'm not hurt." She said brushing herself off.

"I can't do this, not with you."

"Of course not." She mumbled.

"I don't want to taint you."

"Taint me?"

"I don't want to use you, Kali. You're my friend."

"I have to go." She said quickly. She was slightly limping, but she quickly tried to walk away.

"Kali." He called after her, but she didn't turn around. Soon she was out of sight.

Zack looked down at the ground, starting to cry again. He kneeled down when he saw something gold in the dirt. It was her necklace. It had come off, when she had fallen.

Zack sat down on the ground and stared at it. The band had snapped. It was broken.

Chapter 13

Kali:

Kali was walking to class when she felt someone pull on her wrist. She turned, and looked up suddenly. It was Zack. He stood there for a moment looking at her. He was studying her with an air of caution in his face.

His grip was really tight. She couldn't move, as he clutched on to her arm.

"Hi" He said softly. He looked down and let go. Then he rigidly stepped back, as if he was afraid of hurting her.

"Hi." Kali said, distracted. He had seemed to come out of nowhere.

"How are you?" Zack asked.

Kali hesitated. "Ok."

Kali wasn't sure what to do. She walked slowly, and uncertainly, out of the science building towards her next class. Zack walked beside her.

He didn't say anything for a moment. Then he opportunistically, ushered her off the main pathway, into the clearing. He found a random bench and sat down on it.

Kali clutched her folder to her chest. She slowly sat down next to him. She looked at the ground, instead of looking in his eyes.

"I noticed you've been ignoring my phone calls, and texts all week."

"Yeah I've been busy." She said unconvincingly.

"Do you hate me?"

Kali shook her head, although she still refused to look at him. "Why would I hate you?"

"Why *wouldn't* you hate me?" Zack asked incredulously. "If it wasn't for me, your brother would still be alive."

Kali swung her legs back and forth, and slowly shook her head. "That's not true." She told him. "You think I wouldn't just be glad, that someone made it out of that horrible mess alive?"

"Yeah I would" he commented. "But I'm sure you'd prefer it'd be your brother."

"I'm sure I'd prefer not to think about it." Kali countered him.

"So you don't blame me?"

Kali ran her fingers through her hair. "No, of course not." She said blankly. "You blame yourself enough for the both of us."

Zack smirked to himself. "Well, you may not hate me, but you're definitely mad at me."

"For what?" Kali mumbled softly. She started biting her fingernails. She was still looking down at the ground, away from Zack.

"For kissing you? Or for what your brother and I used to get up to? I don't know. Pick a reason. I'm sure you have the right to be mad at me for something."

"Why do you treat me like I'm any other girl?" Kali asked suddenly. "I'm a surfer, and surfers are generally pretty laid-back people. I don't get my panties in a twist about much. I'm sure your hormones got the best of you then. Like mine got the best of me on Saturday morning. I know you have a girlfriend. I know you were just upset." She paused. "I know my brother went off the rails for a while. I know he had a reason too, and so did you." Kali finally looked at him. "It was breast cancer right? Your mother had breast cancer?"

Zack looked away. He seemed completely shocked and exposed. He couldn't speak for a moment, then finally he wiped his eyes, with the cuff of his sleeve. "Yeah."

Kali nodded solemnly. "Belinda finally explained it to me. I didn't know. I'm sorry Zack."

Zack nodded. He shook his head confused. He clearly didn't want to get into this now, but suddenly he couldn't fight it anymore. Tears sprang to his eyes again.

Kali watched him, feeling bad, but there was nothing she could do.

"I've never cried in front of anyone before." Zack admitted. His voice was muffled by the sobs. "Not even at the funeral." He looked at her desperately. "I've cried in front of you twice now."

"It's Ok." She told him softly. She paused for a moment then cautiously put her hand on his shoulder.

He cried and she watched him. She felt so powerless.

Finally, Zack caught his breath. He looked up. He tried to compose himself somewhat. He took a deep breath in. He reached in his pocket and pulled something shiny out.

"This is yours Kali."

It was the gold necklace with the turtle charm. It was the one he had given her on Saturday.

"I thought I had lost that." Kali said shocked.

"The band at the bottom snapped, but I had it fixed." Zack explained. He held him palm open flat, so she could take hold of it.

Kali thought about it for a moment, but then she shook her head.

"Thank you." She said slowly. "It's beautiful, but you should give it to Caroline... She's your girlfriend."

"I want you to have it?" He said exasperated. "It's a birthday present."

"You should give it to her." Kali said, holding her ground. It was hurting her to do it. She wanted the necklace more than anything in the world.

Zack shrugged. "I can't, and even if I could; this would never be for her anyway."

"What do you mean?"

"I broke up with Caroline. In fact, she dumped me."

"She dumped you." Kali said, surprised.

"Yeah. She started yelling at me, about getting sand in her car again. I guess that was the last straw. We got into a fight, and she told me to go to hell. So I guess that means we're not together."

Kali shook her head. "This isn't the first time you have broken up with her."

"Yeah, but it's the last." Zack said.

He suddenly got a strange look in his eyes. He sat up straight, and then turned to Kali, taking her hand. He looked excited about something.

"The stars are aligning Kali. I won't have time for a girlfriend now." He said eagerly. "Tomorrow I start training. I'm going to Hawaii at the end of next year."

"Hawaii?" Kali asked quickly. "You're leaving."

Kali felt weak. One more person who was going to leave her. The thought was overwhelming. It made her feel sick to her stomach.

"No." Zack shook his head. "We are leaving." He smiled at her. "You have to come with me."

"Huh?"

"You're coming with me." He told her incredulously. "I want you to come with me, to Hawaii?" He said again, as if it was obvious.

"You want me to what? Go with you... to Hawaii?" Kali asked confused. She couldn't make the words make sense in her brain. "But I would never be a big wave surfer." She said dumbfounded. "Why would you want *me* to go?"

"The North Shore isn't the only beach on the island Kali."

"But it's the one you're going to surf."

"Don't worry about me. You can surf Waikiki or go exploring. Anything you want."

She looked at him, confused again. "But you would take me with you?" she asked stunned.

"If you want to go."

"But of course I want to go. Why wouldn't anyone not want to go?"

"Beats me?"

"But I mean you would do that for me?" She asked again, trying to clarify. "You would just…take me with you?"

Zack looked in her eyes. "Yes. I would."

Kali had to take a moment. She was simply overwhelmed for a second, and she had never felt so elated before. "But what if you get hurt? Or something happens" She asked him suddenly.

"That's the chance you take." He squeezed her hand. "You wouldn't be human if we weren't scared Kali."

"And you wouldn't look very human if your body smashed into the reef, and you lost all my air on impact."

"That wouldn't happen."

Kali shrugged her shoulders. "Why not? It happens all the time. You live in the real world more than anyone in this school." She cried. "You don't have your own force field you know."

"I'm going to train, Kali. I'll take my chances."

She shook her head vigorously. "And what about me? You want me to stand on the shore waiting, and hoping nothing bad happens to you?" She asked. "You want me to just sit on the sidelines."

"You would be on Hawaii! You would be too distracted to care what I'm doing! You could go snorkeling or go see the turtles."

"You can't bench me Zack. What if I wanted my chance too?"

Zack was caught off guard. "I don't know." He said exasperated. "I don't know if I could let you."

Kali's head was swimming. So many different ideas were suddenly in her head. "I'm not good enough, am I?"

Zack looked at her in disbelief. "This isn't how this conversation went in my head. I thought you would be freaked out because you thought I *wanted* you to surf the North Shore. Now I'm freaked out because you actually want to surf it."

"I don't think I could surf it." Kali mumbled softly.

"Yeah, but you jumped over the part where I had to convince you to go."

Kali shook her head, "You actually think I wouldn't go? If you care enough to take me." Kali asked incredulously. "But I have to go Zack." She told him desperately. "I can't be left behind again."

Zack looked at her tenderly. "I'm glad you'd feel that way." He said, confused. "I didn't even think you'd let me talk to you in the first place."

"I have to go Zack." Kali said definitively. "Please don't go without me." She said, suddenly hysterical. Tears were springing to *her* eyes.

Zack held her hand even tighter. "It's ok Kali. I already invited you."

Kali started crying helplessly. "I accept. Please don't go without me." She said again.

Zack nodded at her, modestly. "I won't."

Kali helplessly wiped away her tears, with her free hand. "But you wouldn't just invite me." She said trying to figure this out. "What about the others? Damien would go. Would Joel go?"

"Joel is going to go, but you can't tell anyone. His dad would never let him take this trip."

"So, he's just going to sneak out?"

"Straight through the window." Zack said ironically.

"Kali made a face. "And Should I train with you guys." She asked still dumbfounded.

Zack looked at her concerned. "Not like we train Kali."

"But some days."

"Yeah" Zack said hesitantly. "Damien could work out an exercise program for you, personally. He's good at that kind of stuff." He looked in her eyes. "So, you'll come."

"Yes. Of course I'll come."

Zack opened his palm up again, in his other hand. "Would you take this Kali?"

He was referring back to the gold necklace in his hand. Kali stared at it for a long time. Then she finally nodded.

Zack laid it around her neck.

Kali held her hair up. Zack fastened the clasp.

Zack bent over and put his mouth near her ear.

"I'm sorry about the weekend, but I can never kiss you again Kali." He whispered, so close to her ear that she could feel his lips touch her ear lobe. "It wouldn't be good: Not for me. Not for you. Not for Damien, or Joel, or for your reputation at this school. I can never do that again."

Kali fell back down to earth.

Zack moved back to his seat. Kali took the gold turtle charm in her fingers and played with it.

"I know." She said sorrowfully.

"But you'll come with me to Hawaii?" He asked again.

"Yes." She caught his eye "I promise I'll go, if you promise you'll take me. No matter what?"

Zack nodded. "Good." He said breathlessly. "It's a deal."

Kali looked at him disorientated as if this was a dream. A really good dream.

Zack nodded. He put his arm around her, and he she rested her head on his shoulder. Kali could feel the warmth of his body. They waited there until the next bell rang so they could go to their next class.

Chapter 14

Kali:

"Hi Kali."

Kali looked across the lane, but Joel wasn't there. He was busy speeding up to the shallow end of the pool. As part of their training, they were swimming laps, to keep fit.

Kali shook her head. It couldn't have been Joel anyway, because the voice had belonged to a girl. The voice seemed to have come from above her.

"What's up?" The voice spoke again.

Kali looked across to the next swimming lane. A young girl slid down into the next row, on her right. Kali didn't really recognize her at first, but it was another girl from her school. Kali looked closer and realized it was a girl in the same year. She was pretty; her name was Rebecca, but everyone at school called her Becky.

"Hi Becky" Kali said shyly.

"Hey I didn't know you swum laps." The girl said. She was fiddling with her hair cap, and adjusting her goggles.

"Oh, I don't usually. I'm…" *just in training to surf with Kelly Slater at the pipeline.* Kali hesitated. "I just, come down here, sometimes." She said evasively.

"Is that Joel Geller over there?"

Kali looked cautiously over at Joel who was sharing a lane with her. Presently, he was heading back down toward her. Steam rolling down the pool. "Yeah" she admitted.

"Yeah I heard about that."

"About what?"

Becky didn't answer her. "It's so much work this year, hey?" She said idly, looking at Kali.

"Yeah, I guess, but it is school certificate time. So, it's bound to be pretty hard." She replied, nervously.

"I know." Becky sighed. "But I'm looking forward to the end of it."

Joel appeared swimming freestyle. He turned quickly and pushed against the wall. Then he was speeding away in the other direction. He was clearly a strong swimmer.

"We're in the same math class, aren't we?" Kali asked.

"The girl shrugged her shoulders. "Are we?"

"I think so." She replied. "How are you going with that Geometry stuff we are doing?" Kali tried to start a conversation, but it rarely worked well.

"I'm ok." Becky huffed. "My mom can explain all that stuff to me better than our stupid teacher."

Kali nodded. Talking about mothers, was a touchy subject.

"Yeah I guess." Kali mumbled. She couldn't think of anything more to say, and that was about as much conversation as she was comfortable with anyway.

She put her goggles down and was about to start swimming when the girl started talking to her again.

"Are you going to introduce me?" Becky asked, as Joel swum back down.

Kali lowered her head. Joel hit the wall, and stood upright against the diving platform. "What are you waiting for?" Joel reached over and slapped Kali on the back. "I've done ten laps, to your one."

"I was just talking to my fr… I was talking to Becky." She looked across at Becky. "Joel this is Becky. Becky this is Joel."

Joel looked confused for a moment.

He tried to catch Kali's eye, but she wouldn't let him, so he looked at the girl in the opposite lane. He vaguely nodded. "Hi."

"Hi." Becky said; falling all over herself to get his attention. "You're pretty fast."

"Yeah I was just finishing up." Joel said, running his fingers through his hair.

"I'm amazed you get the time to come swimming, with all your commitments. Especially now you're in year twelve, and you're the school captain."

Kali nodded and smiled at Joel.

Getting voted school captain, was the one thing that finally helped Joel believe in himself. It was good for his confidence, and self-esteem. It also, finally, helped him prove himself to his father.

The class vote itself had been practically unanimous. Almost everyone at school wanted Joel to lead them.

"Well I guess it's all about will power." he hesitated. "And inspiration." He said finally. "The more you're inspired. The more you can find the energy to do." Joel laughed at himself. "I have a lot to do this year."

"Adrenalin too." Kali giggled.

Joel reached over and touched Kali's shoulder. "Yeah, we're going to need a lot of that." He laughed easily.

Becky's face turned red. She looked at Kali.

Nobody knew about their plan to go to Hawaii, so every time they talked about it, it was like an inside joke. The innuendo seemed to irritate others.

Certainly no one else thought it was funny that Kali was hanging out with the most popular guys in school.

"School captain, swimming and School. I don't know how he finds time for his *girlfriend!*" Kali over emphasized the point since Joel was still going out with Justine.

"So." Becky ignored her. "How are you helping us students, these days?" She tried to flirt with him, while not getting the point.

"Well..." Joel began uncertainly. "We have weekly meeting and.,."

Kali wasn't in the mood for it. She put her head down and pushed against the wall. She started stroking the water and did four laps of freestyle. Finally, she got back to Joel. He was still talking to Becky. He looked very uncomfortable.

Kali stood up and watched him. "I really should be going." He told Becky and then glanced at Kali. "We really should be going."

"Oh, ok, well maybe I'll see you at school then." Becky said. "See you Kali." She gestured, and put her goggles back down. She quickly started a lap of breaststroke.

"Who was that?" Joel asked, digging his finger into his ear.

"A girl in my math class." Kali told him flatly, then she turned around to jump out of the water." I think she has a crush on you."

"One of your friends?"

"No." Kali got out of the pool. She walked over to get her towel from the bench.

Joel followed her, and called out to Zack and Damien. They were swimming in a lane further down the pool.

Kali was supposed to get a lift home with Zack today.

Kali went into the girl's locker room, and dried herself. She got changed into a simple white sundress and a delicate knitted beanie. It was really cold outside so she threw on a blue jacket.

Zack was already waiting for her as she came out of the locker room. He was wearing some track pants and a sweater. He looked so handsome, no matter what he wore.

Damien and Joel had already left. Those guys usually just wrapped a towel around their waist, and took a shower when they got home.

"I'm sorry I made you wait for me." Kali muttered softly. "I think I might walk home."

She didn't wait for him to reply. She walked out through the reception area and stood outside. She hadn't even done her jacket up. The cold air made her shiver.

"Why do you do this?"

"What?"

"Why do you always run away? Why are you so afraid to accept anyone's help?" He said flustered. "I told you I'd give you a lift home. So that's what I'll do."

"I just feel like walking is all."

"No you don't, you're exhausted. Just look at you."

Kali *was* actually exhausted, but she shook her head. "I don't live very far away."

Zack was annoyed. "You look so ominous in that white dress." He shook his head. "Why are you wearing a dress for? It's freezing."

Kali shrugged. "I don't know." He walked over to her, and literally zipped up her jacket, for her.

"I just didn't want to bother you." She told him. "Don't you have a study session with Melissa tonight?"

"Do I?" He asked, then stomped his foot on the footpath. "Damn it, I do to." He looked at Kali and laughed. He stepped back away from her. "Driving you home isn't going to make me late for my study session."

Kali shrugged. "Ok then, fine, take me home."

"Good I will then." He said annoyed.

Kali headed for his car. "It's getting easier." She murmured. "I can do ten laps in a row, and I hardly feel a thing. It used to hurt before."

"Are we putting too much pressure on you Kali?"

"No, I can handle it." She said.

"Look at those clothes hanging off you, you're so skinny." He said that even though he wasn't looking at her.

"No I'm not."

"You're so frustrating." He said. "Why don't you talk to me?"

"I do." Kali stuttered.

"I need to know how you're going. Are you really ok with this?"

"Don't you see how hard I'm trying?" She pleaded with him.

"I do see. That's what I'm worried about - that we're pushing too hard."

"You're not responsible for me Zack."

"Yes I am. I want to be responsible for you. I want to know how you're going."

"I can handle it." Kali said uncomfortably. "What about you?" She prodded him. "What about Melissa? What if, by the time you finish your HSC, you want to take someone else, instead of me?"

"It's a school project with Melissa, not a date Kali. Besides, I'm committed to this."

"But Melissa's one of the cool kids?"

Zack stared at her for a long time. "So are you."

"That girl in the pool only talked to me because I was friends with Joel."

"What girl in the pool?"

"It's all the same." Kali explained obliviously. "When they see me with you guys, they look at me with venom in their eyes. Every time I turn around, some girl is throwing a knife at my back."

"Then don't turn around. Keep your eye on the prize"

"Which is?"

"Us." Zack blurted out. "Your future. This trip."

"It doesn't feel real yet." She blubbered.

"It will be real. It will be *so* real." He assured her.

"I know it will be." She agreed.

"Kali you're coming with us, but it's not going to be easy. You have to want it." He walked towards his car in the carpark, and Kali walked beside him. "No one rides for free, Kali."

"I do want it. I like the training." She looked down at the road. "But I get lost in between your world and theirs."

As they got to his car, Zack stepped forward and grabbed her by the shoulders. "I'll take care of you. You're in my world now." He told her, then looked deep within her eyes.

Then suddenly he leaned down and kissed her on the mouth. He held it just a moment, but just as quickly, he pulled away.

"Sorry Kali…. I didn't mean… Just get in the car. I'll drive you home."

Kali got in the car nervously, then she just heard Zack mumble to himself... She only just heard it.

"Damn it." He grumbled. "I can never touch her again."

Chapter 15

Zack:

"What's wrong?" Zack asked Kali.

This morning, they were all so excited during their airport transfer, but now Kali looked a little lost.

They were currently sitting at the airport, food court counter, eating lunch, and they were just about to leave the country in an hour or so.

Right in front of where they were sitting, were the massive glass panels of the airport terminal. They were looking directly at the brilliant view of the whole airport.

Zack had been watching the parade of airliners that rolled into their gate. They were such massive planes. Zack never fully understood how they could get something, so heavy, into the air.

On the ground there were many airport employees. They drove their little golf buggies around the tarmac. With big luggage trailers, that went right up to the aircrafts. The baggage handlers were all hard at work with their florescent green vests on. They loaded, or unloaded, the luggage in the cargo hold. Depending on weather the plane was arriving or departing.

In the distance Zack could see the runway, and he could literally see the planes progress as they came into land. They touched down on the concrete, and then gradually slowed down, as the pilot slammed on the breaks.

Then there was a blind spot where the plane would disappear behind a building. Then the plane would remerge being towed into its gate.

On the opposite runway Zack could see the planes speed up, and then simply fly up into the air. It was the most fantastic view, but somehow Zack lost sight of it. All he could see was Kali's sombre face reflected in the glass.

It was dark and cloudy outside. That's why her image was so strong, in the glass.

Kali almost choked on a chip she was eating, as she snapped back to reality. She looked up to see him staring at her.

Kali's cheeks flushed red. "Just a little nervous." She said doubtfully.

Zack looked her in the eyes, and smiled. He reached over and took a couple of her fries, from her McDonalds chip container. Zack had finished his meal ages ago, but of course Kali was still eating. She ate at a snail's pace, and she hardly ever finished her meals.

Kali relaxed a notch and smiled back at him.

"The lady at the check in counter, didn't have to be such a bitch about our surfboards." Zack said softly.

"I know." Damien said, flustered. "And why do we have to come so many hours early?" He argued. "I'm so sick of all this waiting."

Kali started giggling to herself. "It's a fourteen-hour flight." She reminded him

Joel started laughing as well, and then Zack joined in. He smirked at Damien. "She's right dude. Why don't you get out your colouring books or something?"

"Fuck off." Damien told Zack. He smiled at Kali. "Just ignore me for the next fifteen hours."

Kali grinned at him. "I do know what you mean. At least when we get on the plane; we can get settled."

"Exactly" Damien agreed.

He laughed for a moment, and then jumped to his feet. "I'm going back for another McOZ. It's my last slice of home for a few weeks." he mumbled to himself, and then disappeared towards the McDonalds express store, in the airport terminal.

Joel jumped up and chased him. "Yeah. I could go another Mc Oz." He cried out. "Wait up." he called to Damien.

Kali stared at Zack, as they were alone together. He took her hand, and she looked incredibly nervous, but excited, and she didn't know which emotion to favour.

"I'm sorry if I was being hard on you, these last few months." He told her flatly.

"I don't think you've been *too* hard on me." She meandered.

"I just needed you to push you. To try harder." He exclaimed. "I needed to push your limits. So you could be prepared for this. I needed *you* to push your limits."

"I know." She nodded. "I loved trying." She tried to explain. "I loved working hard so that I could reach this goal." She paused. "And we could all reach this goal together."

"I just hope I wasn't too harsh." He clarified.

"You weren't." Kali tried to find the words. "Just a little distant." She paused. "But I understood why, and you were *always* supportive of me."

"But I'm sorry if I froze you out."

"You didn't." She shook her head again. "We did this together. I depended on all of you. All three of you were there for me."

"Yeah." Zack continued. He didn't seem to get what she was saying. "I was busy with school, and everything was really crazy."

"It's ok." Kali said softly. "Besides..." She grinned. "I didn't want to cry on your shoulder too many times. I wanted to toughen up."

"We don't want you too tough." He joked, but squeezed her hand. "I care about you. I wanted to be there for you. Not hard on you."

"You weren't hard on me." Kali screamed, trying to make him understand, "And even if you were. I probably *needed* you to be hard on me." She whispered. "Even though you weren't."

"Because you deserve our support."

"And I got it. I found solace in each of you, in some way." She smiled to herself. "Besides, you don't know yourself. You say a lot, without saying anything at all."

Zack grinned, despite himself. "We will all be together on Hawaii." He told her adamantly. "We'll have each other's back." He looked at her hopefully. "Can we do that?"

Kali nodded. "I'd like that…very much." She emphasized.

Zack looked over at her for a long time. "I don't know what's going to happen Kali." he continued finally. "For all I know, you could hook up with some authentic Hawaiian long haired hippy, with a Malibu board, and a pick-up truck, and run off with him."

Kali started giggling.

"I don't know what's going to happen on the waves." He told her seriously, almost desperately.

"That's in God's hands." She smiled at him.

"Yeah." Zack sighed, and nodded at her. "We will keep each other strong." He told her.

Kali watched Damien and Joel come back towards the table. "Ok." She whispered. "We'll keep each other strong."

Part 2
Hawaii

Chapter 16

Kali:

Kali had been here two weeks, yet she had barely even got her feet wet, on this side of the island.

Every second day, one of the boys would take turns, catching the bus to Waikiki with her. They would surf at Waikiki, or go exploring.

On the fourth day, it was Kali's birthday, and they all came down together to Waikiki. They went to the zoo, and the aquarium, and had lunch at the Hard Rock Café. It was such a great day.

The surf, however, on the south side of the island, this time of year, was sloppy and small. She had to share the beach with ten thousand other tourists. Half of them were inexperienced, getting there very first surfing lesson. Yesterday she found a couple of good waves with Damien, but it was kind of frustrating for him, and for her.

Every other day, she would just stay at the North Shore and watch the stellar field of athletes in the water. She would just hang out, or peruse the local surf shops, or take a trip in Haleiwa.

Kali felt like the North Shore was like a carrot that was being dangled in front of her. But she was continuously being beaten with the stick, because she couldn't ride it.

"Damn it." Kali said, talking to herself. She tripped on a rock, as she walked up the driveway of the backpackers resort. She breathed in the salty air, and then exhaled slowly, as she wondered back to cabin 4.

As she got to the front door, she peered in for a long time. She noted what everyone was saying or doing, but they weren't doing much at the moment.

There was another guest staying with them in their cabin. He was taking up one of the 6 beds, and he was young, cute, and really kind of thoughtful. His name was Dane. Kali liked him

Kali sat on the porch steps of the cabin. She sat there for a while looking in at the boys, but they didn't know she was there.

"What a hassle this is." Zack said from inside.

"What." Joel asked. He sat at the table reading his magazine, and eating special K.

"This." Zack held up the tail end of his board. "I've cracked the fiberglass at the end here. I'll have to fix it.

"You're complaining about that?" Joel swallowed a mouth full of cereal. "Poor Dane over there snapped his whole board in half this morning."

Zack glanced at Dane. Dane sat on the couch near the doorway, he looked embarrassed.

"Really?" Zack said, concerned.

Dane was squeamish. He just shrugged his shoulders.

"Don't worry about it. It happens to the best of us." Zack smirked. "Just get Joel to buy you a new one; he's rich."

"Would you stop telling people that" Joel mumbled.

"No seriously." Zack continued to stare at Dane. "You can use one of ours, if you want."

Dane sat up straight. "I've already got a spare, but I might be able to buy a new one."

"With what?"

"I was thinking about getting a job."

Joel almost choked on his food "Minimum wage here in the US is about five dollars an hour for someone your age."

"I know. I live here."

"It would take you about four years."

Dane looked at the ground. "I've got some money saved up." He said unconvincingly.

"Yeah, maybe I should buy you a new one." Joel admitted.

"Are you really rich?"

"I have a six thousand dollar limit on my credit card."

"Wow."

"Yeah, and he hides it somewhere under the floor boards. Or in the wall. So don't bother looking for it." Zack piped in.

"Just keep working on your fiberglass problem over there." Joel called out.

Zack shook his head annoyed. "I'm not doing that right now." He picked his board up and carefully placed it under his bunk, on top of the other one. "So what happened?"

"I don't know." Dane began sheepishly. "I went up to Velsyland, you know, for the first time. The wave I was riding closed out on me."

"You were surfing by yourself? You shouldn't do that."

"Why not? I came here by myself."

"Yeah, and I admire your spirit, but one of us could have come with you." Zack scolded him. "Why didn't you get me? I haven't been to Velsyland yet."

"I don't know." Dane looked up. "You were with Kali."

"Kali?" Zack said awkwardly. "What was I doing with Kali?"

Dane shrugged his shoulders. "I don't know."

"Oh we must have been jogging." Zack lay back on his bed. "Where is that girl anyway?" He sounded aloof, as if he didn't care, but Kali knew he did care.

He was so attentive to her lately. He was always worried about her. He was always so concerned for her safety, as if he was responsible for it.

"She's at the beach. She just stands their ankle deep in the shore break. She won't go in." Joel slurped up the rest of his milk.

"I know that. Where is she?" Zack asked impatiently.

"I think she's at Sunset." Joel called out.

Zack jumped up and hit his head on the top bunk. "Ouch." He looked across at Joel "by herself?"

"No Damien's there."

"Oh." Zack slowly lay back down again. He put his hand to his head and felt a bump on his forehead. "Did anyone see big pipe today? It was going off."

"I saw the pipeline today." Dane jumped in. "That's where Kali is. She's not at Sunset." he said sheepishly. "It's really going off today!" He exclaimed. "Not the biggest I've seen it, but it's really clean."

Kali had in fact seen Dane at the Pipeline earlier today. He had spoken to her for a moment. He was so fun, and kind. She found it really easy to talk to him.

Because most of the conversations around here, revolved around surfing; she found it easy to talk to most people that she met.

"Are you going to watch the contest tomorrow?" Joel asked.

"The pipe masters? Of course I am. I already told you I was going down with you." Zack said.

Joel nodded. "Whatever." He got up and put his bowl in the sink. "I can't wait to see the girls compete. What do you say Dane? Are you ready to be shown up?"

"I don't care. Girls have got naturally better balance than boys do. I bet Kali will be surfing that wave one day."

Kali got up. She opened the door to the cabin and stepped inside. "One day soon."

They were all watching her as she came in. She looked around nervously, and then smiled.

"How are you going Kali?" Zack asked carefully.

"It's looks so big out there."

"Yeah" he agreed.

"Don't say yeah, as if you understand. It's not too big for you." Kali looked around and opened her mouth, but then blushed at all the eyes on her.

"It *is* too big." He answered back. "Why do you think I'm not out there?"

"Because you have a ding in your board."

"How long have you been standing out there?" Zack asked.

"I was sitting on the steps, in the sun." She replied.

"Did you use sunscreen?"

Kali softly laughed to herself. "Yes I used it." She looked at Joel, then walked closer to him. "Girls don't compete in the pipe masters. They surf Maui this time of year."

"Really? How did I not know that?"

"Do you take any interest in girls surfing?" She asked sarcastically.

"I take an interest in yours."

Kali lost her smile, and turned around. "Well I guess you can put that on hold for awhile."

"You can't surf pipe kali. You're not strong enough." Zack tried to reason with her. "You don't have to prove anything."

"Yeah, but it's pretty disappointing."

"What' disappointing?" Damien walked in the cabin and looked around at the group. He looked stoked, like he had just got the wave of his life. He always had that look on his face lately.

"Nothing, Damien, don't worry about it." Kali said irritated.

Damien shrugged. He went back to his bunk, and stowed away his board, and backpack.

"I know, Kali" He began. "You want to get out there, but trust me. I ate it coming off the turn this morning." He told her. "Even I got a weird vibe out there. I had to get out of the water. It's dangerous if you're not ready for it." He smiled at her meekly. "Look I scraped my arm." He held up his arm to show her, and it was indeed, red and sufficiently scraped.

Damien went and got a bowl from the kitchen. He sat next to Joel who already had the cereal, and milk.

"Yeah it's not for the faint hearted." Joel said looking off into space.

"What's up with you?" Damien nudged Joel.

"I'm just sitting here eating breakfast." Joel said incredulously.

"No, something's been on your mind since you got here."

Joel looked at him curiously. "You noticed that?"

"We all noticed that." Zack called over.

"Really?" Joel shrugged his shoulders. He looked away as if he was slightly embarrassed. "I broke up with Justine." He said out of nowhere.

"What?" Damien asked stunned.

Joel shrugged. "I broke up with her." He said again. "She was dogging me after formal. I think she wanted us to get married or something."

"Far out." Zack commented. He got up and walked to the kitchenette. He got himself a bowl, and a banana, and sat down on the other side of the table. He started pouring the special K and nodded sympathetically at Joel. "She was always an idealist."

"Yeah, the problem was; I don't actually love her."

"Joel you don't need to explain it." Zack told him.

"I know. I just feel bad."

"You don't need to feel bad." Zack cried. "If she wants to stick her head in the sand; that's her problem."

"Everything was so intense with her." Joel said exasperated. "I couldn't take it. I knew I had to get out."

Damien spoke slowly. "We were hoping you'd do it before you left." He gestured. "We didn't think it would actually happen though."

Joel didn't seem to hear him. "We had sex after the formal, but it wasn't that great." He informed them.

Zack looked up suddenly. It seemed to be the first time he had heard about this. Probably Damien too, from the look on his face.

Joel had finally lost his virginity, and he hadn't said a word until now.

"It was your first time." Zack mumbled. "It wasn't supposed to be any good."

Kali was listening in attentively. Dane was in the corner lounge, trying to look casual, although he was listening to.

"You should have heard the things she had to say, after we broke up." He recalled. "She literally threw things at me. Luckily she didn't know I was coming *here*." He suggested. "That would have made it so much worse."

"She was just being a bitch." Zack told him adamantly.

"You deserve better." Damien agreed.

"I've been going out with her for over three years. I was ready to let go, but it kind of hurts."

"That's because you care too much." Damien told him. "You're still feeling guilty and worried about her feelings. That's what you do Joel; you over analyze." He explained. "I'm sure another girl on this island can distract you."

Zack nodded. "When you find the real thing, you'll know what you were missing." He said empathetically.

Joel smiled. "I have seen a few girls, out there, who could *potentially* distract me."

"Yeah, to say the least." Damien said emphatically.

Kali went back to her bunk. Talking about other girls wasn't her favorite subject. It made her uncomfortable. She grabbed her wallet. "I'm going to Starbucks." She mumbled as she walked out the door.

Chapter 17

Kali:

Kali's biggest pleasure was going to Starbucks coffee house on the North Shore. She always went there to think and to relax. It was a place where she could indulge in a hot chocolate, and a piece of the most delicious chocolate cake.

She was walking there by herself, but Dane ran after her. He caught up with her at the end of the driveway. He wanted to get a coffee, so they walked in together.

Starbucks was an extension of the Foodland supermarket building. It was located just a few hundred meters up the road from the plantation village backpacker's resort. That was where Kali and Dane were staying.

Kali waited in line and got her hot chocolate, and chocolate cake. She was eating too much junk food lately, but she *did* go for a jog with Zack this morning, so she figured she earned it.

Dane got a latte and a muffin. He guided her into one of the booths in the store and they sat down together. Kali could feel her shyness rising up, but Dane was just so casual. She didn't usually have a problem talking to him.

"You guys are crazy." He said laughing.

Kali was taken aback by the comment. "What do you mean?"

"It's like watching an episode of 'Entourage'. Except with a girl in it. You are all so different, and yet and you couldn't be any closer."

Kali shrugged. "The boys have been friends for ages."

"What about you?"

Kali scooped the chocolate cake into her mouth. She relished it, and then swallowed. "That's a long story."

"I have time." Dane encouraged her.

Kali shook her head. "It's complicated."

"When I first met you, I thought you were Zack's sister... But the way he looks at you... Well you're not. And you're not Damien's or Joel's either." Dane began. "How did it come about that you guys all come to Hawaii together?"

"We're just friends." Kali said being evasive. "We started surfing together." She shrugged her shoulders. "Eventually, we just knew we had to get here."

Dane watched her. "That's it."

Kali nodded initially. Then something provoked her. She finally felt like talking, and for some reason, she felt like she could tell Dane anything.

"You know it's funny." Kali began her story. "We all agreed that the best way to do it, was to not tell anyone."

Dane leaned forward. "Not tell anyone that you were coming to the islands?"

Kali nodded. "Nobody knew. Not our parents, not my sister, not anyone at school. It was just too much pressure and some of us wouldn't be allowed to go anyway. So we didn't tell anyone."

Dane looked shocked. He grinned at her. "How did you pull that off?"

"I don't know." Kali blushed for some reason. "We packed at the last minute. We got our airport shuttle at four in the morning, when nobody was awake. We didn't even go to a travel agent. We booked our tickets online."

"Clever." Dane commented.

"Yeah. Joel paid for the tickets on his credit card. I paid him back with my savings account. Zack had inherited money once, so he was fine." Kali paused. "Damien paid what he could, but we all chipped in."

"Wow." Dane smiled. "Did you at least leave a note?"

Kali giggled. "Yes. We all left notes to our family, and we called as soon as we got here."

"So... Now you're here."

"Yes." Kali nodded. "It's pretty amazing. I love it here."

"But you *won't* go out there." He motioned out the window towards the ocean.

"I can't go out there. They'd never forgive me." Kali told him.

"But you want it?"

Kali shrugged. "Yes, of course I do, but I was talking to these guys the other day." She started explaining. "And they said I am too small, and the wind is too strong. I would bounce of the face of the wave instead of riding it. That's even if I'm strong enough to catch it in the first place."

"And you listened to them?" he asked. "They tell you you're just a girl, and you're not strong enough, and you just take their word for it."

"You disagree?"

"I was thirteen when I rode this place for the first time."

"Yeah, but you live on Kauai. You're used to riding big waves." Kali explained. "And you're used to the conditions. For us it's different. It's not sand under there. Not like at home. It's rock! It's volcanic rock, and if I hit it…" Kali didn't finish the sentence.

"I think you're stronger than that."

"Me, or my bones?"

"I'm probably only a few pounds heavier than you, and I can do it."

Kali shook her head. "Believe me. If I could, I would."

"But you can." Dane argued with her. "Adrenalin, alone, will get you onto your first wave. It doesn't matter how strong you are"

"That can't be true."

Dane shook his head. "But don't you just want to get that one green, hollow, Hawaiian wave?"

"Of course."

"Well then?"

"I can't do it." Kali said again. She cowered. "I don't know how to do it. Or what it would be like. I'm scared." She admitted.

"Yeah, we're all scared, but if all you see is what you can't do. Then you will never be able to do anything."

"But it's so much out of my hands." She cried. "Just getting up on the wave would be hard for me. I pull back all the time. Then riding the wave? It could close out on me, or I'd probably fall off. A million things could happen." Kali huffed. "And taking the wipe out; I get pummeled in Australia, just on the little waves. I'd get pulled from limb to limb. And after all that, I'd never have the energy to paddle back out again. I don't even know if I could duck dive a wave like that."

Dane watched her intently. His flat expression was unchanged. "A wave like what?"

Kali wasn't sure what he meant.

"A wave like the ones you see in the movies. Is that what you're seeing when you look out there?" He paused. "The waves at the moment aren't even that big, and haven't been for a while. Not the ones that I see, and certainly not the ones that I rode this morning."

Kali stared at him, hypnotized by the sound of his voice.

"You've built it up in your mind to be the biggest surf the world has to offer. The most spectacular, the most dangerous: That's what runs through your mind when you go to paddle out?"

Kali nodded.

"Take a step back and look at it for what it really is. It's not always that big. Sometimes it is, sure, but some winters we are bitterly disappointed in the swell. In the summer it doesn't break at all."

Kali Started to understand what he was saying, but she was hesitant.

"When those waves come." He continued. "The ones that you're talking about; you'll know it." He explained. "You'll feel it in the air, and in the vibration of the ground. There will be a buzz on the whole North Shore. Then you'll hear it. You'll know that it is happening. Only the best of the best will be out with their jet skis. It won't be for you, or for your friends, or me."

"So technically, there are waves I could surf. That's what you're saying."

"Yes, Kali, I think so."

"Zack would kill you if he knew you were talking about this."

Dane shrugged. "What? Does he own you?"

Kali was caught off guard by the comment. "No, but he's more worried about me than I am." She paused. About my safety." She clarified.

"Look, all I'm saying is: Keep an open mind. You don't want to regret not going for it, when you had the chance. One day, the waves might be just your speed."

"You're only seventeen Dane, how do you know so much."

"I grew up on the islands. The ocean is my education." He said motioning out the window to the sea again. "I have a difference of opinion to your friends. I think you could do it, and if I didn't, I certainly wouldn't encourage you."

Kali nodded.

Dane shook his head. "You look like he does; I'm not surprised Zack brought you."

The comment seemed to be dangerously close to condescending.

"I look like a guy?" She asked softly.

Dane shrugged. "Intense."

Kali shrugged her shoulders. "Zack was best friends with my brother. That's why I know him so well. That's why he brought me."

Dane drunk a large gulp of his latte. "So, you grew up together?"

Kali thought about that for a moment. "We *are* growing up together."

Dane shrugged. He grinned at her. "You know, there is a twenty first birthday party, at one of the North shore houses on the weekend. I think the locals would allow me to invite you guys. Your little gang from Clover, Australia." He laughed at her. "Do you think Zack would allow you to go?"

"Of course he would." Kali said incredulously. "He looks out for me. He doesn't have the ability to ground me." She explained. "We are always happy to go to a party."

Dane nodded. "Then I'll ask him." He smiled at her. "I'll show you how we *really* do things in Hawaii."

Kali smiled back at him.

Dane took a bite of his muffin. Then he nudged her. "You should buy a dress."

Chapter 18

Kali:

K ali opened her eyes suddenly.

She looked into the deep pitch black. She flicked her head in every direction, but her surroundings were dark. She couldn't see anything.

She could hear it though. She could feel it.

She slowly stretched her legs out in front of her. Then she lay perfectly still on her back. She was lying on the same bottom bunk she had been sleeping on since her first day at the North Shore. The roar of water outside was deafening. She could hear a crashing sound like a crack of thunder, but it sounded every few seconds. There was a rumbling in the floor boards that accompanied the noise.

She felt scared, but excited too. This was the day of the house party. That was her first thought, when she woke up, but that didn't matter at the moment.

This was one of those days Dane had told her about. Every one of her senses told her that the giant waves of Hawaii had finally rolled in from the winter storms of the arctic.

Kali could even taste this feeling. The air was thick with the salty spray that came off the waves.

Finally, she raised her arm and looked up at her watch; it was 4:10 in the morning. No one else seemed to be awake. That didn't mean that they weren't. The noise was so loud. All the other people in the cabin couldn't possibly sleep through it.

Kali wondered if Zack was awake. If anyone could be woken, and inspired, by this constant drum beat of breaking waves; it would be Zack. He always seemed to sense when the good waves would come in.

She listened to the sound for about twenty minutes before she sat bolt upright in bed. She couldn't stay still any longer. It was magic out there. She turned around and looked out the window at the dark blue sky.

The air was cold today.

Kali slowly crept out of bed and sat on the ground. She sat, stooped down, with her legs crossed on the wooden floor boards. She pulled her bag over and as silently as possible, changed into some track pants and a red t-shirt.

It only took a minute for her to change. She reached for a brush and tugged at the knots in her hair.

Her bag had lots of stuff in it. Kali had to dig around for a moment to find her socks. She put them on, slid on her sneakers, tied her hair back in a pony tail, and then she was ready to go.

She felt like she could jog the entire length of the North shore. She could see what was going on at every break. She could get the inside scoop before anyone else.

Kali stood in the main room and looked around before she went out the door. Incredibly no one was awake. They were all comfortably in bed, and every one of them, including Zack, was still fast asleep.

Kali thought that was weird. She walked outside, and the whole cabin site was undisturbed. They were still peaceful under the blanket of darkness in their bed.

Out on the ocean the impressions of rough seas, and the shadows of massive waves could be seen all across the horizon.

Kali stood in the middle of the driveway. She did some leg stretches, and warm ups. She waited to see someone else, but no one came. It was 4:40 in the morning now.

She seemed to be the only one awake and the only one who could appreciate this unusual morning.

Kali slowly started jogging down to the Kamehameha highway. She turned left from the plantation village, and headed in the direction of Waimea. She jogged down the hill and started walking softly through the Waimea parking lot.

There were a few cars around. Kali had a feeling that the people she would see on the beach today would be the same people she would see in the surfing magazines.

Already she could see three jet skis sitting on the sand, but it was too dark to recognize anyone.

All together there were ten people here at Waimea including Kali. Six of them were in the group talking. One guy was talking on his mobile phone. Two others were waxing up their boards. Behind her in the parking lot, there was one guy that had just pulled up in his car

A lot of the boards sitting round had foot straps on them. Kali was anxious to see how the system worked. She wanted to see the dynamics of the tow in.

A whole hour went by. Kali sat against the cafeteria brick wall and watched. She was fascinated as the surfers zoomed in and out to the rapidly shifting line up. They were carried by the jet skis, or the medium size Zodiac boat that they used for rescues.

They looked tiny in the distance against the massive waves.

They were so professional letting go of the rope, but one guy was not so lucky. The wave took him out from behind, and left the others scrambling to perform a dramatic rescue.

Kali found herself holding her breath as she waited for the surfer to be pulled out. Luckily this guy had a bigger lung capacity than she did.

At 5:50 the crowds were gathering. Most of them were spectators. She got up quickly and went to explore the rest of the North Shore.

The pipeline was next. It broke just a few meters from the shore. Kali could see up close and personal how each surfer tackled each of the waves they were riding.

The pipeline was remarkably clean. Wave after wave rolled in and formed the perfect curl. It was calm early morning conditions, just a breeze, nothing to make the water too choppy.

Kali watched the guys make the steepest drop she had ever seen, and then pull in to the pipe. They remerged a few seconds later, with a gust of air, and water, that spat out, just before the wave collapsed in on itself.

Kali had to sit down as she watched the epic wave. It could have been an hour or two that she stayed there. She just lost track of time. Each wave was becoming more, and more fascinating. Each surfer's approach at riding it, was equally as interesting.

Sometimes the surfers got hurt and the life guard were working overtime to tend to them.

A lot of other guys got pounded, and simply paddled back out to find a more forgiving wave.

Kali finally shrugged off the spell and started jogging again up to sunset beach park. This was a different wave completely, it was further out to see. It was hard to see exactly what was going on, but the pace was fast, and the wave was surprisingly uncrowded.

Kali looked out and watched with deep admiration. There didn't seem to be a single person out there who was completely committed to what they were doing.

It was overwhelming, but now the bay was packed. There were too many people around her. Kali decided to go back to the cabin.

A few hours ago, Kali felt like she was one of the only people in the world. Now, however, the beach was so cramped, she couldn't walk two steps in a straight line without bumping into someone.

Tiredness had set in when she got back to the plantation village.

She grew weary with every step she took in the rapidly increasing heat of the day. She was tired but more importantly, busting to go to the toilet. Her full bladder made the walk back to the cabin an uncomfortable one. She had plenty on her mind though.

Yet again there was no one in the cabin when she finally got back. Kali burst into the bathroom with a running push of the door. It didn't even occur to her that it would be occupied. The door wasn't locked or anything.

She halted immediately when she saw Zack.

She stood frozen, and so in shock, that she didn't look away for a full minute. Zack stood with one foot out of the shower, dripping wet, and he was completely naked.

He was clearly about to grab hold of a towel with his right hand, but when she came in, his arm paused in mid-reach. He stared at her for an indeterminate amount of time.

Kali saw everything; everything from head to toe.

The time space continuum seemed to stop. Kali stared at Zack, as he stared back at her. He didn't look embarrassed, or annoyed. He had a blank look on his face, and his eyes were fixated on hers. A moment later he finally shook himself out of the moment. He casually grabbed the towel and just as casually wrapped it around his waist.

"Hi Kali" he said to her.

Kali's body jolted, and she started to walk backwards out of the room. "I'm sorry I didn't know that anyone was here."

She finally shuffled back past the door way, and closed it as quickly as she could. Kali had never seen a naked guy before. Her cheeks were flushing so red and hot, she thought she was going to melt.

Zack walked out, about two minutes later, fully clothed. He was wearing board shorts and t-shirt. He rubbed a towel over his wet hair.

"Bathroom's free" he commented.

Kali didn't' know what to do. Apparently, her embarrassment had not cured her full bladder. She raced back into the bathroom. It was at least five minutes before she came back out.

She decided that hiding in the shower was not going to be a realistic option for the entire duration of her embarrassment.

Zack didn't look up, as she slowly surfaced from behind the door.

He looked different to her now. He sat at the table with a bowl of cereal, and a deck of cards.

He was freshly shaven. He had wet hair. He looked really good and smelled really good. He was shuffling the cards quickly, but he still showed no emotion.

"I thought everyone had gone out." Kali said again, nervously.

Zack sighed. "Don't worry about it Kali."

He turned to look at her for the first time since the incident. What he saw, seemed to surprise him. He was about to speak but thought better of it, and didn't for a while.

"Were you gone all night?" he asked finally.

"What do you mean?"

"I woke up at a twenty to five this morning and you weren't here." Zack explained.

"I went for a jog." Kali said hesitantly.

"You could have left a note."

"I didn't think I was going to be that long."

Zack shook his head. "You can't just take off in the middle of the night and not tell anyone." He snapped at her. "Anything could have happened to you."

Kali had never seen him *this* concerned before. "I just wanted to see the ocean up close." She tried to explain. The waves are really big today. You should see them."

"I have seen them." He told her. "I saw them when I was out looking for you."

"Well I'm right here."

Zack checked his watch. "It's eleven-o-clock in the morning."

"I got caught up in it." Kali exclaimed. She looked in his eyes and they looked solemn.

Zack's stance faltered. He dropped his attitude, and bowed his head. He looked down at his cards. "I've got time for a few games of snap, before I go watch the competition."

"The competition" Kali cried. "That's why it was so crowded down there."

"Are you going to come with me?" Zack asked her.

"Yes." She answered.

She slowly made her way to the table and sat down.

She had just seen Zack naked. The image was engrained in her brain. It was hard to look at him without grinning.

Zack had one hell of a good body, but she always knew that.

"So you want to play cards" he asked her softly.

Kali nodded. She watched him shuffle the cards, then he handed over half the deck and put the cards down in front of her.

Zack was clearly embarrassed. He didn't know what to do about it. Kali didn't either. She was still as red as a tomato.

Kali put the first card down and looked out the window. "The waves aren't as loud in the daytime." She remarked.

Zack nodded. "Yeah, they were really pumping this morning." He commented. "That's why you got up I suppose."

Kali nodded again.

Zack was watching her, watching the ocean, in the distance. "I would have gone jogging with you. If you would have woken me up."

Kali shrugged. "I didn't want to disturb you." She cried. "I know you push yourself to the limit out there." She gestured out the window to the ocean. "I figured you needed your sleep."

"But it was a pretty amazing morning this morning. You could have woken me." He said apprehensively.

"I'm sorry."

"Don't apologize." He told her. "Maybe next time."

They both put a few more cards down.

"Snap." Zack called out finally. As he snapped his hand down over a second King of hearts.

How appropriate, Kali thought to herself.

Chapter 19

Kali:

The first rule of anything was that Zack didn't drink. Not in excess at least. He did drink, but only one, or two beers. Kali had never seen him drink more than two in the same day. It was curious behaviour for a young man, but Kali often attributed it to the death of her brother. Also, Zack was a complete control freak.

Now he was drinking rather heavily, and all Kali could do was watch. Her plan was to stay out of his way anyway. Just a few hours ago she had seen Zack naked. Now she was trying to avoid him all together.

Damien was the one that started drinking. Watching the contest made him feel truly alive. He was buzzing on a natural high. He didn't need the extra effects of alcohol, but he did it anyway. They all did, maybe just to feel normal. Everyone else on the North Shore was drinking.

The fact that Zack didn't drink often, actually worked against him. Just the first two had adversely affected his state of mind. Now he was on his fourth, and he was honest to God drunk.

Kali stayed in the bathroom for a while. She had been attempting to do her make up for the last half an hour. She got the cosmetics at the local chemist. She had no idea of the colour charts and what brands to buy. She bought some foundation, lipstick, mascara and eye shadow. In the end she left off the eye shadow, because she didn't know how to apply it properly.

Now, it was close to leaving time. Kali got changed into her little black dress. When she walked out of the bathroom, the boys were already dressed, and waiting for her.

They were wearing smart long sleeve shirts with collars. They had their best jeans on. They looked very handsome; as they always did.

They all stopped talking when Kali came out of the bathroom. They glared at her. Then Damien whistled at her.

"Someone looks sexy." Dane commented.

Zack shot him a look.

Kali stood in the middle of the room. She felt strange and awkward, like she had just been made up into someone else. Maybe someone who could have been beautiful.

The shoes on her feet made her feel so tall, but they were uncomfortable. They were black high heeled slip-ons, with ankle straps, and a buckle.

"You look gorgeous Kali." Joel winked at her.

Kali blushed.

"But you took long enough." He added. "Let's go." He said, eager to leave for the party.

"Wait I forgot my necklace." Kali yelled. She ran back into the bathroom.

"Oh, come on Kali." Damien whinged.

"I'll catch up." Kali said quickly.

Kali stood in front of the mirror again. She held her necklace up and let it dangle and sparkle in the light. It was a gold necklace that Zack had bought her. The one with the turtle pendent on it.

Suddenly Zack appeared in the mirror, as he entered the bathroom. He moved around to stand behind her. He took the necklace from her hand, then slowly, and carefully, pushed her hair aside.

He very succinctly laid the necklace around her neck and fastened the latch. Zack ran his fingers through her hair and styled it back into place around her shoulders.

Suddenly Zack's hands moved down her waist. He fastened them tight around her. He pushed up against her. Kali felt his warm lips against her neck. He kissed her once, twice, three times, and then his lips were against her cheek. He kissed her once more and she could smell the alcohol. It was so thick on his breath.

130

Zack was holding her so tightly. She couldn't move even if she wanted to. She couldn't say anything either, she was too shocked.

"Kali." Zack said out loud. He drew in closer to her ear, and kissed it. "If that was any other girl: She would have taken off her clothes, and got in the shower with me. You're such a tease."

Kali felt numb. Any other time, she would have wanted Zack so close to her. She dreamed about his hands being all over her, but today it was so cheap and cold. "You're hammered Zack."

Zack dropped his head. "Yeah, I know." He told her. His hands moved slowly up her hips, up her stomach, up on to her breasts. They hesitated there for a second. Then they moved up to her shoulders. Then he moved back, and away.

He nodded at her, as he left the bathroom.

Kali waited a moment and followed him out.

Zack had already caught up to the others. He didn't look back at her. She followed, slightly behind them, as they went to the party.

It was the second party that Kali had gone to. There were a lot of house parties on the North Shore. They were fairly informal gatherings. Everyone just stood around listening to music, talking, drinking, and watching surf videos in the lounge room. There was always a barbeque in the back yard, volley ball on the beach, and skateboard riding on the terrace.

Kali tried to have fun at those parties, but she was awkward at the best of times.

Kali decided that maybe she was frigid. Maybe she wasn't giving herself a chance to meet new people.

She decided adamantly that tonight she was going to do what everyone else was doing: Get drunk and have fun. She didn't care about what Zack said.

She was sixteen now anyway. Her birthday was a few days ago.

It didn't take her long to meet new people either. She met two cute guys and they offered her a drink.

Zack

Zack was having the time of his life. Ever since he had got here to the islands, he had so many interesting people. They came from everywhere, and from all walks of life. Some were educated. Some were well travelled. Some were just adrenalin junkies.

All the people just came from different countries, and different back grounds. They were all easy going, and had plenty of jokes and stories to be told.

Hawaii was exactly the place Zack wanted to be.

The waves were the same waves he had been dreaming about his whole life, and now he was surfing them.

He had surfed Sunset, Waimea and the pipeline. He couldn't get over the fact that when he got home, he could tell his dad that he rode the pipeline.

Honestly, when it came to the crunch, he didn't know if he could handle it. Yet the waves this season had not been very big. Not by Hawaiian standards.

Many were just his size. They were perfect waves, and all he had to do was ride them. There was no school, or parents, or homework to get in the way.

He had no hang ups at all, except for the high prices at the Foodland supermarket and the occasional ding to his board, or scrape to his skin.

Zack wondered if life could really be this good. Especially when his best friends were right there beside him.

Sometimes the pecking order made it hard to get his own wave, but it was to be expected. He was always patient, and respectful, and happy to wait.

Today a lot of people bowed out anyway. The Hawaiians had been frothing at the mouth for the massive groundswell. It had hit the coast today, just in time for the competition.

Zack was at Keoni Mitchell's 21'st birthday party. That was the invitation said. He was standing outside beneath the stars with a group of people he had never met before. He was standing there with a beer and a cigarette, and the conversation was good.

There was plenty of alcohol around. Zack was soaking it up even though he was drunk to start with. Fuck it. Life was too short to be so serious all the time.

When he got to the party earlier, everyone had dispersed pretty quickly. At the moment he didn't know or care less where Damien and Joel were, or even Kali too, for that matter. He needed to be free of her tonight. There was only so much worrying he could do about another human being, other than himself.

Everyone was talking about the heats they had seen that day at the contest. How the level of surfing was holding up to the massive waves.

Zack took a drag of his cigarette. He spied Dane out of the corner of his eye. The guy was seventeen, a year younger than Zack. He was wondering across the grass towards him. Dane looked doubtful. Zack waved him over, to come join the conversation.

Dane came over and quietly spoke to Zack directly. "I think Kali is drinking in there."

Zack exhaled his cloud of smoke, and shook his head. "I'm over it. Let her do what she wants."

"Yeah, but she's not alone." Dane said.

Zack shook his head. "So what?"

He looked around distracted, the North shore house was loud, and the music was blaring. It was built on the ocean side of the Kamehameha highway. It was hard to hear with the roar of water. Zack looked out at the ocean and sighed. "Does Joel have her?"

"No. Joel's been talking to some girl named Jasmine all night. I don't know where they are now." Dane answered.

Zack raised his eyebrows. "Really? Interesting. What about Damien?"

"He's making out with some girl."

"Sounds like Damien" Zack remarked. "Why don't you just let the girl have some fun?" Zack took another drag of his cigarette.

"You mean the fifteen-year-old girl?" Dane sneered at him. "You should go check on her."

Zack ran his fingers through his hair. "No, don't go check on her. Just stay here and enjoy yourself. We don't need to coddle that girl. She can take care of herself for once." He blew out a mouthful of smoke. "And she's sixteen now."

"But she's with these guys in there and ..." Dane protested.

"Just chill out." Zack insisted. "She needs to toughen up. It's the only way we're going to get her into the water."

"You mean you *want* her in the water?"

Zack shook his head. "Only when I'm drunk Dane."

Dane looked hesitant, he got a beer from the esky. He only stood around for another ten minutes. He joined the conversation a few times, but then he disappeared inside again.

Zack stayed put. The conversation had just swung unexpectedly to the charter boat trips to the Mentawais Islands. Zack was enjoying his cigarette, since he hadn't had one in so long.

Dane was probably eager to get back to Kali, since he clearly had a crush on her.

Zack had finished his first cigarette, and had to ask for another one when Dane came out again.

"Zack" Dane called over.

Everyone heard him, and stopped talking.

Zack left the group to talk privately with Dane. Dane had Kali under his arm, and she was swaying back and forth like a tree branch in a hurricane "What is it?" He said annoyed.

"She can't have had that much to drink, but look at her. She's pale she's sweating."

"What?" Zack asked, looking doubtfully at the incapacitated girl.

"I think there is something worse than saying she's drunk."

"Kali would never do drugs" Zack blurted out.

"Yeah but someone could have slipped something into her drink."

Zack looked at Dane. "What?"

"We'll look at her." Dane said annoyed.

"You mean the date rape drug?" Zack said it, as soon as he thought it.

"If the shoe fits." Dane mumbled. He looked down at Kali who was hanging so far down on his arm, she was looking to keel over.

"Fuck." Zack yelled out, flustered,

Kali shrugged, then very slowly straightened her back. "I feel funny" she told him unsteadily.

Zack watched her, trying to stand up straight. She looked like she couldn't do it. She looked exactly as Dane had described her: pale, sweating, she couldn't stand still, and her voice was shaky.

"What's wrong Kali?" Zack asked her.

"I was just talking about the moon with these guys. I was thinking that I could be an astronaut one day."

"What fucking guys?" He demanded. "Did you get a good look at them?" He asked Dane

"No, I think I scared them off. Before I realised what was wrong with her."

"Damn it" Zack said, taking hold of her, away from Dane, or trying to.

"Fly me to the moon Zack" She said spinning around.

She was either sick or drunk. She couldn't concentrate on anything. Zack wasn't in the clearest mind either, but he knew he had to get her home, straight away.

"Sounds like an interesting conversation." Zack commented. He turned to the Dane. "What the hell did they give her?"

Dane raised his arms, as if he had no idea.

Zack had his arms full trying to hold Kali. He tried to grab hold of her, but she kept evading him.

"I don't know, I was just talking." She meandered. "I remembered it was a full moon tonight. Don't you think it would be fun to go to the moon?"

It wasn't a full moon tonight. It was a full moon last night. Zack had to quickly grab her before she fell down.

"And what about the stars." She endeavoured. "We should totally go to the stars."

Zack shook his head. "We can't do that Kali." He had his arm slung around under her armpit, so he was supporting her entire weight.

Zack looked around cautiously.

He was out the back of the house. He started ushering Kali through the house, so he could get to the front, and to the pavement.

Kali halted as they reached the den. "My head feels funny." she told him.

"We'll go outside and get some fresh air." Zack looked across at Dane, who was watching on eagerly.

"No." She said abruptly. "We can stay and talk." She insisted. "I was just talking, and I can't remember what I was talking about. I think it was about the stars."

"That's right." Zack assured her. "We were talking about the stars. We were going to go out and see them. We were going to walk home."

"I can't... walk." She told him, as if she had forgotten how.

"It's ok" he tried to reassure her.

"It's just funny, 'cause I don't remember what I was going to say." She started giggling weakly.

"We're going to go back to the cabin now." Zack told her. He tried to walk with her, but her feet were faltering.

Dane was watching on, annoyed at the turn of events.

"The music is so loud." She shook her head irritably. "Make them turn it down."

"I can't do that Kali."

"God I'm so tired Zack." Kali closed her eyes for a moment, but then opened them again. "Maybe we should go outside where it's not so loud."

"That's a good idea." Zack was finally able to escort her out, but he did it by practically lifting her up off her feet.

She was groggy as they got outside. She breathed in a few gasps of fresh air, and then in a second she just blacked out altogether.

136

He felt a tug of his arms, as her head fell down, and her body went limp. She was like a wilted flower. Her body went floppy and loose. There was nothing holding her up except for his own strength. Zack adjusted her body, and picked her up in his arms.

Dane instinctively put his two fingers on her carotid artery. "It's strong. She's just out." He said wisely, as if he had seen this kind of thing before.

Zack carried her the entire way home. It wasn't that far, and she wasn't that heavy.

Dane didn't say anything, he seemed annoyed at Zack for not believing him the first time. They walked home in silence, and Zack got her into bed.

Zack plonked her down on her bunk, and took off her shoes before he tucked her in. He took a pillow off his own bed, and sat down on the floor, next to where Kali was sleeping.

He would stay with her all night. He felt responsible for this. He *was* responsible for this.

Chapter 20

Kali:

The first thing Kali saw when she woke up was Zack's face. He was sitting beside her bunk, leaning against the wall, looking up at the ceiling of the opposite wall.

It was broad daylight outside. Sunshine was streaming through the window. The birds were chirping. The usual pounding of the waves on the shore, echoed against the valley.

"Zack?" Kali asked disorientated.

He looked worried, tired, his eyes were blood shot. He sat against a pillow, but he had no shirt on. He was wearing a black pair of jeans, sitting low on his hips. He looked uncomfortable. When she spoke his name, he jolted upwards and looked at her.

He immediately kneeled beside her bunk to attend to her.

"You're awake."

Kali checked her watch. She was having trouble focusing her eyes on the clock face. She rubbed her eyes and looked again. It was 11:33. Half the day had almost gone.

"Why are you sitting there?"

He kept staring at her. He didn't answer for a long time. "Just because I am" he said evasively.

"What's going on?" She asked curiously.

"Nothing's going on." Zack leaned down and kissed her on the forehead. "You're ok Kali. You're going to be fine."

Kali watched Zack's facial expressions.

"What are you so worried about?"

"Nothing." Zack assured her. He kissed her again, only this time on the cheek. "I'm not going to let anything happen to you."

"Why would anything happen to me?"

"It wouldn't" Zack said evasively.

Kali tried to think of the last thing she could remember, but she could hardly remember anything at all.

She remembered what Zack had said to her in the bathroom last night. Then after that, it was blank. She was leaving to go to the party, but she didn't remember actually getting there.

"Did we go to the party last night?" She asked blankly.

Zack stared at her for another length of time. "Yeah." He finally said, casually. "We went."

"Did I go too?"

"Yeah." Zack said, shrugging his shoulders, trying to look casual again.

"I don't remember."

"Don't you." Zack asked, curiously, but he also sounded worried.

Kali tried to sit up, but she felt dizzy. She quickly lay back down and buried her head in the pillow. "What happened last night Zack?"

Zack chewed on his lip, twisting his face in a fit of indecision. "We're not really sure. You must have got drunk or something." He said softly.

Kali nodded. "I became a blackout drunk on my first try?" She asked incredulously. "I remember thinking I wanted to have a drink."

"I'm sure you did." Zack commented. "You probably wanted to get blind drunk after what I said to you."

She looked at him. Since Zack had come to the islands, his muscles had gotten bigger, more defined. His skin had tanned perfectly to a golden brown. His brown hair was thick and well styled. He looked so good.

He smelled good too. The aftershave that he had used last night was still detectable. The only thing wrong was that he looked really tired. His face was pale and his eyes were red.

"You were drunk Zack. You never drink that much." Kali defended him. "You didn't know what you were saying."

"That doesn't excuse it though."

"You were embarrassed, and so was I." She told him. "It was my fault I walked in on you."

"It was my fault, I didn't lock the door."

"Then don't worry about it."

Zack nodded. "For what it's worth Kali. I'm sorry."

"It's ok." Kali nodded, she rubbed her head. "I wonder if *I* did anything embarrassing last night?"

"No, I don't think you did." Zack said, a little too quickly.

"Would you tell me if I did?" She asked annoyed. Kali tried to get up again, but she felt so lethargic. "Is this what a hangover feels like? I feel so seedy"

"You feel sick? Maybe we should get you to a doctor."

"Far out Zack. I don't need a babysitter." She said agitated. "Can't you just let me, have my first hangover, in peace?"

"I'm sorry." Zack said, confused.

Kali looked past Zack, at Damien who had moved into the kitchen. He was taking a muffin out of the packet. "What's it like out there Damien?"

"It's massive Kali." He said getting excited. "When you feel better, you should go out to see it. I mean we're talking eighteen feet and over!"

"Wow."

"You really scared us last night young lady." Damien said coming in to stand at the edge of her room.

"What do *you* think happened?" Kali asked, trying to piece it together.

"I don't know." Damien said honestly. "I should have been there, but I wasn't." He looked angry at himself. "We think somebody slipped a drug in your drink."

"Oh, for fuck's sake" Zack yelled at him.

"Well, she should know what happened to her." Damien screamed back.

Kali felt really hot. She wiggled uncomfortably under the blanket. "What kind of drug."

"We don't know." Zack jumped in, throwing a harsh glance to Damien.

"And it blanked out my memory?" Kali asked.

Zack looked at her. "It could have been ecstasy or Euphoria. It could have been speed, or nothing at all." He told her. "You could have just been drunk. We don't know." He shrugged. "It did seem likely that it was a drug."

"Was it Rohypnol?"

"What's Rohypnol?" Zack was distracted as he sat down again on the floor, beside her bunk.

"It's a roofie."

"Yeah and what is that." He said slightly annoyed.

Kali hesitated for a long moment. "It's the date rape drug"

Zack gasped. "What the hell are you talking about, of course not" he looked in her eyes. "Ok maybe. But nothing happened Kali. You were talking to these guys. Dane noticed that you looked a little off. So he went and got you, and I took you home."

"You did that for me."

"*Dane* did that for you." He said remorsefully.

"But you were worried about me."

"Yes." Zack nodded.

"Did you sit there all night?"

Zack nodded his head again "yeah, I did."

"I'm sorry." Kali said disorientated. "I'm sorry I ruined your night."

"No Kali. You didn't ruin anything."

Kali shook her head. "I remember thinking I wanted to have fun last night. I don't know how I acted on it, but I guess I could have gotten myself into a lot of trouble."

"Someone took advantage of you last night. If I knew who it was, I would be taking a fucking baseball bat to their head. This isn't your fault. It's mine. You did nothing wrong." Zack practically yelled at her. "You're entitled to have fun, without someone assaulting you." He paused. "And that goes double for me. For what I did last night."

"What are you talking about?" Damien asked Zack.

"But nothing really happened?" Kali said carefully, cutting off Damien.

"One of us should have been there." He said irritably. "We should not have to rely on Dane. Who we only met last week. To look out for you. We should have made sure you're ok. Especially in a house full of revved up alpha males." Zack said annoyed. He looked at her. "Nothing happened to you. I assure you. Dane got to you before anything could."

"I remember thinking I wanted to go off on my own last night. I wanted to give you guys some space." She looked down. "I don't want to be a burden. Please don't blame yourself for me going off on my own."

Zack smiled at her. "Why don't you just get some rest?"

"Kali laid back down. She didn't want to argue with him again. She still felt a little tired and groggy anyway.

Zack got to his feet. He started climbing up on the top bunk. The bunk of top of hers. "I'm going to get some sleep." He said softly. "If you want anything just call me." He leaned his head down, over the side of the rails "Anything at all."

It was about three in the afternoon when Kali woke up again. Zack was still asleep on the top bunk

She wasn't that hungry, but she thought she would try to eat something. There was a muffin on the bench.

It was a blueberry muffin. As she ate, she realized she could only finish half of it.

"Are you ok Kali?"

Kali turned around, just in time to see Damien jump out of bed.

She thought that she had been alone with Zack, in the cabin, but Damien must have been in his bunk.

Kali quickly wiped at her mouth. "I'm fine."

Damien grabbed her hand "are you sure?" He asked her warmly. "Maybe you should wash your face."

Damien led Kali into the bathroom.

Kali looked in the mirror. Her make up from last night was hopelessly smeared, and she was still wearing her little black dress from last night.

Damien picked up a cloth, rinsed it under the hot water, and wiped her face gently. He handed her the cloth, and she finished wiping around her eyes and mouth.

Damien watched her, with his own, amazing blue eyes. As well as his general amazing good looks. He had blonde hair, and gentle facial features. He looked so concerned.

What's wrong Damien?"

"You know I wasn't even there" He began.

"But nothing happened."

"Yeah because Dane was there." His voice wavered. "I was talking to some girl."

"So, what's new?"

"Yeah, but we all expect Zack to watch over you, and he was seriously fucked up last night. Someone else should have stepped up."

"Wow, I'm really a burden, aren't I?"

"No, Kali. Believe me: You're our anchor."

"So, I don't hold you back. I hold you down?"

"No, you hold us together" he looked off into space. "We would never be here, if it wasn't for you." He sighed, not explaining what he meant. "Kali, do we put too much pressure on you?"

"No." Kali said quickly.

"What about when we were training?"

"No, I loved the training."

"Yeah but look at those clothes hanging off you, you're so skinny."

"No I'm not." She cried. "I eat all the time."

"Are you really ok with all this?"

"I wanted to come?" She pleaded with him. "I'm fine."

"Yeah, but you're a girl, and I don't know how far you can push a girl. You get sick every month."

"I get sick?"

"You know what I mean."

"If I couldn't handle this I wouldn't be here." She tried to explain.

"Ok." He smiled at her, but quickly changed the subject. "Dane told me, what he talked to you about, at Starbucks." He shook his head. "He's got some nerve that kid."

"That kid is the same age you are." Kali told him bluntly.

"Be honest with me Kali. Do you want to be out there? Do you want to surf the North Shore?"

"Yes." Kali said softly. "But I don't know if I'm good enough." She shook her head. "Why aren't you honest with me? You've been watching Damien. You're the most proficient surfer here. Tell me, am I good enough? Can I ride a wave on the North shore? Would I be able to ride a big wave, when the pressure is on?"

Damien took a deep breath in. "It varies Kali." He told her. "The waves, the tides, the wind, the swell. The crowds. It depends which break you want to surf. Sometimes it doesn't take much. Other times it pushes you to your limit."

"But if I had help, finding the right place, at the right time?" She asked softly.

"Just think about it Kali. I'd rather you not. Only you can make that decision." Damien quickly changed the subject. "So how do you feel?" He asked.

"Better." Kali whispered.

Damien moved closer behind her, and took her brush from the shelf.

"I feel a lot better." She said truthfully.

Damien surprisingly started brushing her hair.

He patiently unbundled the knots in her long locks. Kali's spine tingled as he did it.

"I can't believe anyone would try to hurt you." He mumbled. "Zack would have never forgiven himself if anything happened to you. Neither would I."

"I remember that I wanted to make new friends last night." Kali said softly. "I wanted to try and have fun, and be fun."

"Fun is overrated."

"No, it's not." She argued. "We just have too many issues to experience it properly."

Damien laughed to himself. "I guess you're right."

Kali closed her eyes. It felt like he was giving her a head massage. He brushed her hair for about five minutes, and it was bliss. Kali slowly reached back and grabbed his arm. She pulled the brush out of his hand, and put it on the sink.

In one motion, at the same time, she leaned back and rested her head on the curve of his neck and shoulder.

"Thank you."

Damien kissed her on the cheek. "You're welcome."

She enjoyed the moment, as he held her.

Finally, he spoke again. "I didn't want you here, originally, Kali." He told her, out of nowhere. "I thought it was too dangerous for you, and you would get in our way."

Kali looked sadly down at the ground. Damien put his hand under her chin and forced her to look up.

"But, while we prepared for this," He added quickly. "I couldn't imagine you *not* coming. You're the one who gave Zack the focus to train for this. You're the one who inspired Joel to defy his father and make this trek. You're the one who makes me feel like I can do anything."

Kali smiled humbly. Damien tightened his grip on her. She was looking in his eyes through the mirror, since they were standing in front of it.

"I wanted to take care of you." Damien continued. "Just like Zack does. I wanted us all, to have this opportunity, together."

"We are." Kali said, bewildered.

"Yes, little Kali." He said smiling at her. "Now the dreams come true. I can't believe I'm living it."

"Neither can I" She smiled

Damien kissed her on the cheek. "You should go back to bed. You still look tired"

He let go of her, and squeezed her hand, as she walked away.

Kali did, amazingly, still feel tired. She crawled back into bed, under Zack's bunk, and fell asleep straight away.

Chapter 21

Kali:

Kali jumped out of bed and stood up. She looked at Zack as he slept dead to the world on the top bunk. "I want to go surfing."

Even in his sleep the word 'surfing' meant something. Zack's breathing changed. He rolled over, onto his right side, so that he was facing her.

She lightly nudged him with her finger. "Zack, I want to go surfing."

Zack looked groggy, and confused as he woke up. "What."

"Now! Today! I want to go surfing."

"You can't go now." He looked at her as if she had just escaped the local mental institution. "You've got to rest."

"I don't want to rest anymore, I've been resting for three whole days now. I read an entire book. I kept down all of Dane and Damien's cooking. I feel fine." She pleaded.

Zack wasn't convinced. At that moment, Damien came in the front door. He paused as he looked up to the back room. Kali saw him too. She turned around.

"What's it like." Zack called out.

"It's calmed down over night. Six to eight, and it's clean, but there's a storm predicted tonight, and the wind will get into it by midday."

"See I told you. We have to go now." Kali winged at him.

"What is she talking about?" Damien asked, interested.

"I want to go surfing." Kali cried out.

"Down at Waikiki?"

"No." she pleaded. "Don't patronize me. You had to know this was coming. Six to eight feet is nothing to these shores. It's nothing I can't handle."

"What do you think?" Zack asked Damien.

"I think she's up for it." Damien said coolly. Looking Kali in the eye.

"You really mean that?"

"It's what she wants." Damien looked back at Zack. "I've never seen a better time than now."

"You sure." Zack looked in Kali's eyes.

"I want this." Kali said defiantly. "Where should we go?" Zack asked Damien.

"I'll take her down to sunset."

"I should take her." Damien interrupted. "You only just got to sleep. After who knows, how long."

"I'm going." Zack snapped at him.

He jumped down from his bunk and put his hand on Kali's forehead to feel her temperature.

"I feel fine." Kali said. "Stop worrying." she waved his hand away.

Zack stepped back. "Are you sure it's not that big. I mean those waves can look awfully deceiving sometimes."

"We'll, they're going to be big. Especially for her, but like I said: it's only about six - seven foot."

Zack still looked doubtful, but finally nodded. "We can go up to have a look, but I don't want you to feel pressured to go in."

"I want to go in." Kali said excitedly. "I'm ready for it now, I know it."

Zack sighed. "Joel! Dane! Get out of bed."

It was like paddling in the middle of the ocean. The break itself was a quarter of a mile out to sea. They were all paddling with her. Like a pack in the water.

It was easier to paddle, than she thought it would be.

The initial paddle was out through the rip. The water was relatively calm. It was just daunting as she paddled away from the safety of land.

It was kind of like she was disconnected from her body. Kali was paddling, but it was completely natural, as if by sheer force of habit. Her body was strong, and she felt fit.

All of the resting and sleep lately, had done her a world of good.

For her training; she had jogged, jumped skipping rope, and rode Waikiki. The whole time she was just itching to get into these waters.

Now she was surfing the North Shore! The feeling was more than physical, it was spiritual. It felt like she was out of her body, looking down upon herself.

She could feel the choppy water underneath her as she sliced through it. It felt strangely calm. As she looked down on herself, she could see the ocean, and she could see her friends. Zack was just an inch away. He paddled so close to her, they often bumped into each other.

Kali had her navy board shorts on, and a bright pink rash shirt.

Damien had bought her the bright pink rash shirt. The vest had long sleeves, and you could see it from a mile away. That's what Damien wanted. He had spoken to the lifeguard on duty, and made it very clear, that the young girl in pink, was the one to look out for.

They moved across from the rip. Suddenly a big wave loomed up out of nowhere.

"Duck dive now Kali." Zack yelled at her.

"Holy cow."

It was like a wall of water in front of her face. Kali took a deep breath in. With all of her might, she pushed the board down. Way down under the crest of the wave. She pushed the back of the board down with her foot, arched, and resurfaced behind the breaking wave.

"Kali" Zack shouted at her.

"I'm fine." The lineup was fast approaching. The sets were thick and fast.

They tried their best to paddle around the waves, but there was no guarantee where they would break.

Damien was right; it had calmed down over night. The waves were probably about six foot high. That was seven foot Hawaiian though. They had a bigger scale over here.

Kali breathed in deeply and resumed paddling.

She was scared and exhilarated all at the same time. She wouldn't back down from this. She couldn't even if she wanted to. She was already out.

Zachary Cummings was not Clark Kent. He could not save her from what was about to happen. She had to do this on her own. She pushed through the water. Simply keeping up with the boys beside her.

It happened faster than she could assimilate it. She paddled, and paddled, harder and faster. Thee auspiciously strong current gripped her like a floating twig and carried her out, and around to the lineup. There were masses of people already out. They were waiting for their very own wave.

If a freak set came out of nowhere, they would all have to paddle out further. The trick was to get over, under, or around it, before it broke on top of them. Kali worried about that. She kept an eye out on the horizon, but for now, they looked good. Kali sat in the lineup waiting, and watching what the other guys were doing.

Dane, Damien, Joel and Zack didn't say a word. All of them were to weary and nervous, and that included Dane; who didn't even know her very well.

The sun was high in the sky. It reflected on the water yet the glare wasn't too bad. Kali sat for few minutes, quiet and in thought. She closed her eyes, made her decision, and reached out to grab Zack's wrist.

"I'm ready."

Zack looked in her eyes. "Are you sure?"

Kai nodded. "Yes." She lay down on her board. She spun it around, into a prime position, facing the shore, at the angle the waves had been breaking. Damien and Joel didn't follow but sat up quickly and alertly on their guard. She sat up again.

Kali looked around at the people in the lineup. "If I can get one in the next set. I promise I'll commit to it." She told Zack.

Zack nodded. He looked around, and started talking to the guy next to him. She couldn't hear all of the conversation, but they were talking about her. She heard the guy's name; it was Mathias.

Mathias had thick, curly brown hair. A narrow face, and a five o'clock shadow. Kali couldn't help but check him out. There were plenty of good looking boys out here.

This guy looked like he was from Brazil, or Argentina, or some South American destination. He spoke in broken English with a heavy Spanish accent.

"Alright Aussie" the guy said, staring at Kali. "She's a bit young, isn't she?"

Zack shrugged. "She just wants one wave, and it's not that big."

"So it isn't."

"She made me bring her out here." Zack told him. Speaking loudly, so Kali could hear it too.

Mathias nodded and whispered something to the guy that was next to him. "You're up Aussie girl." He laughed.

"Tell me when to paddle." Kali pleaded, tentative suddenly. The second wave of the set had just passed under her. Someone had already coveted it.

"Now" Zack screamed "Now Kali. Now!"

Kali paddled as fast as she could. Zack, Damien, Joel and Dane all paddled beside her, but then they all pulled back at the last minute.

They were blocking for her. Making sure no one got in her way. They were also making sure that someone would think twice before paddling for a wave that already had five people on it. Some of the locals used the tactic it to intimidate the 'tourists'.

It worked. She got the wave to herself. For a millisecond, she hesitated. It was like paddling on the top of Niagara Falls.

She tried to feel the speed and power of the wave, then paddle to the rhythm of it. Then it picked her up. She flew forward, pushing her chest up with her arms, and then jumped to her feet.

It was so steep. She tried desperately to hold her position. She angled straight down the face, but the wave jacked up so ferociously. It was going so fast. Kali foot slipped. She lost her balance, and fell off.

The wave pummeled her. It pulled her round and round, in every direction.

It simply grabbed hold of her and slammed her forward into the churning white wash. She rolled forward, instinctively holding her breath, waiting for the ride to stop, and then it finally passed over her.

Kali opened her eyes. She was treading water, gasping for a few breaths of air. Then without warning it happened again. The force once again overpowering her, like a freight train. She got tossed around like a rag doll. Her board was gone. She was upside down when the second wave passed.

'What do I do?' Kali thought to herself.

She was still under water. It felt like it was happening in slow motion. She didn't even realize what positon she was in.

'I'm upside down. I have to go up' she thought to herself. She quickly spun around, and paddled to the surface.

Kali took a solid breath as she broke through the surface. She raised her arm. It was the only thing she could think of.

As she looked around, she was significantly closer to the shore. There was someone paddling towards her, it was the lifeguard.

She was out of the impact zone, relatively safe, or safer. The lifeguard paddled over on his rescue board and quickly grabbed her.

"How are you going, pink girl?"

"I'm good." Kali coughed a little as she spoke.

The lifeguard paddled her back to the beach.

As the rescue board hit the sand, Kali tried to stand up, but she couldn't locate her legs. She fell down on the beach.

"Are you ok?"

"I couldn't do it." She murmured softly.

"You did fine." The life guard assured her. "How do you feel? Did you swallow any water? Any nausea or dizziness."

Kali thought about it for a minute. "No, I don't think so."

"Sit there for a minute and catch your breath" He told her.

"Thank you for rescuing me." She said earnestly. There were a lot of people standing around, watching her, but she didn't feel embarrassed though, she was alive. She had never felt this alive before.

"Congratulations you just rode a wave at Sunset Beach." The lifeguard stared at her.

"I had a wipe out at Sunset beach."

"I saw you. You got up."

"For about two seconds"

"Sometimes it's like that. Two seconds is all you get."

"You don't think I'm a kook?" She asked humorously.

"Having a wipe out is part of the fun, around here." He assured her. "Especially your first one."

"I guess that's true."

"Everyone does it." He assured her. "You just have to get back up on the horse."

Kali felt disorientated. "My horse is probably broken, or half way back to Australia by now."

"No, just keep an eye out. The boards usually get washed up on the beach."

Kali looked up and saw Zack paddling towards the water's edge.

"Are you ok Kali?" He yelled at her.

Kali wiped at her eyes. "I wiped out." She called back.

"I saw you get up. You were doing good." he told her. He got out of the water and flipped his board up under his arm. He kneeled down next to her

"That's what I told her." The lifeguard sympathized.

"It was such a lame attempt."

Zack shook his head. "You did great baby, a lot of people wouldn't have even tried." He leaned over and kissed her on the forehead. Then he glanced over at the lifeguard.

"Thank you." He shook the guy's hand. "I'm Zack."

"Michael." The lifeguard looked at him closely. "Is this your girlfriend?"

Zack actually blushed for a moment. "No, she's my good friend."
Michael nodded.

"Thank you for saving her."

"She didn't need saving." Michael smiled at Kali. "I just gave her a ride."

Kali blushed.

"Zack's right you know." Michael began. "A lot of people wouldn't have even tried it. A lot of people wouldn't have even got to their feet." He informed her. "I get to watch it all with my binoculars. You should see all the kooks nose dive on there first try."

She giggled. "Really."

"I was on duty when Damien had his first surf here. Trust me, it wasn't a pretty picture."

"He told me he was styling" Kali said.

"Trust me, he wasn't."

Kali giggled. "Maybe I could try it again."

"When you're ready" Zack said.

"You'll be fine." Michael urged her. "Just tell Damien you can't wear his pink, glow in the dark, shirt anymore. You'll attract sharks." He tugged at her rash vest. "I've got binoculars. I can see you in *any* old, plain colored, shirt.

"Yeah, now you mention it." Kali looked down at her bright pink rash shirt.

Michael laughed and motioned out to the ocean "this is the perfect size for you now." He got to his feet and scanned the horizon quickly, looking for any signs of trouble.

Kali took Zack's hand. She climbed up beside him. Suddenly she felt overcome with emotion. "That was awesome."

"Kali!"

They all turned around quickly. Damien was running up the beach, he was yelling at her. "Nice wipeout Kali." He joked.

Kali shrugged her shoulders. "Yeah it was." She couldn't wipe the smile off her face.

Chapter 22

Joel:

Joel looked down Kali, lying on the bottom of his new bunk. His new bunk was in the back room of cabin four, of the plantation village, backpackers resort. The same cabin he had always been in. This was just a different bed.

Yesterday she was out surfing Sunset Beach. Today her muscles might be a bit sore. She might feel a bit stiff. Paddling out in the North shore, was like paddling out into the open ocean. It was a tough, and strenuous. It took a lot out of you.

The girl was sleeping peacefully on top of her sheets, and blanket, because it was quite warm today.

She was huddled up on her side. Her knotty hair lay all over her pillow. She was wearing a Mickey Mouse nightie, and she looked very sweet.

Kali opened her eyes, she looked at him, but she didn't move.

"Hi Joel."

"Hi Kali"

She stared at him, so he felt compelled to say something more. "How are you feeling?"

Kali shrugged. "Ok, I guess."

"There's a new guy in the cabin, so I'm taking the bunk above yours." Joel told her quickly.

"Ok."

"I like your pyjamas."

Kali raised her head and looked at the Mickey Mouse print on her blue nightgown. "Thank you." She giggled. "I'm a big Disney fan."

"Me too, I like Aladdin." Joel volunteered.

Kali eyed him suspiciously. She seemed to be waiting for something. "I like Cinderella."

"I was really proud of you yesterday."

She looked away discouraged. "It was a lame attempt."

"It was a good attempt Kali. You got up. You were out there."

Kali shook her head and smiled at him. "It was just a fleeting moment." She shrugged her shoulders. "It was like a dream."

"No, it was all too real."

"I surfed one wave for zero-point-two seconds, but you're out there everyday Joel. You can tell me. What does it feel like? What is it like surfing the North Shore of Oahu?"

Joel sat down next to her bed and rested his hands in his lap. He looked into space for a moment "It's a moment of magic Kali." He began slowly. "You sit out there and you wait. You wait for your turn, and you wait for that wave that's travelled across the ocean to find you."

He elaborated. "You look behind you, and you see the swell lines, and how quickly they turn into waves, how quickly they travel. You have to think fast. Then you put aside your fear, and your hesitation, and just go for it Kali. You go for it with all of your might."

"You have to paddle fast and jump faster. If you're on the pipeline, before you know it you're freefalling. If you're at Waimea, you have to sail down the wave smoothly before you can even pull off your first turn."

"But the force, and the roar, and the speed, it's all just a killer rush Kali, and we don't even ride the big waves. Not the really big ones." He shook his head. "It's just amazing. It's such a miracle of nature." Joel nudged her. "You got a taste of it. You know what I'm talking about."

"Sort of." Kali said.

"You're all alone out there. It's a hundred percent personal. No one can say they're better than you. Or tell you how to do it. It's all up to you."

"And you go for it."

"Yeah." Joel nodded. "You go for it."

"I wasn't alone yesterday." Kali said reflectively. "Everyone told me what to do. They steered me when I paddled. They told me what wave to go for. Zack negotiated my spot on the pecking order. You all paddled with me on to the wave before you pulled back." She sighed. "It was easy, just doing what I was told. I wasn't scared, with so many people around me."

"We're glad to be there for you." He shrugged his shoulders.

"That's the thing." She cried. "I didn't feel anxious, when I knew you had my back. And I only got one wave, before I got out of the water. I probably could have held on, but I fell off. I think it was just a novelty to me. I even knew the lifeguard was looking out for me. You guys made it so easy. I don't know if I could do it on my own"

"I wouldn't want to do it on my own." Joel told her. "You must have noticed that I go surfing only about half as often as Damien and Zack do. I don't go by myself like they do, or Dane does. I don't ride the size that they have achieved. I'm a little more gun shy than they are, but I'm still out there. I can still honestly say I rode the North Shore. I'm getting better, and braver. It's just what you're comfortable with. You start out small and work your way up."

"Yeah I guess." Kali said hesitantly.

"A taste is more than most people will ever get." He tried to explain. "I just... I just think Zack is right Kali. I don't think you're strong enough yet. The conditions were perfect yesterday, but today it's about sixteen feet."

"I know." Kali nodded. "I was kind of blessed yesterday."

"You know I never expected this Kali." Joel started to say. "When I was a kid I never thought I'd be popular, and have such good friends. I certainly never thought I'd be a big wave surfer in Hawaii. I was kind of shy and goofy as a kid. I never thought my life would be this exciting."

"That's why you surf goofy foot." She giggled. "Because you were goofy."

"I met Zack, and Damien, and then we all met you." Joel hesitated. "When Zack told me he was bringing you to Hawaii, I thought he was crazy, but I never had a chance to say no. If he was going to bring this little girl here to the islands. Then the least I could do, was be man enough to do what she could do."

"I don't do anything."

"You trained pretty hard for this Kali." He insisted. "You put your heart and soul into your preparation. I think that at the time, we never even believed that it was going to happen for real."

Kali shrugged. "It never quite felt real." She agreed. "Until we got the airport."

"Now it feels too good to be true." Joel commented.

"Yeah it does." Kali smiled at him, but she quickly changed the subject. "You know, I saw you this morning."

"Sorry?"

"I saw you this morning." She repeated. "I saw you with Jasmine. You were together."

Joel looked at the ground. He didn't say anything.

"You were sitting by the big tree, outside of the Waimea parking lot." Kali continued.

"You saw us." He asked.

"You were kissing her."

Joel held his breath for a moment. "Was I?"

"Yes, but you never told us you were going out with her." Kali queried him

Joel scratched the back of his head. "It's just new. I'm getting to know her."

"For three days, after the party, I hardly saw you. I knew you were with her, but the other guys don't know that."

"I was going to tell you, but I wanted to make sure."

"Sure about what?"

"Sure about myself and about her. I don't know it's complicated." He said squeamishly

"But you're in love with her?"

"How do you know that?"

"The way that you look at her." Kali said softly.

Joel sighed. "I suppose, but it's not going to last very long. She here on holiday with her family and she leaves a couple of days after we do."

Kali smiled. "It's good to see you so happy. It's interesting to see at least one of you in love."

Joel thought that was funny, Kali was in love with Zack. Zack was in love with Kali. The electricity that passed between them could light up every island of Hawaii.

Kali chewed on her lip for a minute. "The other girl you went out with in high school. You didn't love her?"

"No." Joel said softly.

"But you went out with her anyway?"

Joel grinned at her. "Are you psycho analysing me Kali?"

"Why did you go out with her?" Kali asked curiously.

"Justine was rich, I was rich. Our parents expected us to go out together." He said wearily.

Kali hesitated. "Your father put a lot of pressure on you?"

"Sometimes" Joel said evasively.

"And he hit you?"

Joel inhaled suddenly. He was caught *so* off guard. "Don't go there, Kali."

"You're father's an idiot." She whispered at him.

"Don't say that. He's my father."

"You did everything he asked you to." She persisted. "You got all good grades. You became school captain. You went to all of his lawyer events. You social climbed for him." Kali shook her head. "I hope he appreciated all of it."

"He pushed me Kali." Joel defied her. "He put a roof over my head, and gave me a car, and he pushed me to get good grades. He was demanding on me, and I succeeded because of it."

Kali looked at him for a long time. "Ok." She finally acknowledged.

"Don't worry." Joel assured her. "You guys help me break free, and he's mostly all bark, and no bite anyway."

"Mostly?" Kali queried, but she didn't push him on the subject. "But now you want to follow in his footsteps and be a lawyer?"

"I want to do corporate law."

"That's what you want, for yourself, and not for him?"

Joel nodded and shook and his head. He was smiling. "Kali, I follow my own dreams. I promise! You don't have to worry about me."

Kali smiled back. "You all worry about me. I just want to return the favour."

"Well you can stop. I always wanted to be a lawyer...of my own volition."

"Good." Kali nodded. "I was going to say. I think you should bring Jasmine by sometime so we can all meet her. I'm sure everyone will love her."

Joel smiled. This was actually the encouragement he was waiting for.

"I want to get Jasmine a gift to remember me by." He told her suddenly. "I was hoping you could help me."

Kali started to smile again. "Help you pick out something for Jasmine?"

"Yeah, if you wouldn't mind"

"Of course, I will. We can go to that big mall on the island. What do you think she'd want? Something from the Disney store?"

"I was thinking more along the lines of jewellery" Joel explained.

"Oh" Kali shrugged her shoulders. "I don't know much about jewellery."

"You're always wearing that beautiful gold necklace around your neck. Maybe I could give Jasmine something like that."

Kali took the gold necklace, and pendent, in her fingers and started playing with it. "Yeah, I guess this does mean a lot to me." She said softly.

"See." He nudged her. "You know more than you think you do. So, you'll help me?"

"Can we go tomorrow?"

Joel smiled at her. "We have to go soon. We don't have much time left on the islands."

Kali nodded. "I guess it's all going to end soon. We should try and make it count."

"Yeah, back to reality soon."

"You guys have your future to think about. I'm sure everything will change."

"Not that much."

"It will." Kali said softly. "You guys are going to go your separate ways. Everything is going to change."

Joel chewed on his lip for a moment. He was distracted looking out the window, at the distant waves. "We'll be around Kali."

Kali shook her head. "No, you won't." She said softly.

Joel wasn't sure how to respond to that, so he didn't. He pretended he didn't hear her.

Chapter 23

Kali:

Kali kicked her legs up under her, and huddled into the couch. She was in the corner of the cabin on the sofa. She had her diary on her lap. As usual she was writing *all* the things that had happened, in *all* the hours of the day.

When she found a moment alone, she would get the old diary out. Everything on the island was incredible, and she wanted to preserve it, and evaluate it, in her precious written words.

Today however, she found herself frustrated. She didn't feel like she was doing enough.

"Good morning Kali."

Kali looked up from her notebook and saw Dane walking past her. He went to the kitchen and poured himself some cereal and milk.

He wasn't even wearing a shirt. He only had on some board shorts, and they were pretty low on his hips.

Kali watched him. There was something about him today. The fluidity with which he walked and moved was fascinating.

All surfers had a gracefulness to them.

They were strong and fit. They were carefree. They put their life in God's hands every day. It didn't bother them, nothing did. They were so casually cool.

"Hey." She said.

"You're writing in your Diary again." He commented

"I write in it all the time."

"Yeah, I know. I've seen you."

"I don't have much to write today." She said, exasperated.

"Why. Is something the matter?" Dane asked casually. He sat down at the table to start eating.

"Cabin fever." Kali said bluntly.

"Yesterday we went snorkelling. Didn't you enjoy that?"

"It was amazing. But that was yesterday morning. I finished writing about that yesterday afternoon. "

"So, you're full of beans today?"

Kali laughed softly to herself. "Yes." She said emphatically. "The guys are out surfing twelve foot waves. I should be doing something."

"I don't know what they're doing out there. It's choppy as shit today."

"They're getting some last minute waves." Kali sighed.

"Why don't you go out and do something."

"I want to." She said sincerely. "But I don't know what to do."

"It's not that big out there you know." Dane said suddenly, changing the subject. "The rain created a pretty choppy swell. It's pretty messy out there, but strangely not very big." Dane looked up her smiled. "I think it will clean up by this afternoon. Most people will write it off and get drunk by midday. It might be uncrowded later on. Maybe you can think about giving it another try."

Kali smiled awkwardly "You think I could?"

"Yeah. Why not." He shrugged his shoulders, as if it was so easy.

"But you said later on this afternoon." She commented. "I'd psyche myself out if I had to think about it all day."

"Why don't you go to the movies or something?"

"I don't want to go by myself." She said, frustrated again.

"I could go with you." He said casually.

"You would do that for me?"

"It's not the biggest favour I've done for anyone." Dane shook his head. "You know I like you right? You're my friend."

Kali huffed. "I tried to meet new people at that party and someone stuck a drug in my drink. Apparently, I have to be unconscious for anybody to want me." She said miserably.

"Kali. You wouldn't have done anything at the party." Dane smirked to himself. "You wouldn't let anything go too far. You wouldn't have done anything to cheat on Zack, even though, you're not going out with him. You don't notice anything, or anyone on this island who isn't Zachary Cumming."

"What?" Kali asked, unsure.

"You're hopelessly devoted to Zachary Cummings." Dane told her.

"What?" Kali asked again, shocked.

"You're in love with him." Dane declared. "And the other two as well."

"We're just friends."

"Are you serious? Zac Efron could be standing next to you, hitting on you, and you wouldn't notice. You're too busy waiting on *them*."

"So?"

"Maybe you should get out from under their shadow? Maybe they are holding you back."

"I think it's the other way around."

"Have you ever thought of living for you, and not for them?"

"No. They're my friends. I owe them everything."

"See; that's what I'm talking about. What if you don't? What if you don't owe them anything? What if you could do whatever you wanted, and not worry about what they thought?"

"How would I do that?"

Dane got up. He walked towards her and sat down next to her on the couch. "I want you to come surfing with me this afternoon" He told her softly. He took her hand, and squeezed it tight. "I want you to come and surf Sunset at sunset."

Kali bit her lip. She looked amazed at *his* hand, as it clutched *her* hand.

He was a pretty amazing guy. He was telling her about something amazing, that she should do, before she left. Maybe something she *had* to do before she left.

"You've never experienced anything so beautiful in your life." He continued.

"I can't surf those waves." Kali said wistfully.

"Yes you can. You have no idea what you can do. Besides; you really have to see it to believe it. Sunset at sunset. It's so warm. Then the sky goes orange, and then red. Then it's dusk and it's beautiful. You get out of the water just as the sun's lowering in the sky. It's amazing."

Kali nodded "I tried and I failed."

"Then try again. Don't worry about anyone else. I will take you out."

"I don't know." Kali said softly.

"Do you trust me Kali?"

He was still holding on to her hand. "Yes." She nodded.

"Then all you need is a little bit of faith."

"And a bit of skill."

"And a bit of passion." He countered her.

Kali turned around. She checked her watch. "If you want to come to movies with me. We should probably get going?" She said quickly, as a statement and a question, at the same time.

She was about to get up. He grabbed her hand again, to stop her.

Kali shook her head. "We're going to miss our movie."

"Come on Kali. Say you'll do this with me."

Kali looked down. Then she looked in his eyes again.

Dane was young. Just like she was. He had blonde hair and brown eyes. Truthfully, he was still a little immature. Still a little unsure. They were just kids, trying to be grownups. Never the less, he saw something in her. There was a spark of excitement in his eyes.

Dane was all about taking chances. Kali was all about playing it safe. If he hadn't convinced her the first time, she never would have paddled out on the North Shore.

He was completely different to Zack and Damien and Joel. Their duty was to protect her. Dane's duty was to make her reach for the stars.

Everything about him, felt like she was doing the right things for the wrong reason. Or doing all the wrong things for the right reasons. Right from the beginning; being around him made her feel alive.

He was right though. She stayed aloof up till now. Kali didn't want Zack to see her partiality towards Dane.

Now he was asking her if he could take her on the ride of her life. At twilight no less. He would show her things she had never seen before. He would force the independence out of her.

She finally submitted and nodded.

"Yes!" Dane nodded back and briefly kissed her on the cheek. "You need this Kali, you just don't know it yet."

It was about four thirty when they got back to the North Shore. Kali ducked into the cabin unseen. Nobody else was in there. She quickly changed into her board shorts and blue rash shirt. She grabbed her six-foot-eight-board, with a block of sticky bumps wax.

Dane grabbed all of his stuff as well, and they headed out. It was about two hours before the sun completely disappeared behind the water.

What Dane had said this morning about the surf conditions was true: The surf had cleaned up. The waves were not very big, nor especially very crowded.

Kali was even fortunate enough to have the same life guard on duty. She waved at Michael as she went past and caught his eye.

"Going to try again *pink girl*?"

"You know it." She yelled back. Although she was not wearing the pink shirt.

"I'll be watching out for you." He laughed to himself. "Try to hold your position this time."

"I'll try my best."

The sky was really turning orange, as they both hit the water. It felt warm, and it felt peaceful.

Kali followed Dane out through the rip. She once again circled around to the line-up. He spoke to her as they paddled. It kept her distracted enough to ignore the big breaking waves, so close to her.

"Not bad for a rom com." He laughed.

Kali tried desperately to keep up with him. "Yeah, it was fun."

"It was fun watching you try to eat sushi." He laughed.

Kali paddled hard and didn't' take her eyes off the water in front of her. "It was fun ditching my plate of sushi and going to Pizza Hut instead."

They were both furiously trying to get through the water. They had to duck dive the same wave. Kali was trying to avoid the rogue waves that came out of nowhere. "I must admit; I liked that part too." Dane called out. He was slightly in front of her.

It was very quiet out the back. Almost mystical. There were only a dozen people out, including herself and Dane. It seemed like magic show.

She was sitting in the golden evening, watching the other surfers perform their tricks.

Perfect conditions, perfect company, and Sunset at sunset was the most beautiful thing Kali had ever seen. Dane was right about that.

Kali listened to some of the other surfers talk amongst themselves. Everyone was in the same jovial mood. The sky around her was turning pink. She and Dane gradually made her way to the centre of the line up to get their own waves.

"You go first. I'll catch the one after you."

"Ok." Kali said softly, feeling strangely ready for this.

"Wait till this set is over. Take the first one of the next set." He told her, as if he some sort of sixth sense about this kind of thing.

Kali nodded again.

She waited.

Then it came for her. She *knew* this was her wave. She paddled with all he might.

Somehow the other held back, and let her have it.

She was a little more relaxed. She looked back for just a second before it picked her up. Then she jumped.

Kali could feel the thrill. She kept still. She balanced herself evenly. The board flew down the face. She tightened her body. She leaned back on her back foot. She made the turn.

She concentrated hard, as she kept moving across the face, trying not to get ahead of it,

She was careful and crafty. She made quick, small turns. She carved up the face, so she didn't go over the falls. She was agile and fluent, so the wave didn't swallow her whole. She rode the wave as far as it would take her.

Then she bowed out, and fell back into the water.

It was the exhilarating. The most exhilarating thing of her life.

Kali couldn't believe that she had did it. She paddled back into shore. It seemed so easy, like she was meant for this wave, and this wave was meant for her.

Kali looked up at the sky and smiled. "Thank you, God."

Kali briefly saw Dane surfing the next wave, but she had to concentrate on getting back in. She paddled steadily, and as she neared the shore, he had already caught up to her.

"You did it!" He flipped his board to the side and waded out of the water. "How did it feel?"

"It felt amazing." Kali emphasized the word. "It was brilliant! Fantastic! Amazing!"

"It was indescribable?" Dane asked her.

"Yeah, that's what I was trying to say." Kali beamed. She looked up at the tower and waved at Michael the lifeguard. He grinned at her as he waved back.

Dane threw his board on the beach next to Kali's. He stepped closer to her.

Kali looked up at a couple of twilight stars. "It was so great." She screamed. "Let's do it again."

The sunset was a dark purple now. The shore break was lapping behind her. The island was indulging her; everything seemed to fall into place.

"It's a bit too dark now Kali."

Kali peeled off her rash shirt, and stood there for a moment in her bikini top and board shorts. "Thank you for this."

Dane took her hand. He stared into her eyes, as if he was asking her permission. She nodded.

Kali felt Dane's arm go around her. She felt his soft embrace. She felt his warm body heat up against her. Then he kissed her.

His mouth was soft and warm. His body was strong. His embrace was tender. Kali had never felt anything so tender. The only other guy she had ever kissed before was Zack. That had been forceful, desperate, and almost violent. Dane's kiss was sweet, slow and affectionate.

His kisses were all so passionate and unassuming. She had received a perfect ride and a perfect kiss all in one afternoon. Life was so good sometimes.

Kali melted into his embrace. She couldn't believe she was so happy. She couldn't believe she was going to leave tomorrow afternoon.

Part 3
Back at the Ranch

Chapter 24

Joel:

Joel looked around the lounge room in his somewhat, high state of mind. His friends were passing around the hash pipe, and they were using it to get stoned. He wasn't the biggest fan of marijuana, but he did it anyway because you were only young once.

He wasn't allowed out of the house today, but he came anyway. He was at his friend Adam's house. He was helping Adam set up for a party that he could in no way attend.

Because of his dad's abject fury at him going to Hawaii, incognito. He was grounded from the moment he got off the plane, till the moment he turned 18. Of course it didn't help that he was the last one of his friends to turn 18.

When he snuck out of his house today, he told his parents he was going to Woolworths for some school supplies, or should he say, university supplies.

Adam was having a pre-university party, to celebrate the end of summer, and basically the end of their childhood. It really just meant his parents were out of town.

Joel's parents were furious for many reasons. They were 'angry' that he broke up with Justine. They were 'angry' he went to Hawaii, and they were 'angry' that he took a fifteen year old girl with him.

Looking at it from his parent's perspective, he could, sort of, see their point.

Considering what happened, at the North Shore party: Kali being drugged and all. Not to mention, things could have gone very adversely wrong. Anyone of them, including, if not especially, Kali, could have got seriously hurt surfing the North Shore.

Kali had ridden only that one wave, but she *did* have a wipe out. She could have smashed into the reef. She could have been caught in an underwater cavern. She could have drowned. They all could have.

Joel had certainly bounced off the reef a couple of times.

Thank goodness nothing happened.

Joel was a Christian and he prayed many times for a good holiday, and a safe return. It turned out, God had smiled on them.

Joel accepted his punishment with an air of triumph. Going to Hawaii was worth it. It was worth any kind of punishment. It was the time of his life!

Joel had to sneak out today because Damien had insisted that he come to Adam's house. For whatever reason he was very enthusiastic about it. He had some sort of announcement.

When he got to Adam's house, Adam was the one who cracked open his baggie full of Marijuana. Joel went along with it. He had a few cones, so far, but he was doubting himself.

Now, he wasn't *just* going to go home, hours late. He was going to go home smelling of marijuana smoke.

Joel looked at each of the people in the room.

They were sitting in Adam's lounge room. Joel was sitting on one recliner. Zack was sitting on the other recliner. He was sitting with his new girlfriend. She was on his lap, and leaning all over him, chewing gum.

Zack had had a new girlfriend since ten minutes off the plane. Her name was Miranda, and Joel really didn't care for her.

Adam sat on the couch, next to Kali.

Kali had come in five minutes ago. She looked somewhat nervous as she entered the room. A little edgy that they were all smoking pot. She must have felt like she had walked into the twilight zone.

Zack didn't initially know she was coming today. He didn't know that Damien had invited her.

He was mad at all of them, because they were exposing her to drugs again. Zack and Damien had just had a twenty minute argument about it, before she got here.

Damien was sitting on the floor with a tray, a bowl, and a pair of scissors. He was chopping up the green plant they were using to get high.

"Do you want a cone Kali?" Adam asked suddenly.

Zack looked up at the speed of light. "No she doesn't!" He snapped at Adam. "She just came to blow up balloons and stuff. Right?" He continued. "Damien only invited her, because he has some sort of announcement."

"No, I'll have one." Kali defied him.

Zack glared at Adam furiously.

"I'm sure she's been around marijuana before" Damien argued. "Right Kali?"

"Right." Kali mumbled. She was looking at Adam, packing hash into the pipe.

"Ryan wouldn't have liked it." Zack scoffed, for the third time in an hour.

"Ryan's not here." Kali said vacantly.

"I ordered Chinese for lunch." Damien told Kali, trying to lighten the mood. "I'm going to go pick it up soon."

Kali glanced over at Zack. He was smitten with Miranda on his knee. "Did you get me honey chicken?" She finally asked.

Damien nodded. "You know I ordered you honey chicken." He told her. "How could I forget your favourite meal? You'd get mad at me, and never come back."

Kali giggled. "You know me so well." She sighed. "That will be the nicest meal I've had in ages."

Joel looked her up and down. It could have been the *only* meal she had had in ages.

"I'm glad."

Damien looked at Kali. He continued laughing, to try and keep the mood light.

Kali looked at Zack, and his girlfriend, as if they were aliens.

Zack had his hands around Miranda's waist, but he was embarrassed at having both Kali and Miranda in the same room.

"Kali, you remember Miranda." He said softly

"Hi." Kali said politely.

Miranda shook her head, and gave a sour look to Kali. "Hi." She said with an exaggerated tone.

Joel couldn't help but stare. Apparently Miranda couldn't even say hello to someone, with giving them attitude.

He had no idea why Zack was going out with her. She had orange hair and she was pretty, but that was the extent of her good qualities.

Miranda was in the year above them at school. She was one of the mean girls that Kali avoided like the plague.

She spoke all the time, with hardly any point to her sentence structures.

Joel turned his attention to Adam. Adam had already filled the hash pipe and given it to Kali. He held the lit flame, over the pipe, and she inhaled the smoke from it.

Then she coughed a little.

"So you guys all went to Hawaii together." Adam asked.

"Not me." Miranda piped in.

Zack looked up, and so did Kali. It was somehow taboo to talk about it with other people.

"Yeah we did." Zack changed the subject. "So, how is year 11 going, Kali?"

"It's only my second week, but it's fine." She said feebly.

"Year 11?" Miranda jumped in. "Gee, Zack. I can't believe you still hang out with high school kids."

Zack raised his hand. "Kali's my friend." He told her.

"I was just kidding." She sobbed.

Zack closed his eyes. "And how is your family?"

Kali stared in his eyes. "They're fine."

Miranda watched the two of them, staring at each other. She nodded disapprovingly.

"So I start my nail artistry course next week, Zack" She said, conspicuously changing the subject. "One of the girl's in my class was one the girls from your year. Jane Spelling or something. She was the one that tripped, in front of everyone in in the bus bay, and went flying, so you could see her granny undies." Miranda joked, viciously. "I still remember how funny that was."

Zack's shook his head. "What."

"Jane Flemming" Joel said, irritated. "She was a nice girl. She was a friend of mine."

That wasn't exactly true, but Joel was eager to defend the poor girl, from the nasty comment.

Damien and Kali both shook their heads.

Zack *wasn't* listening. He was violently staring at Adam.

Adam was sitting next to Kali and flirting with her. He was taking it upon himself to do all sorts of things to her. He was whispering in her ear. Putting his hand on her leg. Making her laugh. Then he was packing a second cone for her.

Kali put the hash pipe in her mouth, and smoked a second one. Adam held the lit flame over the funnel, while she inhaled it back.

Joel was so high he could do nothing but stare. He was too high to move.

Damien didn't look impressed either, but he didn't say anything. Zack was watching Adam like he was a bull, and Adam was a red flag.

As she finished inhaling. Adam whispered something into her ear, and she started giggling.

Joel's eyelids were so droopy. He suddenly wanted to go to sleep, but he continued watching Kali. He couldn't look away, even if it meant that he had to watch on, as Kali got deflowered in front of all of them, by sleazy Adam.

If Adam's hand got any further up Kali's skirt, Zack was going to rip it off.

Finally Damien got up. He walked around and stood in front of the room. He demanded their undivided attention. "I have an announcement." He told them, with an overly animated expression on his face. "I got a spot on the qualifying circuit. I'm joining the tour." He told them, so excitedly.

"What?" Joel asked.

"I going to start on the qualifying circuit. I'm going to be a professional surfer." Damien said again.

Zack's mouths hung open. Kali looked like she had just been hit in the face.

"Congratulations." Joel said slowly.

Zack got up and shook his hand. "I knew it."

"This is huge." Joel said. He got up and shook Damien's hand as well.

Kali got up and gave Damien a warm hug. "That's amazing." She said softly. "You're going to do great on the tour." She told him. "I'm so proud of you."

Joel took a stop back. He was reeling.

Kali was right. Everything was going to change.

Chapter 25

Joel:

Today was Joel's birthday. The week after he started University.

Things were so different now.

Damien was gone. Joel's life was hectic. His dad was still mad at him. His first week at University left him swimming in the deep end.

He headed over to Zack's house at nine o clock at night because he was going to a night club for the first time, for his birthday.

"Why did you come so late?" Zack yelled at him. "Kali fell asleep waiting for you."

"I had to do my readings." Joel said, distracted. "I thought she was coming over tomorrow."

"So did I." Zack admitted. "She came over to give you a birthday present, on your birthday. It seemed important to her. So I told her to stay."

Joel looked down at the sleeping girl on the floor. She looked so peaceful. Joel thought, she was *his* girl, just as much as she was Zack's. "I wonder what she's dreaming about."

"I don't know." Zack smiled at him. "Probably about some guy she likes."

"She likes you Zack" Joel said flatly.

"Don't go there." Zack made a face.

"I have no idea what's going on lately." Joel said honestly. "Why did you take her to Hawaii, if you're just going to ignore her afterwards? You've practically abandoned her lately."

"Abandoned her?" Zack said indignantly. "We're at university now. You're in law school. We are all busy."

"Yeah, but she's here now." He said exasperated. "We can't really take her to the club with us."

He looked at Kali again. The girl lay asleep, on the floor, by the hearth of the fireplace. She was wrapped in a pair of blue Levi's Jeans and a white cable knit sweater. Her long golden brown hair lay carelessly down her back. Her sweet face was turned away from the fire, and nestled into a soft cushion. The flames at her back, made her look all the more sensual.

Seeing her like this, she was so natural and serene. Not so inhibited and apprehensive, like she usually was.

"I wonder about her sometimes." Joel walked up and down the room closing all the blinds.

"What about?"

"She's blocking us out. She's turning into an ice queen. It's like she's hiding something." Joel suggested. "Did anything really happen between you two?" He asked bravely. He was trying to satisfy a curiosity that he had had, for long time.

"What? Are you serious? Did anything happen between us?" Zack repeated the question. He shook his head in disbelief. "No." He said adamantly.

"Then why are you avoiding her?"

Zack readjusted himself on the couch. He sat forward, and buried his head in his hands. "Don't start Joel."

"That is a, very, vulnerable girl there." He tried to explain. "We are not there to take care of her anymore."

"Did we ever really take care of her? She's not your daughter Joel. She's two years younger than you are."

"Yeah." Joel shook his head. "I just feel like there is something going on. You're being such a dick to her lately."

"Why am I such a dick?"

"Ever since you came back, it's like you have fulfilled your obligation to Kali Lockhart. You just tossed her aside on your own person scrap heap."

"I got a job, Joel. I'm trying to start a new life. My best friend left to go on the global surfing world tour" Zack said exasperated. "My dad is on my back about doing engineering as my major. I have to figure out what I want to do with the rest of my life. What the fuck do you want from me?"

"I want you to give a shit." Joel said irritated.

"I do."

Joel shook his head. "When she comes over, you always disappear. You never take her to Nikita any more. You can tell she's not eating properly, and her grades suck."

"How am I responsible for all that?" Zack yelled.

"Because you promised her. You told her you'd be there for her."

"Why don't you write an essay on her Joel?" Zack snapped at him. "You can give it to me, so I know everything I'm doing wrong" He paused. "Besides, I went from eighteen foot waves, to two. I don't go surfing as often anymore, and for the record, there are two of us here. You can hold her hand for the rest of eternity?"

Joel thought about that for a moment. "I would. Except, now she's pushing *us* away. She's avoiding me, too."

"Everything has changed. How do I reach out to *her* when everything has changed for *me*? I hang out with new friends. I have a girlfriend. My school hours are different."

"Yeah, but I'm still kind to her. No matter how busy I am. You look at her like she's gum that is stuck on your shoe."

"I do not." Zack yelled at him.

Kali stirred on the floor. Realistically, they were yelling too loudly, for her to possibly still be asleep.

Joel didn't know at which point she actually woke up. She straightened her body and looked around at them.

"Please don't fight" She said earnestly.

"Sorry Kali." Joel said to her quickly.

"I never wanted to come between you guys."

"We're just arguing Kali." Zack started to explain. "We did that long before you showed up."

Kali looked Joel straight in the eye. "Zack took me to Hawaii because he feels guilty about my killing my brother." She said out of nowhere. She put her head back down on the pillow and closed her eyes.

"What?" Joel turned his head and looked at Zack.

Zack waived his hand. "I'll tell you later." He looked back at Kali. "That's not true. I took you there because you're my friend, and I care about you."

"If it never happened, my brother would have been in that plane seat instead of me."

Joel looked between the two of them. He once again, had no idea what was going on. Kali was speaking directly to Zack.

"If he was still alive he would have brought you anyway." Zack argued. "That was your destiny Kali, whether you believe it or not."

Kali ignored the comment. "Do you think I'm an ice queen Joel?"

"What." Joel did a double take. "I meant, I thought you were guarded lately." He explained softly. "That's all."

She shook her head sadly.

She was like a little kitten on the floor, waiting for someone to drop down a ball of string, so she could play with it. She slowly sat up and bended her knees, close to her chest.

"Nothing has ever happened between me and Zack." She said, glaring at Joel.

Obviously she had not been asleep at all. She had heard everything.

"Then why don't you date someone else." Zack asked, a little too bluntly.

"You mean other boys? Kali asked sarcastically.

"Well, why not." Zack said.

"Because no one would want me. Half of our school thinks I'm your groupie. The other half think I'm a loser."

"Don't be ridiculous." Zack said defensively.

"Am I?"

Zack shook his head. "You're a beautiful girl Kali. Plenty of guys would want to be with you."

"Like you would ever think about it."

"Guys your own age will be lined up around the block for you." Zack said

"Could that be any more of a cliché? Besides, I don't want just any guy, I want it to be love. Not like you and your flavour of the month."

Zack was caught off guard. "I never wanted you to be like me. That's why I'm backing off."

"I guess if I go out with someone else. I'll no longer your problem?"

"That's obviously not what I meant." Zack said irritated.

"I came over for the weekend so that we could hang out, and go surfing. I didn't come so that we could toast marshmallows by the campfire. I certainly don't want to stop you from going to the club and drinking beer." She explained. "I'm glad your dad let you out Joel. I *want* you guys to have fun at the club. You deserve it."

"Well it is my eighteenth birthday. He had to cut the shackles sooner or later." Joel mumbled.

Kali got up. She went to her school bag and got out a small gift wrapped item. "Happy birthday Joel." She said, handing it to him. She leaned over and kissed him on the cheek.

Joel unwrapped the gift. It was the latest Nickleback CD. His favourite band.

"Thanks Kali." He put his arms around her, and hugged her briefly. She felt so feeble in his embrace. He stepped back. Then he grabbed her arm. "I have to talk to you Kali."

He guided Kali into Zack's room. Zack was left behind looking disorientated, as Joel took her away.

Joel ushered her inside the bedroom and closed the door. "Kali you know we'll be around if you need us, right?"

"How can I believe that?" she mumbled to herself.

"I can see all the mixed signals that Zack gives you. He pulls you closer with one hand, and pushes you away with the other."

Kali shook her head. "No, it feels like he's pushing me away with both." She shrugged. "But you guys are right. You are both really busy. If you never said anything: I could have just disappeared. I'm *trying* to give you your space."

"Yeah, that's fine, but Zack's turning into the guy he used to be before he met you."

"What is that supposed to mean?"

"Zack was distant, angry, he was a mess. Now he's scared. His charisma won't save him anymore, and he knows it."

Kali nodded. She looked around Zack's room. She looked at his books, and his CD collection. "What do you think I can do about that?"

"You should go easy on him."

"He stopped talking to me Joel. He's barely even polite anymore."

"I know he's a stubborn mule. I know he takes the easy way out every time. He dives head first into a relationship, for safety. A relationship that is not necessarily good for him, but he tried so hard with you."

"I explained about that. It was all guilt."

"Yeah, about you brother... I'll get to the bottom of that later" Joel raised his eyebrows. "But that's not what I'm talking about. He really does care for you. You have to be the one to take the high road."

"I'm tired of banging my head against a brick wall. I don't know what the hell he wants from me."

"He doesn't know what he wants either. If he was brave; he would be on the world qualifying circuit with Damien, but he's not brave." Joel sighed. "So he just doing what society tells him to do: Get into university, and get a cute girlfriend."

"So he's just sleepwalking through life? He has been to Hawaii. He has good friends, and he's now he's lucky enough to get into university?"

"He's never been happy Kali." Joel tried to tell her. "Not until her met you."

Kali thought about it for a moment. "I know how hard his life is." She finally admitted. "I guess I can try to be nicer, but I don't believe that."

"You can believe anything you want." Joel told her. "But *you* have to be there, for *him* now." Joel smiled at her. "You know what?" He continued. "The longer you stay in here. The more it's going to piss him off."

"What do you mean?"

Joel laughed to himself. "He's jealous."

"Of what?"

"Of us being in here together."

"What are you talking about?"

"I've known him for a long time."

"And he'll get jealous of *us* being in his room?"

"He gets jealous if I look at you."

"I don't believe you."

"He masks it in contempt."

"Maybe we should step out there, and start making out." Kali giggled.

"He'd want to fight me, for your honour."

"Kiss me goodbye then. I'll see his face." Kali suggested.

"He'd never talk to me again."

Kali giggled once more.

Joel opened the bedroom door. He walked out with Kali, beside him.

Zack looked at them suspiciously.

He looked at them for a long time, and then finally spoke "Adam just texted me. He is on his way." He kept glaring at Joel. "We should wait outside."

"Alright." Joel shrugged. He looked at Kali. "You can keep the fire going for us." Joel said. Assuming that she was going to stay the night. "We'll go surfing tomorrow morning."

"Ok." She nodded at him. "Have a good night."

"Thanks." Joel nodded.

He caught Kali's eyes, and then smirked to himself. Then he did what she told him to do: He leaned down and kissed her on the lips. He held it for a moment.

The strange thing was; it felt good. A little too good.

Zack caught sight of it, and stared at them breathlessly. His mouth hung open.

Joel finally stepped back. He felt disorientated.

Kali stepped back grinning, as if it was the funniest thing in the world.

Joel shook his head. "Alright, I'm ready."

Zack looked pale. "Let's go."

Chapter 26

Kali:

K ali heard Zack and Joel talking, outside, as they waited for Adam Camden to come pick them up. They were talking about the weather, or something lame, but not about what had just happened.

Kali was glad that Joel was finally standing up to Zack.

She got up and walked over to the fireplace. She threw another log on the fire and prodded it with the poker.

She decided to take Joel's lead. She would stay the night, and go surfing tomorrow. (If that actually happened, depending on how hung over they were.)

Kali was all alone in Zack's house. Zack's father had gone to visit his own father.

Kali moved to the kitchen.

There was a bowl of fruit on the top counter. Kali picked out an orange, and then got a knife to peel it with. The knife was shiny and silver. It reflected the light above her.

It wasn't so long ago that she cut herself with knives like these, at moments like these. When her mom was gone, and her brother was gone, and she used to piss off the people that were left.

Kali pulled off her watch, and picked up the knife with her left hand. She rested the blade across her right wrist, and pulled back the handle.

She only made a thin cut.

She took the knife away. There was no blood. The blade wasn't that sharp. There was hardly a scar, but at least this way, she could punish herself.

Kali looked at her wrist for a long time. She put the knife back in the sink, and put her watch back on. She decided she would peel the orange with her fingernails. She took it back to the carpet, and ate it, in Zack's quiet lounge room. She attended to the fire until she fell asleep again

Kali shivered as she woke up in the early hours of the morning. It was quiet now and peaceful.

She could hear the ocean from where she sat on the floor. Zack's house was just a few blocks away from the beach.

Kali had fallen asleep on Zack's lounge room floor. She had woken up with a sleeping bag over the top of her.

The air was cold and icy. A salty breeze snuck under the doorway. It was refreshingly cold. Her hands and face felt like porcelain.

The embers in the fireplace still held a faint glow. The curtains over the windows were drawn. The room was black. Kali's eyes readjusted just enough, so that she could make out most of the things around her. She slowly climbed to her feet and looked around the room.

It was a rectangle room, except for the fireplace, which ran diagonally, across the far corner. There was a TV and a coffee table. There was a couch and recliner chair.

Joel was with her. She knew it. She knew it from the moment she woke up. The soft snoring was the giveaway.

He was huddled up on the couch. His body under the covers of a meagre blanket. His clothes slightly smelling of alcohol. He was slightly twitching. Like he was too cold to be comfortable, but too tired to wake up.

Kali turned to the fire, assessing it. Then she quietly scrunched up some newspaper, and stoked the kindling. Then she placed another log on top. She watched the orange flames dance around the wood, and somewhat light up the room.

Kali picked up her sleeping bag and wrapped it tightly around her shoulders. She carefully walked in front of the couch, and tried to get a better look at Joel. He shifted uncomfortably as she realized his blanket had gone astray.

"Good morning Joel." She whispered, as she evenly laid the blanket over the top of him. He didn't stir, or hear her.

There was another noise, it was soft and strange at first, but as she walked past the bedroom it became crystal clear what he was listening to. The moans, the deep breathing, the rustling of bed sheets.

Kali tried to get away from the door, before it made her sick.

She wondered what *hussy* was in there this time. Zack would have never slept with Kali. He would have slept beside her. Put his arms around her. Curl his fingers round her long hair. He had kissed her on the trampoline over a year ago, and yanked her around ever since.

He would certainly never do anything that would make her sound like the girl in the bedroom.

It was too awful to hear. Kali walked into the bathroom and locked herself in side. She stepped towards the bathroom cabinet and peered in the mirror above the sink.

She cupped her hands under the tap, and brought the refreshing water up to her lips. It tasted nice as it ran down her throat.

Finally Kali looked back in the mirror and lingered there frozen and unsure. The light from the full moon beamed through the open window, and she could see herself quite well.

Brown skin and golden brown hair. She thought that she could have been considered pretty. Not as pretty as the girls in those magazines, but still a modest untamed beauty about her.

She stood there for a long time, staring into a dark mirror.

Finally she opened the door and stepped inside the hall. It was too dark to see, but she didn't want to see anything, or hear anything else.

As she walked past Zack's bedroom, she heard a whispering voice from inside. It was a female's voice, but there seemed to be no reply. Zack had probably rolled over and gone to sleep. Even while the girl was talking to him.

He always did that. He fell asleep so easily when he was tired. He would push his mind and body to the limit. Then he would simply curl up somewhere, and drop like a lead balloon.

Kali did not want to be in the same house as that.

Her board like most of their boards was in the foyer near the back door. She silently retrieved her steamer wetsuit from the hall closet, along with a pair of swimmers that she kept in there. She suited up in both of them.

She grabbed one of Zack's coats with hood and the fur lining, and put it over the top of her wetsuit. She picked up her board on the way out, and headed to the beach.

The sun would be up soon. A few other surfers would be out to go dawn patrolling. It didn't matter about the cold. She didn't even really feel it, except for the pavement under her bare feet. She ignored that. Her feet were pretty resilient now.

She walked along the sidewalks turning down each street that led to the bay. The town was historic but also had lots of new and flashy buildings, like the new surf shops and cafes. It was a nice place to live.

It was a perfectly fresh and crisp winter morning. There was still a light mist in the air, and a heavy dew on the ground. Kali made her way to the beach, and carefully set her board down on the sand. She watched the spectacular horizon, as the sun rose from the ocean.

There was someone else there at the beach. She hadn't noticed him at first. He was silent and still, sitting down, with a blanket wrapped around him. He was watching the waves, or maybe he too had come down for the sunrise. A surfboard was still in its cover, and it lay beside him.

He didn't stir as she looked across at him, although he obviously knew she was there. His eyes dreamily watching the waves. His powerful physique, sitting up straight, with his legs crossed.

Everything beyond the bay was utterly quiet. The rest of the world seemed to disappear. He turned to look at her. She could feel the weight of his stare, yet he seemed fairly indifferent about her arrival. She smiled awkwardly, but quickly looked away embarrassed.

She heard him move, the arch of his back straighten, as he finally acknowledged her. A thin smile on his lips. He got up, and walked over to her. He hovered there for a moment. "Do you mind if I sit down?"

"No, not at all." Kali told him.

He dropped down next to her, and sighed to himself. "Your Ryan's little sister."

Kali froze for a moment. "Yeah."

"And now you're Zachary Cummings best friend." The boy looked around. "Where is he?"

"I came alone today."

"Oh, I'm Shawn."

"Hi." Kali said hesitantly.

"It's nice to meet you. I've heard a lot about you."

"Really?" Kali smiled. "It can't be all true."

"So you're the one …"

"That they play with."

"I wasn't going to say that. I didn't believe any of that." Shawn pronounced. "Zack was friends with your brother. I assumed that Ryan introduced you to Zack."

Kali stared at Shawn. "Not many people knew about that."

Shawn motioned to the beach around him. "Zack and Ryan were here often enough. Always laughing, and hanging out."

"Were you friends with Ryan?" Kali asked curiously.

Shawn shrugged. "Yes, I was. Back in the day. It seems like a long time ago." He gave Kali a sombre glance. "I felt really bad when …."

"How well did you know Ryan?" Kali cut him off.

"We were best friends in primary school. As Ryan got older, he got more popular."

"So you guys drifted apart?"

"No, not exactly. In the beginning, we always hung out here, at the beach. Ryan was a good friend, right until the end...there was just a time in the middle when..."

"When he started hanging out with Zack?"

"Yeah exactly, one day he just disappeared. They stopped coming to Nikita beach, and started hunting the Crystal beach scene."

"Where they could get into mischief." She smirked.

Shawn bit his lip. "More than you know." He said reflectively.

"No, I do know." She told him. "I know why they stopped being friends."

"Shelly?"

It took on a whole new meaning when the girl had a name. "Yeah." Kali said quickly. As if she already knew that.

She wanted to change the subject, but it was interesting. Shawn was on the *inside*. Her brother had confided in him. "Are you friends with Zack." She asked suddenly.

"I don't know." Shawn shrugged his shoulders. "Zack was a year younger than me. I guess we are acquaintances. We both come here to Nikita. He's a little intimidated around *me*, which is surprising. He always takes the time to say hello. "

Kali laughed. "Yeah, I'm constantly surprised by what intimidates Zack."

"He's a wild card. I guess the girls go for that kind of thing."

Kali giggled, but she couldn't exactly deny it. "What was my brother like in high school?"

"Wow." Shawn smirked. "This is taking me back."

"Sorry." Kali said.

"He was a good guy. He was nice to everyone. He was charismatic. Just as laid back as you could get. All he needed in life was a box of cereal, a girl, and a surfboard."

"I only remember him having one girlfriend, and it didn't last very long." Kali said confused.

Shawn nodded. "Actually you're right." He remembered suddenly. "He wasn't as lucky in love as people thought. He kissed a lot of girls at dances and parties, but he *did* only have one girlfriend. In fact, his love life was a bit of a disaster. When he wasn't high, or drunk, he would actually get shy around girls."

"Really." Kali laughed.

"Yeah." Shawn sighed again. "He just got carried away with Zack. Then one day, he just snapped out of it."

"Yeah." Kali nodded. "I get it."

Shawn smiled. "When I found out that Zack and the boys were in Hawaii. It blew my mind. That was Ryan's dream, and they took you as well! I was green with envy." Shawn paused. "Zack certainly knows how to take the ball and run with it."

Kali shrugged her shoulders. "He's a bit unpredictable." She agreed.

"Yeah."

"I think Zack's going off the rails again." Kali said sombrely. "I know he had a one night stand last night. He was with some girl, but it wasn't his girlfriend. His girlfriend is on a snorkelling trip with her family at The Great Barrier Reef."

"Is that really any of my business?"

"I don't know." Kali said idly. "Would you ever go home with someone you don't even know?" She asked out of nowhere.

"Is that an offer?"

Kali burst out laughing. It was so funny, she couldn't stop laughing for a couple of minutes.

"I've never had a one night stand." Shawn finally admitted.

"Yeah because you're thoughtful. Zacks been a mess since Damien left."

"Well, that's sort of understandable." Shawn suggested. "He lost his mom, and Ryan, and now Damien. He's probably just trying to push away everyone else. Before they push *him* away."

"I guess." Kali smiled. "That was pretty insightful."

"I'm doing a Psych minor at university."

"Well somebody needs to talk him off the edge. That's what Damien always did." Kali said wistfully.

"What was it like in Hawaii?" Shawn asked suddenly, changing the subject. He clearly didn't want to talk about Zack all day.

Kali breathed in deeply and then exhaled. "Amazing." She paused. "The surf was unreal! But for the record, I attempted only two waves. I only, really, rode one of them."

"That's two more that I've attempted." He sighed. "I don't know if I'll ever be that brave."

Kali blushed. The sun was rising, and it was beginning to shine down on them. She felt warm as she listened to the sound of Shawn's voice.

"I didn't think I would either." She said, obviously. "But something happened, and someone gave me the courage to try, and I went for it."

She smiled again. "Sometimes you're in the right place at the right time and Hawaii invites you in." She shrugged. "It kind of mystifies you like that."

"Sounds pretty amazing."

"It was."

"I can only imagine." Shawn was quiet for a moment. "I guess I'll have to contend myself with Nikita."

"Nikita is still the best beach in the world." Kali said happily.

"Maybe we should hit the waves before it gets crowded. This is our beach right?"

"Yeah." Kali stood up and yawned, stretching her hands up in the air.

Shawn got up and started unzipping his board bag. "You can tell me more about Ryan." She said hopefully.

Shawn held up his board and examined the wax on it. "I can tell you what I know."

"That's good enough for me." Kali nodded enthusiastically.

Suddenly Shawn leaned over and kissed her on the cheek. "He was a lot like you."

Kali beamed. She stretched again. Then as she did, she looked behind her. She nearly fell over, when she saw Zack was standing there.

He was a fair way behind her, but he didn't have his board with him. He was just standing there, staring at her.

Their eyes locked, and the space between them seemed to disappear. His expression seemed blank. A perfect poker face.

"I'll race you in." Shawn nudged her. He didn't see Zack. He was facing the other way.

Kali leaned down to do up her leg rope. She felt shaky. "Ok."

She looked around again but Zack was gone. She wondered if he had been there in the first place, or if it was her imagination playing tricks on her.

For a moment she hated Zack, what was he doing here?

Chapter 27

Kali:

K ali walked back to Zack's house after she went surfing with Shawn, and she felt smitten. Shawn was such a warm and thoughtful guy. She was so glad she met him.

As she entered Zack's back door. She put her board in the rack, and returned the coat to the closet. She threw a t-shirt over her head, and put her jeans back on.

She was surprised to see that there was no one in the lounge room. There was no one in Kitchen either. She slowly came to the doorway of Zack's bedroom and peered inside.

"Hi Kali."

Zack sat on the bed, in a position, as if he had just been meditating. There was a book beside him. The cover was all crinkled, and the pages were torn and dirty.

He had just had a shower, and his hair was still damp. The skin on his face was clean and smooth, like he had just had a shave.

He had a pair of blue jeans on, but he wasn't wearing a shirt. Kali wondered why he sitting like that, when it was unusually cold

"Hi Zack."

"How are you going?" He asked politely.

"I'm fine. Did you follow me today?" She asked bluntly.

Zack looked at her incredulously. "You walked past my bedroom window, at five in the morning. It spiked my curiosity. Yes I followed you."

"I hoped I didn't interrupt you getting laid."

"Did you get any today?"

"What do you mean?"

"With Shawn?"

Kali refused to back down. "I don't kiss and tell."

"I know that."

"What?"

"You and Dane."

"What?" Kali asked, again.

Zack stared at her intensely. "I followed you on Hawaii too."

Kali stared at him curiously.

Zack explained further. "We got back to the cabin on the second last day of Hawaii. You, once again, weren't anywhere to be found. You could have left a note." He said annoyed. "We were sitting up on the tables at the barbeque area. Worried about you. When you came back with Dane. You went in the cabin, snuck back out carrying you board. With your rash shirt on." He hesitated. "Damien and Joel didn't see you, because they were facing the other way. I saw you though. I followed you."

"So what?"

"So I saw you ride that wave at Sunset Beach. I saw you kiss Dane. I saw you, like you were a whole different person. Why didn't you tell anyone?"

"Because it was a secret, with Dane. It was our secret."

"So, you don't care enough to tell me? Or Damien, or Joel?"

"I wanted my own memory of Hawaii." Kali tried to tell him. "Like you must have so many memories of your own. Without me in them."

"Just how *little* do you think of us Kali?" Zack overruled her. "We would have been so happy for you."

Kali shook her head. "Zack, you felt responsible for everything I did. You would have worried. You would have tried to control the situation. I wanted to do something for myself."

Zack raised his eyebrows. "And what about Dane? Were you sleeping with him?"

"No." Kali cried out. "No I didn't. I only kissed him a few times."

"And Shawn?"

"What about Shawn?" She asked incredulously

Zack glared at her. "I saw him kiss you today."

"On the cheek!" She screamed. "He was just being sweet. I only met him today. I was just talking to him."

"It looked like more than that to me." Zack grimaced. "It looked like you were meeting him there."

"Does it bother you that he kissed me, or does it bother you that it was Ryan's ex-best friend that was kissing me? Someone who knows all your dirty laundry. Someone who took Ryan away from you. Someone who could take me away from you, too."

Zack seemed confused by the question. "We're just friends Kali."

"I know we're friends, and you told me to start dating."

"I told you, you were old enough to find the right guy. I didn't tell you to go hook up with the first guy you saw."

"I take my cues from you. If you can't see the distinction. I don't see why I should have to."

"You're better than me, and he has a girlfriend."

"I know he has a girlfriend! I just talked to him a little bit." Kali cried. "He's a really nice guy. Why are you being like this?"

Zack breathed in and exhaled slowly. He closed his eyes. "I followed you this morning, because I wanted to apologize to you."

"Oh." Kali said, surprised.

"I was pretty hard on you last night." He said softly.

Kali nodded, not knowing what to say.

Zack repositioned himself on the bed, but as he moved, he yelped involuntarily.

He instinctively put his hand on his side. Kali saw how vulnerable he looked. She walked closer to see what was wrong, and she couldn't believe she had missed it so far. The massive bruise on his side. Plus the red cut on his back.

Zack saw her concern, and shook his head. "It was just a wipe out, it doesn't hurt."

"The fin hit you on the back?"

"It's ok."

"You should go to a doctor."

"It's fine." He mumbled. "There was no blood."

"But there was a lot of pain, I bet."

"It will be ok, in a few days." He dismissed her.

"I'm not sure about that." Kali leaned over closer, and lightly touched the cut on his back. "You came through Hawaii, relatively unscathed, and then you do this in Clover?" She asked.

"I was distracted." He mumbled. "I went to Crystal beach to clear my head."

Kali sat on the side of his bed. She kept caressing the bruise with her fingers. It really did look red. "Did you tell your one-night-stand, before you left? Or did you just leave." She asked ironically.

Zack looked down, as if he was ashamed. "We had breakfast." He murmured softly.

"Why don't you roll over, I'll give you a massage?" Kali asked him. She was worried that he might have internal bleeding or something.

Zack stared at her for a long time. Not knowing what to do. He was completely caught off guard.

Kali was too. She didn't mean to ask that. It just came out.

Zack shook his head a few times, confused, but then he doubtfully stretched his body out, and laid face down. With his head on the pillow.

She started massaging his shoulders.

Not really knowing how to give someone a massage. She just rubbed into his skin deeply. Then after a length of time, she worked her finger over his upper back. She slowly made her way down to where the bruise was.

"Shawn is kind of funny." She told Zack as her fingers worked their way around his back. "He told me about the stuff that he and Ryan used to get up to."

"Yeah. They were best friends."

"He seems really down to earth. I like him."

"I *am* friends with Shawn you know." Zack told her.

"He said that you're acquaintances." Kali said hesitantly.

"I suppose he had nothing good to say about me."

"He wasn't that interested in talking about you."

"I suppose not" Zack noted. "He is definitely a better man than me."

Kali shook her head. "You're both good, just different."

"A guy who pushes you away with one hand, and pulls you closer with the other?" He murmured.

"You were listening last night?"

"No. I forced Joel to tell me what you guys were talking about." Zack admitted. "Once he got drunk. It wasn't that hard."

"You can push me away." Kali said, idly. "But you won't succeed. I won't let you. I'll never let you leave me." She remarked to him.

Zack nodded. He moaned despite himself as she hit a solid muscle. "That feels so good."

Kali concentrated back on the massage.

He buried his head in the pillow, but he kept moaning every now and then.

She was working her fingers over his cuts, and bear skin. Digging deep into muscles, but soft over the affected bruise area.

Zack kept moaning.

Kali eventually got up and went to the bathroom, for the disinfectant. She dabbed at his back with diluted Dettol.

He stopped talking to her, but his moans said it all.

After a while, he went silent. Kali thought he was asleep. She slowly started to get up, but he suddenly grabbed her wrist as she tried to move away.

He turned on to his side, to face her. Then he pulled her down onto the bed with him.

Kali wasn't sure what to do. She simply laid down next to him.

She was facing him.

He smiled at her, and put his hand on her waist. "Just stay with me." He said wistfully.

Kali blushed nervously.

She really had nothing better to do today. Except homework, and that didn't really interest her. She just nodded as she lay next to him. Her head on the pillow, just a few inches away, from his.

He closed his eyes.

Kali exhaled, and nodded again.

She was tired from her early morning surf anyway. She eventually just closed her eyes, and rested. With his hand on her waist.

She only had her eyes shut for a couple of minutes, when Zack started talking to her again.

"You still have your bikini top on." He called out suddenly. "It's still wet. You must be freezing." He told her, seemingly worried.

It was true. The cold bikini top was starting to bother her. It was starting to chafe as well.

Zack, without asking, reached under her shirt, and undid the bikini strap, around her back.

Kali followed his lead and grabbed the strap around her neck and yanked the whole thing off from under her shirt. She dropped the bikini on the floor, behind her.

Now she was just a girl in a wet t-shirt though.

"You must be freezing." He literally put his arm around her, and pulled her whole body closer.

She was now right up against him. His body heat was so warm.

He held her like that, for some indeterminate amount of time. She lingered in his amazing embrace, but after that, it seemed like the most natural thing in the world when he started kissing her.

It just happened.

It was soft and slow kissing. Like Dane had kissed her.

They were just passionate kisses, and he was holding her.

He was kept kissing her, and kissing her, and it felt so good.

He kept pulling her closer and closer, if that was possible.

Kali had to bite her own tongue, not to scream out with desire. She moaned.

Then, suddenly, as quick as that, he was gone.

"I can't do this Kali. I'm sorry." He told her. "Your brother would hate me for this. You should go."

Somehow Zack had detached himself, and jumped out of bed, in one leap. Then he was suddenly walking out of the room.

Kali heard him go down the hall, and then the bathroom door slammed shut.

Kali felt exposed, and vulnerable.

She got up and ran out the door, out of the room, and out of the house. She ran home, more confused than ever.

Chapter 28

Kali:

"I don't want to live without you. I don't want to live without you. I could never live without you, live without your love."

Kali lifted her head up and realized she was singing. It was a hot, humid night. She was so restless. She was lying on Damien's bed, waiting for him to come home, from oversees. She was lying on his soft mattress, in a pink Roxy t-shirt, and a pair of denim shorts.

Tomorrow Damien was coming home from the tour. Kali was going to stay the night at Damien house. When he got home at five in the morning, she was going to be there, with Zack and Joel, to surprise him.

Zack and Joel were supposed to be here already, but they both pulled out at the last minute. Zack had to work as a night filler at his supermarket job, and Joel had to study again for his exams.

It was hot and sticky as she lay back on the bed now. Damien's mum was asleep in another part of the house. The nice lady had, welcomed kali with open arms. Mrs Grisham, was a kind, and big hearted woman. She was always worried about her son.

Outside it was sprinkling spring rain, but it was nothing more than a light mist. Today had been one of the hottest days October's history.

Kali closed her eyes and listened to the late night love songs, on the local radio station. The songs were seductive and deep, making her mad with desire. She wiped the sweat of her brow and leaned over to turn the radio down. She thought she heard talking outside, but couldn't be sure.

It could be anyone out there. She didn't know the neighbourhood very well.

The talking stopped. Kali heard a door slam. Then a car started up. Then she heard it drive away.

"Well." Kali said out loud before turning up the radio again. She tried to remember the daydream that she was having. It was probably about Zack, it was always about Zack.

She remembered the lyrics to the song. "I don't want to live without you." She began talking to herself. "But I have to go, because we can't live like this." She serenaded herself, smiling, although it didn't make her happy.

"I love you and you ignore me. What could I ever say? That you would ever want to hear? I just want to look in your eyes, because then I don't have to say anything at all."

She was practicing her words for the final speech she was going to give Zack; before her family left town.

That's right! Kali was leaving town. Her dad got a job in Sydney. She was moving. She was leaving Clover.

"My dad got a job in Sydney, close to my sister." She began talking to herself again. "Now I'm going to leave town, and go far away." She sighed. "I have to leave, and hopefully leave you wondering. Maybe you can feel the hurt that I feel…. When you turn your back on *me*."

Kali knew that she would never actually say these words out loud. But she liked to pretend. She liked to practice a speech where she could say anything she wanted, and she could finally say how she felt.

"There's appears to be a girl in my bed."

Kali jumped a mile high. She looked over to the door way, and Damien was standing there grinning at her.

He had a giant board bag hanging off one shoulder, and a big duffle bag, hanging off the other. He had a smaller back pack as well. Damien was wearing a long sleeve, button down, rusty shirt with blue jeans.

He looked *so* good.

"Damien!" she screamed jumping off the bed.

Damien inched his way inside the room and dropped his stuff off on the floor. He sighed as the heavy load fell to the floor. Kali didn't give him time to take a breath. She jumped on him. He twirled her around as her hands clung around his neck.

He put her down, and kissed her on the cheek. "Are you sure this is loud enough." He said, winding down the volume dial, of the radio. "I could have been a burglar robbing the house, and you wouldn't have noticed."

Kali was stunned. "I thought you weren't coming home until tomorrow."

"No." Damien shook his head. "Zack must have got the dates mixed up. It was today." He said simply.

Kali smiled. "Couldn't wait to see me huh?"

"No as a matter of fact I couldn't." He kissed her on the cheek again. "What are you listening to?"

"Late night love song requests."

"That's your kind of music." He commented.

Kali grinned. He was right. She did live for love, and anything that would remind her of it.

"So, you came back now."

He closed his eyes and ran his fingers through his hair. "I came back because I missed you kali: You're my girl." He looked her up and down, like he was seeing her for the first time in years, rather than a few months. "So where is everyone else?"

"I assume Zack's at work. Joel's studying."

Damien smiled. "No surprise there. Are you still fighting with Zack?"

"We were never really fighting." Kali tried to explain. "We just stopped talking to each other."

Damien sat on the edge of the bed, and patted a spot next to him. "He does this Kali. You have to reach out to him."

"I don't know how to do that." Kali contended. "Besides, Miranda would always get in my way, if I tried."

"Yeah I know." Damien rolled his eyes. "I don't understand what's going on there, but you've always been the one to pull Zack out of the quick sand." He conferred. "You have to do it again now, before it gets over his head."

"Not me." Kali laughed. "I'm the complication that he could do without." She shook her head. "You've been talking to Joel!" She accused him. "Joel told you to say that."

"No. He didn't. I just agree with him." Damien sighed. "And you're not a complication, Kali." He defended her. "And you mustn't know Zack very well, because he prefers the teen angst."

"You say that like you're an adult now."

"Hotels, planes, competitions, different cultures. I think it's fair to say I've grown up a little."

"But how is it? It must be so much more than that."

"I love it Kali. I really love it." Damien confided in her. "It's exciting, and overwhelming, and scary, but it's so rewarding."

Damien looked around his old bedroom. "Sometimes it's lonely, but there are some really great guys on tour that I've made friends with. People I can bunk with." He looked her in the eyes again. "I love the tour Kali, and I've done pretty well too. I can't believe I'm saying this, but it's easy for me. It's just second nature."

"I'm so glad for you Damien."

Damien sighed to himself. "You should see some of these waves Kali." He emphasized the point. "Some great right handers that would be perfect for you." He fell back on the bed.

He was lying on his back, with his legs still hanging over the side. He tugged on her arm, and pulled her back, onto the bed, next to him.

"There's this great spot in South Africa. I wish you could have been there with me." He looked over at her. "I could have shown you so much."

"Did you take photos?"

Damien looked back up at the ceiling and shrugged. "I took a few." He smiled. "It's not the same. We'll have to go together. South

Africa is amazing. It's so beautiful. I even went on this safari. You haven't lived till you see a giraffe up close."

Kali giggled. "We could go to the Zoo."

Damien nudged her with his elbow. "No, trust me. Africa is better."

Kali giggled again.

"So we're here alone are we?"

"Yeah" she nodded.

"I can't believe how long your hair has gotten."

Kali flicked at her curls. "I like long hair."

Damien grabbed her wrist. "You're a bit thin aren't you? Have you been eating properly?"

The question was starting to get on Kali's nerves. She pulled her arm back and looked up at the ceiling. "I eat all the time."

Damien gave her a funny look, but changed the subject. "And how's school going?"

"Horrible."

Damien saw that she was serious, and didn't push it. "You'll be fine." He told her.

Kali didn't want to talk about herself. She wanted to hear about Damien's adventures on the tour. "So what happened in Europe? Tell me all about all the stuff you get up to."

Damien lifted his head, and then dropped it again. "I can't even think at the moment. I'm too tired for that right now. Let's just lie here." He smiled at her, then curled up on the bed, and closed his eyes.

Kali did as she was told, and eventually started to get sleepy herself. She was lying there for about ten minutes, and she was about to fall asleep, when Damien did something completely surprising.

He curled his arms around her upper body, and dragged her backwards, so that she was right up against him. He put his arms around her, and held her tight.

Kali wasn't sure what to do, so she just waited.

"Things are strange when you get back to reality." He said contemplatively.

"What do you mean?"

"It just feels strange." He meandered. "Like my family." He told her. "And my friends. You're all a million miles away. Then I get off the plane, and my dad gave me a lift home from the airport." He sighed. "Apparently, my sister's up to her old tricks again."

"I'm sorry to hear that." Kali said doubtfully.

"Then I get home, and you're here." He kissed her on the cheek one more time. "I'm glad you're here." He paused, but then kept talking idly, as if he was desperate for someone to talk to. "My standing on the tour is way up there, in general, but I didn't do so well, in my last competition." He sighed again. "When you're not doing well, you adrenalin drops, and it gets a bit lonely."

Kali nodded. "It must be really hard on you." She said, trying to be thoughtful.

Damien's squeezed her body tighter for a second. His arms were already straddling her rib cage, and his head was so close to hers, on the pillow.

"It's like any job I guess." He mumbled. "You have your ups and downs."

"But your job is a little more extreme." Kali empathised.

She was lying there for another few minutes, before she turned to lay on her back. Then he did something even more surprising. He kissed her.

Damien kissed her on the mouth.

"What was that for?" Kali asked confused.

He let go of her waist. "I don't know." He said, looking up, slightly bewildered.

"You're really nostalgic about being back." She gestured, embarrassed.

"No." He said, looking at her "I'm not sure that's it." He told her, uncertainly. "I don't know what it is." He shook his head again. "These late night love songs are killing me Kali."

"Yeah they're good aren't they?"

"No, that's not what I mean. Yes, they are good, but they are making me crazy." He tried to tell her.

Kali giggled at him, but in all truth, she was desperate to be kissed again. She leaned over and kissed *him* on lips.

Damien smirked, marvelling at the situation. "That what you want?"

Kali looked in his eye for a moment, and then nodded.

Damien took a deep breath in. "Really?"

Kali nodded her head again. As she continued to stare deep in his eyes.

Damien turned to lay on his back, and stare at the ceiling. He exhaled slowly. "You're so dangerous Kali." He said idly. "You're so dangerous." He said again. "If I crack under the pressure tonight, then Zack will massacre me in my sleep, no matter how much I want it."

"Just because you kissed me?" Kali giggled.

Damien's voice was so strong, he didn't flinch. "No." He told her. "Because I'm about to make love to you."

Kali breathed in very slowly, and then out again. "Are you."

I don't know."

"Would you?"

"Maybe." Damien answered, uncertainly again. "For crying out loud?" He said, frustrated. "Do they have to play so many Foreigner songs? Foreigner is anyone's Achilles heel." He said referring back to the radio play list.

Then it happened, out of nowhere.

His mouth was on hers.

His body was wrapped around hers, and he was kissing her, with all of his strength.

Kali laid back. She felt the tender touch of his lips against her skin. He kissed her collar bone. Up to her neck. Up to her face. Then this mouth was on top of hers, kissing her, and caressing her, was all his might.

Meanwhile Foreigner's '*I want to know what love is.*' was emotionally tantalizing both of them. Making this situation ten times more intense.

Damien's love was so open and giving.

It wasn't like Zack, who couldn't reciprocate his feeling, without feeling guilty. Damien didn't let guilt tear him apart, with each touch.

Kali closed her eyes. She felt the wonderful joy of his body on top of hers.

Her skin was so euphorically exposed. Damien's other hand was exploring every inch of it. His touch was so strong, but delicate. He knew exactly what he was doing. He was practiced in this art.

Damien was so gentle, even while he was being so passionate with her.

Kali was overcome with pleasure. She surrendered herself to the rhythm of his body: And he did the rest.

He slowly, and tenderly kissed her, undressed her, positioned her, caressed her, and then he was inside of her, and it seemed to go on forever.

His tenderness engulfed her. His athleticism was breathtakingly apparent.

She experienced every emotion inside of her.

The melodies of several intense, and painfully passionate love songs spurred them on. The people who were making the requests, certainly knew what love was.

She experienced, an amazing amount of pleasure, until it stopped.

She lay there overwrought, trying to catch her breath. Damien lay down next to her. He smiled and looked in her eyes.

Finally he spoke. "You're only sixteen Kali. He's going to kill me."

"Not if he never finds out." Kali said softly.

"I do love you Kali." He said adamantly. "I hope you know that."

Kali smiled back at him. She put her head on his shoulder. "Everything is changing anyway." She said, without explaining.

He held her close. His body, and his emotions were so warm, and Kali was so excited that it had finally happened.

She never imagined this would happen, but it was the best thing that could have ever happen.... before she left for good.

Part 4
4 Years Later

Chapter 29

Zack:

Zack stumbled across the dance floor, and barrelled into the boy's toilets. He tripped his way into the stall, and hung his head low over the toilet bowl. After a moment of felling sick to the stomach, he finally threw up.

He slowly put his hands to his face. He felt the husky whiskers over his chin, and the unkempt dark curls that grew in his hair. It had been so long since it was last cut.

Adam ran into the bathroom after him. He stood in the doorway looking down amused. "You can't hold your alcohol at all can you?"

"I saw her there! It was her, I swear it was her."

"You saw who?" Adam took a sip of the beer stubby he was holding.

"Kali you idiot, didn't you see her?"

Adam slapped him on the back of the head. Zack lurched forward to throw up again. "Kali who?"

Zack got his breath back. He wiped his face, with the cuff of his sleeve. He quickly got to his feet, and turned around, grabbing Adam by the scruff of the neck. He slammed him back into the bathroom wall.

"You know who she is; Kali Lockhart. She was sitting on you couch when you practically felt her up. Don't pretend you don't know what I'm talking about."

"Let go of me." Adam pushed back on Zack's chest and Zack stumbled backwards.

"How long have you been saving that up? I hardly even touched her, and even if I did, at least I was getting some play. You never touched her." He shook his head. "Talk about hopelessly devoted; she would have been your performing seal. You could have done anything you wanted." Adam paused again. "And you didn't even touch her." He repeated.

Zack straightened up. He looked at Adam for a moment before he swung his fist back and punched his friend in the head. "Fuck you."

Adam touched his eye and he stepped back. He looked shocked.

"It wasn't her Zack. It was a figment of your over active imagination. How many times have you thought you've seen her, and it turns out to be someone else? For crying out loud, it's been four years. She's not coming back Zack. It's never her. All the wishing in the world isn't going to make it her."

"I could have sworn…"

"What is she? Twenty now? You wouldn't even know her. If you saw her."

"She's twenty-one! And of course, I'd know her. She the same person." Zack retorted.

"Yeah, but she will always be a kid to you." Adam answered. "And for the record: Why do you care so much about this girl? They're all the same."

"You know that's not true."

"What I know is that you're being a wimp. You're the one that created the sexual tension. You could have just fucked her and be done with it. Now it's built up in your mind as the, be all, and end all, of civilisation. It's the question that was never answered." Adam shrugged. "The flame's not going to go out, until she puts out."

"That's poetic." Zack's anger boiled over. He could feel his cheeks flush red. He drew back his fist but he stopped himself.

"Put Psych one-o-one aside for a second." Zack tried to reason. "She just ran away Adam. She just left without saying goodbye. What kind of person does that?"

Adam cautiously watched Zack withdraw his hand. Zack rested it at his side before Adam answered. "You don't know anything about her. You never did. She was just a fantasy. You're staying true to the idea of her."

"No."

"Come on Zack it's your twenty-third birthday. You're clearly having some kind of melt down." Adam shook his head. "And you're also drunk."

"It's my twenty-third birthday." Zack repeated. "Look around you. I'm throwing up in a disgusting bathroom in a pub. Damien and Joel didn't even show up tonight, and I'm seeing the ghost of a girl, who probably right now, is in the arms of another guy."

"Then pick another girl for yourself. There's plenty more fish in the sea." He made a face. "Especially if your name is Zachary Cummings."

"I don't want another fish. I just want to see her again."

Another patron of the pub walked in to the bathroom at that moment. The guy looked awkwardly between the Zack and Adam. Zack instantly got annoyed. He tugged the door open at light speed and made his way to the nearest exit. There he stood outside on the street. He breathed in deeply, trying to get some fresh air.

He stood staring up at the starry night sky, tired and weary. He wanted to be some where quiet, so he could think.

Adam caught up to Zack in a few minutes, on the street. "What are you doing out here? The party in in there."

"I'm not drinking anymore. I'm sick of it."

"It's your birthday celebration! There are ten guys in their waiting for you to chug down another Jim Beam shot."

"Well let them wait."

"Why don't you just get your act together, and go back in there."

Zack breathed in the hot summer night. "Has Joel come yet? Is he in there?"

Adam exhaled slowly. "No, he's not in there."

Zack nodded. He turned around. "I just want to be on my own. My birthday never meant anything." He said solemnly. He started walking away.

"Anna's in there Zack" Adam called out. "She's looking pretty hot tonight."

"You can have her." Zack answered. He started walking down the lighted streets. The brisk sea breeze wafted past him. The stars shined bright in the sky. The night was full of them.

He walked not far before he reached a coffee shop. It was still open at this late hour. There were only four other people inside including the cashier.

It was quiet and peaceful in the coffee shop. He looked at all the patrons. There was a couple by the corner. They sat together and talked softly to one another. Sometimes they started giggling. They were clearly in love. Zack watched them for a moment. He was jealous of the way in which they cared for each other.

The other customer was an old man. He was sitting by himself at a table. He was staring into his cup of coffee. He looked so deep in thought there could have been an earth quake at that moment and he wouldn't have noticed.

He looked like a kind and worldly old man. He had white hair, and a white moustache. He looked gentle and knowledgeable; like he had a whole bitter sweet life time to reflect on. He just sat solemnly, late at night, in a small coffee shop.

And then there was the girl at the counter and Zack recognized her immediately. Her name was Amber. She was in a few of his classes in high school. He had never really spoken to her before, but he had always noticed her.

Amber Manning was kind of like Kali Lockhart. They kind of looked the same; long brown hair, brown eyes, they were both slender. They were both pretty. They were both shy.

"Hey Amber, how are you going?" He reached the counter and looked at the girl standing on the other side of it.

Amber looked shocked for a moment.

"Hi Zachary" she said finally.

It was so cute that she called him Zachary. Nobody ever called him Zachary any more.

"What can I get you?"

Zack looked up at the menu. "A hot chocolate."

"Would you like a cup or a mug?" Amber asked softly.

"A mug."

Amber smiled. "Full cream milk?"

"Yeah, thanks."

Zack suddenly had a fantastic idea: He should ask her out.

"So how are you going Amber?"

"I'm good thank you." She took a mug from off the top of the coffee machine and worked her hot chocolate magic behind the counter.

"What have you been up to?"

"I'm just working here, and hanging out" she shrugged "nothing too exciting"

"You look really nice" he told her.

Amber looked shocked, as if it was the last thing in the world she expected to hear.

"Thank you." She smiled. "It's nice to see you're still living here in Clover."

"Clover is my home. I don't think I could ever leave."

"I know what you mean." She said slowly. "That will be two dollars eighty."

"And two choc chip cookies as well." Zack got his wallet out of his coat pocket. "Why don't you make it three?"

"I didn't think you were a cookie man Zack."

"I have always been a cookie man. The cookie monster was my favourite Sesame Street character."

Amber giggled.

Zack opened his mouth to ask her out. At the last minute he had to stop himself. On her finger was an engagement ring. A flood of disappointment overcame him. He looked away. "Damn it" he swore underneath his breath.

"What did you say?"

"I was going to say… it's good to see you." Zack said earnestly.

She looked confused by the comment, but he was still thrown by the ring. He walked away to sit at the booth, at the very back. He sat down and sulked.

"Why did you leave me Kali?" He asked the air around him.

Zack drunk his hot chocolate, slowly, while he also tried to sober up.

He kept thinking about the girl that had left him behind.

When he finally finished the cup, he looked up. He was the only customer left. He was alone except for Amber. She was sneaking up towards him.

"We actually close at midnight." She whispered gently.

Zack checked his watch one more time. He realized it was a quarter past.

He instantly jumped to his feet. "I'm so sorry." He looked in Amber's brown eyes. She smiled at him.

"No, it's ok." She told him.

"You should have said something." He cried.

"You looked kind of deep in thought." She tried to tell him. "I just let you sit there. While I cleaned up."

"Sorry Amber." Zack scratched his head. "I'm screwing up everything today." He said pensively, as he started to walk out.

"Wait. You don't want to forget your cookies." She called out.

Zack turned around. She handed him the small paper bag, with his two remaining cookies. Then Zack felt something in his eyes. They were tears.

He was not crying because he missed Kali. He was crying because he had made Amber late.

"What's wrong?" She said worried.

Zack wiped away his tears, embarrassed. "Nothing."

Then he looked in Amber's eyes. He decided he'd go for it anyway. Fiancé be damned. He cupped her face in his hands, and kissed her.

At first, she kissed him back. Then suddenly she pulled back. For a moment she could not respond. She was too shocked. Finally, she shook her head. "I...I'm engaged Zack."

"I don't care. Come back to my place with me."

She looked at the floor. She shook her head slowly.

"I can't do that to him. It's Richard, Zack. My fiancé is Richard Sampson your old biology partner. You know, the one with the pimples, and the glasses. You were nice to him. He was your friend. One of your less popular friends." She added bitterly. "I think you should go."

Zack walked out of the coffee shop. He trudged slowly, along the road, to his new townhouse.

The hot summer night was stifling as he walked alone. He was sad and drunk.

There were still a few tears falling from his eyes. He was supposed to be happy. It was his birthday, but he wasn't happy.

He tried to stop himself from crying, but the more he tried, the more the tears fell, and the more humiliating it all became.

The snuffling had somewhat cleared up, as he got home. He walked inside, away from the desperate heat outside. His town house was just as messy as he had left it.

He didn't even make it to the bedroom. Instead he flicked on the television, and settled himself on the couch with a blanket and a cushion. There was an old movie on the screen. He started to watch it.

The movie was about a young girl and a horse race. It had Mickey Rooney in it. It was a really good movie. He ended up watching the whole thing. Then he fell asleep where he lay.

Chapter 30

Kali:

"Kali Why did you leave me?"

Kali awoke suddenly. Someone was calling her. Someone was screaming her name so loudly. But it was not someone in the waking world; it was in her dreams.

She lifted her head, from the pillow, on her bed, and looked around the room. It looked so hot outside and the sun was streaming through the window. The book she was reading had fallen out of her hands. It sat face down, and open on the floor.

It was going to be a fine day, as expected.

Kali sat up with her legs crossed and listened to the sounds of the house, but there were none. The house was empty. There was nothing but a residual silence.

When she closed her eyes, she could hear the ocean, but it wasn't real. Living in the suburbs, she never actually heard that sound for real anymore.

A cool shower was what she needed.

Kali's wrist watch; the one that Joel had given her for her sixteenth birthday, said that it was 11:08. Kali couldn't believe she had slept so late.

She had to be at work in just over an hour. That meant she had to get ready. Kali walked over to the Kitchen and got a drink of water. She collected her work clothes from her bedroom, and went into the bathroom.

Something didn't feel right.

The feelings wouldn't go away. She stood exposed, and alone, under the hot shower. Her emotions were overpowering her, she felt like crying.

She closed her eyes and let the hot water scold her skin. She finally figured out what it was.

"It was Zack's birthday today."

*   *   *   *

"Are you ok?"

Kali looked up from the magazine in her hand and studied the boy in front of her. She pulled the sleeves of the blue knitted jumper over her hands, and wiped at her eyes with the cuffs.

One minute she was walking to work. The next, she had made a pit stop at the local newsagency. She had made her way, by sheer force of habit, over to the surfing magazine section.

Those habits were suppressed, but not dead inside of her. A big pile of brand new Australia's Surfing Life magazines sat predominantly on the shelf. That was her favourite magazine.

She quickly picked one up, and opened it up. She scanned through the introduction, and all the glossy pages. Then something unexpected caught her attention. It was an article in the middle of the magazine.

The picture was unmistakable. The article was about a guy she knew. It was someone she had loved. Someone who had loved her back. It was about the only person in the world who had ever made love to her.

An entire article had been printed in the magazine, about a young, up and coming, South Coast surfer: Damien Grisham. It was an article about his life, his prospects, and how he was a rising star in the art of surfing.

Kali couldn't believe it. It was him. It was really him.

The article was positive, and hopeful, and amazing. Damien was so articulate in his expression. He was so honest, and thoughtful, in his interview.

His picture was of the boy she remembered. He had not changed at all. There were no visible piercing or tattoos, His hair was just as long, and just as blonde, as when she left him. If anything, he looked better than before.

Suddenly tears started falling from Kali's eyes. She couldn't help but remember what it had felt like to be in Damien's arms.

"Mam are you ok?"

Kali looked up suddenly "Mam?" The newsagency store employee was tapping her on the shoulder. She looked up at him disorientated. The boy was young and fit. He looked at her surprised. The guy was about her age, or a little younger. He had ginger spiked hair and freckles. He must have thought she was crazy

She was crying, and staring off into space. Her tears were falling down her cheeks, splashing onto the magazine pages.

"The surfers make the girls crazy, but we usually don't get such a violent reaction to those magazines."

Kali laughed. "I was going to buy it." She told him quickly.

"That's ok." He smiled. "I haven't even bought my copy yet. They only came on sale today."

"Really?"

"Yeah it's funny, they were supposed to come out tomorrow, but they got here a day early."

"That is funny." Kali slowly wiped at her eyes.

"So what upset you?" The boy asked gently.

Kali closed her eyes and looked down at the article. "Do you see the surfboard he's riding in that picture?"

"Yeah."

"It's mine."

"What." He said stoked. "You know Damien Grisham?"

"I went to Hawaii with him."

The boy's eyes widened. "What? You've been to Hawaii?"

Kali nodded looking at her surfboard getting air with someone else on top of it. She wondered why Damien was using it at all.

"He must have been pretty close to you."

Kali shrugged. "It's been a long time."

"You're not Kali are you?"

Kali was shocked. "How do you know my name?"

"I must confess, I've been reading the magazine, at the counter, in between customers and you see that passage there?"

Kali nodded. He pointed at paragraph of writing in the article. "Yeah." She said weakly, rubbing at her eyes.

The boy started reading the passage out loud. "It Sais *'It always seemed so easy for me to get into professional surfing, but I couldn't have done it without my best friends; Zack, Joel and Kali.'*"

The boy emphasized Kali's name.

Kali's mouth dropped open when she heard him say it. "He mentioned me." She smiled stunned. "I can't believe it."

"Well it's a little blurry, but it's in there." He said, commenting on the tear stained pages.

"You know my name, but I don't know yours." Kali said suddenly.

"It's Jake."

"Nice to meet you." Kali shook his hand.

"And you." He smirked. "I'm captivated. What are you doing in suburbs on such a beautiful day?"

"Same as you, I'm going to work."

"At Woolworths?" He guessed looking down at her uniform.

Kali nodded her head slowly. "Yes."

"It sucks living so far away from the beach, doesn't it?"

"Oh, I'm not a surfer."

Jake's face went blank. "You're not?"

Kali shook her head. "I used to be. I'm not anymore."

"You gave it up?" He asked perplexed.

"Yes."

His mouth hung open. "Why?"

"It's a long story."

"I can't imagine any story that would result in giving up surfing."

Kali nodded, she felt weak. "I think I'll buy two of these." she said trying to change the subject. "The one I ruined, and a fresh one. So, I can hang it on my wall."

"You know, Damien's doing really well, on tour. I've been following him a little bit. He's rising up the rankings, and he's in one of the latest surfing movies."

Kali nodded "Great; I'll have to get it." She looked up at the counter. Someone was waiting in front of it. "You've got a customer." She told him.

The boy turned quickly and returned to his post.

Kali scoured the magazine article. She noted that Damien's next big event was in Manly; in fact, it would start in a few days.

She followed the boy to the counter and bought her two identical magazines. As he handed her the change, he picked up a pen, and wrote his name and number one of the covers of the magazines.

"I've got a spare board if you ever want to give it another shot."

"Thank you. I might try that." She paused. "But I think I want mine back first." She smiled warmly at him, as she exited the store, and headed to work.

Chapter 31

Zack

Zack opened his eyes and looked around his living room. It was dark, the curtains were drawn. He couldn't tell what time it was. There was a noise, and it had woken him.

Zack could have sworn someone had been talking to him. He was almost positive that it wasn't a dream. It sounded much like Damien's voice, but there was no one there. Damien wasn't even in the country.

In front of Zack, on the coffee table, there was a paper bag with the cookies in it. Suddenly last night came crashing back down on him.

It was so humiliating.

Zack had hit on that poor girl, last night. He even knew that she was engaged, and he tried to pick her up anyway. Zack hated the person he had become.

He looked across at the television, but it was turned off. There was *no* old movie on now that was going to make him feel better.

There was also nothing to stop him from feeling the full force of this hangover. His eyes were sore. His throat and lips were dry. There was a pounding in his head that felt like a drum solo to a Red Hot Chilli Peppers song.

It was a Saturday morning. He still had the whole weekend to recover, but even that wouldn't be long enough. He felt so alone.

He knew that he was just going to lay here, for the rest of the both Saturday and Sunday; watching DVD's, and eating junk food. He had already decided on ordering Chinese for dinner.

His birthdays always did this to him. The rest of the year he could bury the past in his subconscious, where it belonged; but his birthday made him remember.

It was the answering machine! It came to Zack in a flash. Someone was talking to him, but it was on the answering machine.

He slowly got up and shook off his blanket. He walked over to the phone. There was one message flashing on the answering machine and he pressed the button to hear it.

"Hey Zack" Damien's voice began "Happy Birthday! How was the party last night? Did Joel come? I'm here in Hawaii. I'm just getting some practice. The competition was sick. I came eighth overall in the Triple Crown. I'll be back tomorrow, then I'm heading up to Manly for the Coke classic. I won't have time to come home."

Damien seemed distracted by something on his end, but then he started talking again. "It's still the twenty sixth over here, but I know you're like a day in front of me, so happy twenty-third. I can't believe we're that old. Anyway, save a piece of cake for me and I'll see you later."

"I can't believe we're that old?" Zack said to himself. "We're only twenty-three, is that old?" He asked softly, talking to himself.

He lifted his hand, and put it to his forehead. He had a slight fever and his headache hadn't gotten any better.

Suddenly, someone started knocking on the door. Zack spun around and practically ran to answer it. He didn't know who it was, but hoped it was someone he cared about. Maybe it was Kali.

Joel was at the door.

"Hi." Joel said. He was dressed in a pair of jeans and a black Jacket. He was clean shaven and he had a new haircut. He looked immaculately groomed; the way he always looked.

Zack felt instantly retarded. He had forgotten that he was wearing his boxer shorts, and the same vomit ridden shirt, that he was wearing last night.

Zack hadn't shaved in a few days either. He put his head down and nodded. "Hi Joel."

Joel looked him over, and raised an eyebrow. "What kind of party did you have last night? You look terrible."

"Thanks." Zack said, being under enthused. "Didn't you come?"

Joel looked around in both directions. He stepped back, shaking his head. "Don't you remember?"

"Not really, but I wasn't there for that long. I take it that you didn't show."

Joel shrugged his shoulders and spoke exasperatedly. "I was busy with work."

"I'm sure."

"I have been really busy lately."

"With work?"

"Yeah."

"She wouldn't let you come, would she?"

"I had a business dinner." Joel said defiantly.

"At eleven o clock at night?" Zack breathed in. He looked up at the sky as he slowly exhaled. His eyes were sensitive to light. They started hurting, badly. "So, how's the family."

"Oliver's teething, he never stops crying."

Zack wasn't sure what to say to that. "And how's Justine?"

"What do you care?"

"I don't."

"Then don't ask. I don't know why you have to be so smug. She's my wife and I love her, I've told you that a million times. I don't know why you're so qualified to judge other people's relationships." Joel yelled at him.

"I've seen what you in love looks like. This isn't it."

"We have a few problems, but every couple does. You should know that better than anyone."

"I do know her problems better than anyone. She was your girlfriend in high school. We got to know her problems 'real' well. And then you went back to her."

"Suck it up Zack." Joel said spitefully.

Zack shook his head. Justine had taken advantage of Joel. He was a little drunk one night, or really he was blind drunk. He went home with her. Then she was pregnant. Then he married her.

"She's a bitch. You don't know what she's doing to you."

"Since you speak of those qualities; that reminds me of Miranda Dempsey. Are you sure you're not having flashbacks?"

"Miranda didn't get pregnant. I thank God for that every day." Zack flew back at him.

"I come over here to say happy birthday, and you end up arguing and insulting my wife…again."

"What can I say, I'm incorrigible."

"Yeah and you're also an arse hole. I've been tiptoeing around you since I was thirteen. I'm sick of dealing with your shit."

Zack looked at the ground again. He deserved that and he knew it. "I miss her Joel."

Joel nodded. He knew who Zack was talking about, but he asked anyway. "Who?"

"Kali." Zack said bluntly.

"I haven't heard you use that name in a while."

"I wouldn't think so."

"Then why today?"

Zack didn't answer. "Why did she leave us Joel?"

Joel stared at him blankly. His expression was hard to read because he was wearing a pair of white Oakley sunglasses that covered his eyes. He also looked away every now and then, as if he was distracted. "You pushed her away Zack."

Zack ran his fingers though his hair. It was perfectly obvious, but the bluntness was a little hard to absorb.

"Thank you, Joel, for that in depth analysis. Is that how you argue in court?"

"You push people away Zack. I don't' need to be Sigmund Fraud to figure that out."

Zack closed his eyes. "She could have left a note."

"Yeah but she didn't." Joel said simply. "She'll be back when she's ready."

"It's been four years." Zack tried to rationalise. "I don't think she's coming back."

"No, this story isn't finished yet." Joel sounded so wise when he said that, especially for someone who got trapped into a shotgun wedding. Zack hadn't forgiven Joel for marrying a girl he didn't love.

Joel was holding a wrapped gift, behind his back, and he handed it to Zack. "Happy Birthday."

"My birthday was yesterday."

"No, it's not, it's today. Your party was yesterday."

Zack realised his friend was right. It was his birthday today.

"Oh yeah." He admitted while opening the gift. It was aftershave. "Thanks."

"Can you put some on right now?" Joel joked.

Zack laughed despite himself. "I think I might go to Coke classic in Manly." He said out of nowhere.

It was an idea that had been forming in Zack's mind, ever since he had got Damien's message on the answering machine.

"What?" Joel asked confused "when?"

Zack shrugged his shoulders. "I was thinking about Monday, or Tuesday. I want to go join Damien. I just want to see him. He's in Hawaii at the moment, but he'll be in Manly in a few days."

Joel stared at him for a long time, and then nodded. "I might come with you."

Chapter 32

Kali:

Kali slowly walked the length of sand of Manly Beach.

The day was warm, but the water was chilly. Kali could feel the cold, wet sand, squidge underneath her bare feet. The shore break ran up, over her ankles, up to her calves, and then receded back into the sea again.

It was the big contest day today. Half of the Coke Classic Surfing tournament had been run a few days ago, but then the event had been put on hold because of small surf.

The delay was much to Kali's advantage. It gave her the time she needed to get to get the courage to come and see Damien. He was competing in the contest today.

Kali took the train to Manly this morning and the big surf was finally predicted today.

The small surf had been accompanied by drizzly rain over the contest waiting period. Today, however, as she woke up at five in the morning. The clouds were gone and there was nothing but blue sky, and streaks of golden sunshine.

The possibility of seeing Damien again was more than she could hope for.

But, who was Damien now? Did he have a girlfriend? Was he married? Would he still care about her?

The day was warming up. Kali wondered around the beach, thinking of what it would be like to see her friend again.

She wore a blue t-shirt, and a white skirt, with the blue flowers printed on it. She also had her purple baseball cap on her head. She carried her white, slip on shoes, in one hand, and there was a little black backpack strapped on her shoulders. It contained some money, a chap stick, her wallet, and a mobile phone.

She watched the surfers in the water and the feeling was nostalgic. She remembered what it was like to be out there.

It caught her completely off guard when she saw something in the distance.

It couldn't be real, but it was.

It was just a few guys mucking around on the sand, but it seemed so familiar. A feeling of de jar vu swept over her. Kali closed her eyes, but when she reopened them, it was the same.

They were just three figures on the beach playing football. They were good looking guys; very athletic. The same characteristics that she had once memorized on three boys, were now amplified on three young men. Even their mannerisms were the same. Everything about them was engrained in her memory. It was them. Just by looking at their hazy outline from a distance, she could see who they were.

Kali wondered if she was hallucinating. She walked further towards them and they were still as complete in body as they were in spirit. She stood at a distance and stared at them, while her feet soaked in the shore break.

Joel had dark brown hair and hazel eyes. He was taller than the other two, maybe a little lanky, but he had style and definitive good looks. Joel had that sharp, well-groomed, Wall Street look about him. That was something you could see from his clothes, and jewelry.

Damien had that blonde-haired, blue-eyed, surfer look about him. Zack was somewhere in the middle, light brown hair, with amazing green eyes, and a clean cut, almost military like posture, and physique. The boys were wearing board shorts and loose t-shirts. None of them was wearing shoes. They had the tan, the sun-bleached hair, and they were still so good looking.

Their faces were so gentle, like they were still kids playing with that football. They were mucking around, and running, and tackling each other. They didn't notice her at all.

The boys of summer.

Kali was too stunned to move. Her first reaction was to faint, but she managed to stay conscious. It couldn't possibly be them, except it was.

There were three boys, and three surfboards, stuck nose first, into the sand. And there it was; the proof if she needed any. One of the boards was hers. The one from the magazine.

It was Kali's surf board and Damien was using it, habitually, apparently.

After ten minutes of subtly watching them, they stopped their game, and came together. They were panting and stretching. One of them started speaking excitably.

"I can't believe you guys came!" Damien told them.

Kali turned and looked directly out at the ocean. She sat down on the ground and put her arms around her legs. She kept staring at the ocean, so she could hear them, but she couldn't see them.

"We came for moral support." Zack said, with a dry wit.

"Yeah, but you just showed up. You didn't even call."

"It was a split-second decision." Joel said. "But let's face it. You need us."

"Yeah right. Like I haven't been doing this on my own, for years."

"Yeah, but we have always been there in spirit. Now we are here in person."

"Good on you." Damien laughed and lightly punched Joel in the shoulder. "But, no seriously guys. I'm feeling good about today." Damien said cheerily. "When I woke up. I felt like I could take this whole thing out."

"Well then, great, do it." Joel encouraged him.

Kali was trying to listen carefully, but she couldn't catch every word. As they came together they started talking more softly, she couldn't hear much of it.

She looked down at the sand. She felt so confused. Was it now or never?

She got up and turned around.

She stared straight at Zack. It took a moment to get his attention. Zack noticed her, looked away for half a second, and then looked back.

Then he blatantly stared back at her. He took one step forward, away from the group, and glared at her as she moved closer.

"Kali?" He asked, incredulously.

Kali nodded.

She didn't say anything. She couldn't make her lips move.

"What." Damien stopped talking to Joel. He looked around, distracted. He saw her. "Is that really you?" Damien asked.

He didn't wait for a reply before he raced forward, picked her up, and twirled her around. He put her back down on the ground. Then he unexpectedly kissed her, on the lips.

Kali smiled. "Hello."

Damien looked into her eyes. He seemed so confused. Kali kept his gaze. She had no answers for him.

Finally, she looked away. She looked back at Joel.

Joel was cautious. He hesitantly, and slowly, walked towards her. He reached out and took her in his arms.

She hugged him back tightly, even thought he was tentative. It was so comforting, when he held her.

Kali slowly looked over at Zack. He stared at her with curiosity, but even more with contempt. Then he looked away. "It's been a long time Kali."

Kali nodded. "I know."

Kali, again, noticed her board not far away. She walked over to it. Her prized Richo 6'2 stick.

"I always kept it." Damien said staring at her. "I use it on the tour sometimes; it's good luck."

A quarter of the way down the board, Kali had written the words 'Kali's board' in purple crayon. The words were still there. The board had probably been reglassed, so they would be there forever.

No one said anything. No one knew what to say. Kali looked down at the ground, trying to escape their gaze.

"What are you doing here?" Zack asked finally.

"I came to watch Damien surf."

Damien looked up. He smiled cautiously.

"Why did you just leave without saying goodbye?" Zack finally asked. "Where the hell have you been?"

"In Sydney. The suburbs."

Kali looked away. She felt Zack's pain, but all three of them were starting at her.

Zack was angry with her. He wanted to know why she left things so unresolved; but he was always the one, who constantly, kept them that way.

As for the other two: Damien had made love to her one minute, then the next minute, she was gone. He must have been so terribly confused. Joel was hurt because he was vulnerable. Joel couldn't always do it on his own. Sometimes he would crumble, when no one had his back.

Kali looked up. Zack had hurt *her* too. He hurt her emotionally, every day. She was in a constant state of pain for the last four years thinking about it. "What do you care? You were with Miranda."

"Miranda?" I've never had a serious girlfriend before, why would I start with Miranda?"

Kali shook her head sadly. "To send me a message."

"And what message would that be?"

"For me to back off."

"I needed some space Kali. I didn't need you to disappear without a trace. One day you were just gone." Zack told her, solemnly.

Kali thought about that for a long time. "I needed some space too." She said back, almost whispering. "My dad got a job in Sydney. I had to leave."

"Yeah, I noticed. I went to your house because I heard you hadn't been at school for the last five day. Turns out, you had changed schools, and there was another family living in your house."

"We didn't sell our house, we rented it out." Kali said softly. "It was all done privately."

"Yeah, well. I felt kind of stupid. People I have never met before, telling me that you had moved on. I felt like I had just imagined our whole friendship. I might as well have."

"I always thought you were better off without me." Kali said idly. "I have no idea why you kept me around for so long. It was only a matter of time before you cut me loose" She paused and looked in his eyes. "Just like you did to all the other girls."

"So, you thought you'd what? Teach me a lesson?" He asked incredulously. "You said you'd never let me leave you, but then you left me first."

"She was just a kid." Joel yelled at him.

"And so were we, when she left in the middle of the night, without so much as a note." Zack turned around. "She's not the girl you think she is."

"I'm exactly the girl you think I am." She shook her head. "I didn't have a choice. I had to leave."

I can't do this." Zack turned around. He started walking in the direction to the car park.

Kali made a face. She should have known he would walk away. He would never stay to face her, but then again, she ran away, a lot, too.

"So you came to watch me surf today?" Damien asked her slowly.

"I didn't expect you to see me doing it." Kali admitted.

"But I'm glad I did." He looked upon her. "I wanted to see you." He paused. "I was waiting for this."

Kali smiled. She looked in Damien's eyes. She remembered what it was like to have his hot breath against her neck. The feeling almost overcame her.

"I've been waiting for it too."

"Forget about Zack." Damien said suddenly. "We can do this." He continued optimistically. "I can take this thing out, without him."

Joel shrugged. "Zack will be around. Watching. He won't leave before the competition."

Damien nodded. "I know." He stared at Kali again. "It's going to be a really good day."

Kali looked him dead straight in the eye. "Will you surf on my surfboard?"

"Of course." His deep blue eyes were so engrossing. They swallowed her whole. "Will you be here when I get back?"

Kali nodded slowly. "Of course."

Joel stepped forward. "Yes." He looked at Kali. "She'll be here with me. She will keep me company."

Kali smiled at Joel.

Damien grinned. "Then it starts again now."

Chapter 33

Damien:

The night was black, even blacker than usual because the cloud cover had returned. It looked like it was going to rain again. Damien went to open the door to his hotel room. Someone had knocked on his door. It was some time ago. The visitor had to wait for a while because he was getting the shampoo out of his hair.

The girl looked a little nervous as he opened the door. He saw her standing there awkwardly. He was just wearing a white bath towel, around his waist. His hair was wet. His chest was bare.

"Holy shit. Sorry Kali. I thought you were Zack or Joel."

Kali giggled. "It's ok."

Damien smirked at her. "It's good to see you again…*so quickly.*"

Kali grinned. "I know." She kept laughing. "I know I said goodbye to you after your heat. After you WON you heat. But I don't want to go all the way home. It takes too long on the train, and I didn't want to come all the way back tomorrow morning, for your finals. I thought, maybe, I could crash here tonight… I don't mind sleeping on the floor." She said quickly.

"Sure." He nudged her. "But you don't have to sleep on the floor, and you know that."

Kali blushed. "You were amazing out there today."

"I felt amazing out there today." Damien said, nostalgically. "Every wave was the right one."

"The judges certainly thought so. I thought so. It was like poetry in motion."

"I'm sure you're better than me by now." Damien said thoughtfully, but he wasn't sincere.

"I don't really go surfing anymore." Kali told him flatly.

Damien shrugged. "Yeah, I know." He admitted. "You're way too pail. It looks like you haven't seen the sun in a decade."

Kali nodded. She turned around and looked out the window. She didn't reply to his comment. When she started speaking again, her back was to him. "I saw your article in surfing life magazine."

"Did you?"

"Yes." She told him. "It was an amazing article."

Damien twitched a little. "I used to want everyone to know my name." He paused. "But now I want to make it to the top, before I jinx myself, into getting there."

"You're already at the top." She said softly.

Damien walked over to her, and came face to face. She was looking down nervously. He put his hands on her shoulders. He kneeled down, so he was looking directly into her eyes.

"Why are you so nervous Kali?"

"I was always nervous."

"Not to me, you weren't."

Kali shrugged. "I expect you to be angry at me, like Zack is."

"I'm not mad, just confused." Damien looked out the window. "I remember holding on to you that night. We were so close. Then a few days later you were gone."

"Everyone was going their own way. I felt like I was going to drive you guys apart."

"We were getting older." Damien told her. "People grow apart as they get older."

"Yeah, but you guys had it so good before I came into your life. I made everything such a drama." Kali insisted. "Like today. When you were having fun playing football. Then you saw me, and I ruined it."

"Kali, that's ridiculous." Damien touched her face, and forced her to look into his eyes. "What do you think was going on, in our lives? Zack was so lonely. He was wagging school every second day.

Reading every vampire book he could get his hands on. Don't ask me why. He was carrying around a secret that was tearing him to pieces. It would have destroyed him." He said emphatically. "I was terrified about my future and Joel was practically manic."

Kali stared at him.

"If it wasn't for you, I never would have gone to Hawaii!" Damien pleaded with her. "Going to Hawaii gave me the courage to join the tour."

"I'm sure that's not true."

"Oh my gosh, Kali. The only reason Zack went to Hawaii was because he is fulfilling Ryan's dream of taking you there. Seventeen-year-old high school students don't go to Hawaii on a whim. Especially the way we went. We didn't even tell anyone we were going, but it was our destiny. You made it all happen."

"It's called schoolies, Damien. Of course, you would have gone!"

Damien smiled sadly. "Joel might have ended up with Justine anyway, but at least we had his blood pumping for a while. At least he tasted the sweet victory of Jasmine. At least he rode waves that were higher than his house. At least he lived on the edge for a while."

"Joel ended up with who?" Kali asked, stunned.

"Far out, Kali. Don't get me started. I'll tell you later." Damien sighed. "The problems didn't start when you came. They started off again when you left." He desperately tried to make her understand.

Kali was taken aback by his revelation, but then she spoke slowly. "You would have ended up on the tour." She whispered. "You were half way there when I met you, but thanks for saying those nice things."

Damien shook his head. Kali always had such low self-esteem. It was maddening not to be able to get through to her.

"When we fell asleep together that night." He looked in her eyes to get her recognition. It was so intimate. I'm not sure I've ever felt anything so intimate." He sighed. "Do you ever wonder about us?"

"All the time." Kali looked away. "I think about it all the time, but I can't imagine us dating" She said, uncertainly.

"No." Damien said softly. "Zack wouldn't have let us date, and even if he did, it would have been futile. You were Zack's girl." He explained. "We could have been together though, for some time. You could have been my good night girl."

"What is that supposed to mean?" Kali giggled.

"No." Damien started laughing. "It's just a song on my IPod: *Goodnight girl*. Every time I hear it, I think of you."

Kali giggled again. "I don't understand any of what you're saying. Why was I Zack's girl?" She argued. "He always had a girlfriend, and I wasn't it. He had no claim to me. He's can't just put a hold on me, like I'm a library book. He never even wanted me."

"Yes he did." Damien smiled at her.

"No he didn't." She grumbled.

"What is that necklace hanging around your neck?"

Kali looked down at her gold necklace with the turtle charm: After all this time, she was still wearing it.

"It's just a necklace."

"Yeah, and who gave it to you?"

"You're telling me this necklace is Zack's claim to me."

"That necklace is all Zack needed to claim you as his own. Everyone knew Zack gave it to you."

"That doesn't make any sense."

"Then why are you still wearing it?"

"Because I like the turtle charm." Kali said hastily.

"You were Zack's girl, and everyone knew it. No one would have looked sideways at you."

"You did."

Damien laughed again. "I just got back from overseas. I was emotional."

"And I was your goodnight girl?"

Damien nodded. "You still can be."

Kali started laughing, and so did Damien. It was nice to hear her laugh.

"Does Zack know that we were together?"

Damien took a deep breath in. Then he let it out. "No. He doesn't."

"You kissed me at the beach." She blushed again "on the lips."

"That was an accident." Damien said slowly. "I haven't told Zack or Joel. I've always thought it's better for Zack, if he doesn't know."

"But why does Zack have the final say?" Kali persisted. "I'm telling you, you're wrong. I'm not Zack's girl." She tried desperately to explain.

"Come on Kali. You know you are." He sighed. "You are the only one who can fix him. You know it better than anyone. Look me in the eye and tell me that *you don't want to be* Zack's girl."

"But I'm not." Kali shook her head sadly. "I'm known it every day since I met him. I knew it today when he walked off on me."

"He'll get over it."

"And I'm just supposed to wait around?"

"You mean by tomorrow, when he comes crawling back?"

"He won't. He's angry. Please don't say things like that." She shook her head. "What if I want to be my own girl?"

"Have you been?" He hesitated. "These last four years."

Kali thought about it a moment. "Not really." She admitted, softly.

Damien looked at her, trying to get her focus back. "That's cause you're too busy hiding." He tried to explain. "Is it *so* hard to believe that you could be pretty, and smart, and resourceful? You don't believe in yourself. You just hide from the world."

She shrugged her shoulders. "I never fit in." she wiped away a tear. "We both know what I am."

"And what is that."

Kali turned away, desperately wiping back the tears. "Weak."

Damien shook his head. "But you're not." He stepped closer to her. "You are beautiful." He told her, and stepped closer again. He kissed her on the left cheek.

"And smart." He kissed her on the right cheek.

Kali's eyes fluttered, and her cheeks lifted, almost a smile.

"And resourceful." He kissed her on the lips.

Kali looked around, astounded for a moment. Then she kissed him back... Like a freight train, she was up against him. So passionately.

It was Kali that jumped *on* him, and twisted herself around, like a pretzel.

One minute her feet were on the solid ground, then she was in his arms, and he was holding her up. Her legs twisting around his waist, and he was kissing her.

He was kissing her, and tasting her, and walking backwards until they both fell on the bed. Then he was lost in her.

Nothing felt more desperate.

He was kissing and grasping at her to fill the void. The void that had been there for so long.

He had never felt so lustful or energised to have something and someone, and have her underneath him. But at the same time, he was careful with her, because it was Kali.

The same Kali from all those years ago. The same anguish filled girl from his youth.

Tonight, this girl belonged to him. Her lips, her face, her long brown hair, her body. This tempting, mysterious and awkward girl child was his possession, and he was tearing into her.

His towel, and most of her clothes, were long gone.

Damien was running full steam ahead, with his mouth, and hands, enveloping her. Then he heard a knock at the door.

It took a moment to register.

"What?"

Kali looked around as if she just came out of a trance.

Damien looked at her disorientated.

Kali started back, then she jumped slightly, and sat up. Then, out of nowhere, almost instinctively, she ran into the bathroom.

Damien, shook his head, confused. He took a moment and tried to compose himself. He picked up his towel and fastened it. He went over to the door and opened it.

It was Zack on the door step. Damien jumped, he moved smoothly into the hallway, and closed the door behind him.

He still felt very strange.

"What's going on?" Zack looked at him agitated.

Damien thought about it for a moment. "Nothing."

"You wouldn't be cheating on Danielle, would you?"

Damien gritted his teeth. "Don't worry about it Zack. What's up?"

"Did I screw up today?" Zack asked sincerely. "I shouldn't have left. Does she hate me?"

"Kali doesn't hate anyone. Least of all you." Damien said carefully.

"You know how much I care about her, right?"

"You mean you love her?"

"She was too young before. I thought I had more time, but if she's back… I just want to talk to her."

Damien felt a stab of guilt.

"I'm sure she'll be there tomorrow. You can talk to her then." He mumbled.

Zack nodded. "Good." He looked around awkwardly. "You know I was walking past a jewellery store today. I saw *this* in the window, and then I found myself buying it." He huffed. "I have no idea how it happened…but it's perfect for her."

Damien began to feel faint. "Is that an engagement ring Zack?"

"No. It's not!" Zack snapped. "I don't know what it is. I don't know why I bought it. I just wanted her to have it. If anything ever happened…I wanted her to know…." He didn't finish the sentence.

Zack incoherently waved around the small box and flicked it open and shut. Damien finally had a good look at the ring. There was a diamond, and an ocean blue stone in the setting. It was understated, but Zack was right. Kali would love it. It was Kali all over.

Damien felt lost for words.

Zack was embarrassed, he put the small box back in his pocket. "Just forget I showed you that."

"I'll try."

"Anyway, you were killing it today!" Zack encouraged him. "I was in the crowd. Off the cliff, watching. The other competitors didn't know what hit them. You had the inroads to all the good waves."

"Yeah. I was in the zone today." Damien agreed, breathlessly.

"Sorry I walked off."

"It's ok." Damien said swiftly.

"I was always going to stick around for your heats." Zack assured him.

"I knew you were around."

"And you talked to Kali today."

Damien held his breath for a second. "She's fine Zack. She's doing well. I didn't have much time to talk to her, but she's doing good."

"Alright. I just had to talk to you. I don't want to disturb you from whoever is in there."

"Huh." Damien made a strange noise with his mouth. "There is no one in there."

"Yeah, sure, that why you're talking to me in the hallway, of a hotel, with only a towel on." Zack gave him a funny look. "And I heard two voices talking before I knocked on the door." He paused. "Don't worry. I won't tell Danielle. Although I'm surprised."

"Yeah. I didn't expect this." Damien murmured.

Zack slapped him on the back. He shook his head, and then walked off down the hall. He was in the same hotel as Damien, but he was two floors above.

Damien exhaled, and walked back inside. Kali was sitting on the bed, looking humble again.

"It was Zack" He said flatly. "And he still loves you." Damien walked over to the bed and put his hand up against Kali's cheek. "He's staying in room 12:02. You can go after him if you want. We don't have to do this."

Kali shook her head. She looked at him. "No." She said adamantly. "No." She said again, thinking about it. "Finish what you started." She nodded, and looked around. Then she raised her head and looked deep into his eyes. "I want you to... This moment is ours." She told him.

Chapter 34

Kali

Making love to Damien was so wonderful. It was the time of her life, but Damien didn't take her seriously.

To him, she would always be Zack's girl. Their passion was only good for an illicit one-night stand. Like a volcano, that had to erupt once or twice, in its lifespan, to clear out the old emotions, and start anew.

A relationship between them, could never have lasted. Damien was right. She was Zack's girl, and that's why she had to see Zack today.

Kali had caught the train down the coast and got off at Clover. She walked to Zack's new townhouse and knocked on his door. Damien had given her directions to this place.

Zack and Damien were co-owners of these amazing side by side, town houses. They had two identical, two-bedroom, units.

They bought the place together. It was both a place to live, and in investment, and it suited both of them. Damien made the deposit with the money he earned on the tour, and Zack was able to invest because he still had his mother's inheritance.

Joel had brokered, the deal. He wasn't quite out of law school yet. None the less, he had ghost written the deal. Drawn up the contracts. Got the seller down to the lowest price. Edited the partnership agreement, and oversaw the bank contracts. Zack and Damien didn't care less. They just signed what Joel told them to sign.

Now they had their very own place in Clover.

None of the three boys ever wanted to leave their home town. They were very business savvy about getting their own property there. The three of them made a great team.

Kali put her bag down on the front porch. She looked around. The clouds were black and low in the sky. There was a distant rumble of thunder in the foreground. It made her feel nervous.

Kali was wearing a pair of bootleg jeans. A new pair of black rock boots, and a white cable knit cardigan.

She felt good. She was working out in the morning now. Seeing Damien surf the coke classic had really affected her. She wanted to be fit enough to get into the water.

Zack didn't know that she was coming to his house today.

Kali stared at the front door, for about five minutes, before she finally knocked on it.

She was nervous to see him again.

"Kali?" Zack said, confused. He answered the door with an apple in his hand. It was half eaten.

"Hi." Kali nodded.

Zack stared at her, confounded. He stood there for a long time, just trying to figure out what to do.

Kali waited for him to say something.

"What can I do for you?" He asked her. His tone was icy cold. He kicked her bag with his foot. "Did you run away again?"

"No." Kali said softly. "I came to see you."

"Why."

"I wanted to talk." Kali said softly.

"It was never really your strong suit." He said spitefully.

Kali nodded. "I could always talk to you."

"Better the devil you know, right?" Zack asked her.

Kali nodded meekly. "I wanted to talk to you. I have to tell you something. I have to say it now, before I come back and everything changes."

"What is it?"

"I love you."

Zack jolted back. The look of surprise on his face, seemed to overwhelm him.

"Don't you think I've always known that?" He said, trying to act cool, although he was completely caught off guard.

Kali closed her eyes. "Yes, of course you've always known it." She yelled at him. "That's why you toyed with me so often. "She picked up her bag, and started walking away. "Nice to see you too, Zack."

"Kali" Zack screamed at her, as she strode away. "What do you want me to say? I don't know you anymore. So much has changed."

Kali felt her lip quivering. Tears were clogging her eyes.

She stopped short, but she didn't turn around. She was deciding whether she should keep walking or not. She didn't want Zack to see her cry. So she kept going. She took two more steps.

"Stop Kali. What do you want from me?"

Kali stopped again. Her crying turned to anger. She dropped her bag. She put her hand up around her neck, pushed her hair away, took off her gold necklace, and then threw it at him. It landed on the ground in front of him. "Nothing! I don't want anything from you."

With that, Kali turned around again. She was so confused. She left her duffle bag on the end of Zack's drive way and started running. She didn't know where she was running to. She just ran.

She ran for about twenty meters when he caught up with her.

She heard his footsteps behind her. He reached her so easily. He was hardly breaking a sweat. Then he caught her. She felt his arms around her rib cage and she got pulled up.

"I'm sorry Kali." Zack whispered in her ear. He tightened his grip around her, and held her painstakingly close. He kissed her on the neck, and then on the cheek. "I'm sorry."

Kali desperately tried to ward back the tears before they could fall. She stood there in the midst, and warmth, of his embrace. He held on to her, for a little while longer.

Finally, he stepped back, and let her go.

"I'm coming back Zack. I'm coming back to Clover. My whole family is."

She looked at Zack. He stared back at her. Then they were interrupted. A crack of thunder boomed so loudly, it shook the ground she was standing on. It pierced her ear drums.

It started pouring down rain on them. Zack grabbed her hand. He pulled her back towards his town house. As they ran together, he stopped to pick up her bag, before he ushered her inside.

"Welcome home." Zack said after a moment of silence. They stood there in the small foyer, both wet and cold.

He looked down at her bag. It was still in his hand. "I think your stuff might be wet."

"It's fine."

Zack stared at her breathlessly.

"I'll get you a sweater." He said softly.

Kali's clothes were a little damp, and it was getting chilly quickly, with the storm. He toddled off down the hall, to his room, and she followed him.

He riffled through his closet, and threw a cable knit sweater at her. He got out a black jumper for himself, and threw it over his head.

Kali slowly put the warm sweater on. It was nice. She looked around his room.

Zack's room was pretty big for a townhouse. It was pretty charismatic for a bachelor pad.

His bed was had blue sheets with a dark red doona. To one side there were a few windows and a desk with lots of personal papers, and a lap top computer. On the other side there was a cupboard and shelves, with some books, and blocks of wax on it.

He had a skipping rope sitting on one shelf, and a skateboard propped up against the wall underneath. There was a large chest pushed up against his bed.

It was a great room, scented with a hint of aftershave.

The room said a lot about Zack. He could not be tamed. He was independent and dark. Passionate and soulful. Anyone who came in here, came at their own risk. They stood the chance of getting hurt... emotionally, and pleasured beyond their wildest dreams, physically.

"It's perfect for you" Kali whispered.

"What is?"

"This place. This room."

"Thank you." He nodded at her. "Come out to the lounge room. We will have a drink."

The storm was still loud and raging outside. Thunder echoed across the sky. Kali shivered again. She sat on one of the cushions of the couch. Zack emerged from the kitchen. He had two glasses of red wine, in actual wine glasses.

Kali accepted her glass nervously, and stared at it for a moment. Zack sat across from her on the recliner.

Kali looked at him. "You never wanted me to drink this before."

"I suppose you're old enough now." He noted.

"I suppose I am." She murmured.

Thunder roared again outside. The storm was getting violent. The reflection of lightning in the windows flashed every few seconds. The thunder was so loud. Zack leaned across and lit a couple of candles on the table. The flames flickered in his eyes. She watched the flame dance around in the cold air.

"How have you been Kali?" Zack asked.

Kali shook her head. She didn't like that question. It was too generic. He could have just looked in her eyes to know the answer to it. "I'm ok." She said softly.

"It's been four years." He said sceptically. "That's it? Just ok?"

"I didn't stop being me when I moved." She said softly. "I'm still shy in Sydney."

"Yeah, but you're driven. You're not afraid to go after what you want." Zack tried to encourage her.

"I don't know what I want." She said, looking at the candles again. "I just wanted to earn money for my future. I have no idea what my future looks like."

Zack smiled. "Anything you want it to be."

"I'm glad you think so."

And what about surfing?"

"I'm not a surfer anymore."

"Why not."

Kali shook her head. She didn't answer the question, because she didn't have an answer.

Zack got up suddenly. "There is something that I want you to have."

Zack left the room. He was gone for a moment. He returned quickly with Kali's 6'2 thruster surfboard. It was the same one that Damien was using on the tour. It had orange streaks, and black writing. He held it out for Kali to take, but she wouldn't grab hold of it.

Zack went and threw it on the lounge beside her. "I believe that belongs to you."

"It's pretty."

"Kali." He yelled at her.

"I wouldn't even know how to ride that anymore."

"THAT?" Zack couldn't believe it. "That used to mean more to you than anything, or anyone."

"No it didn't. It means more to *you* than anything or anyone." She shrugged her shoulders "To me it's just foam and fibreglass."

"I don't believe you."

Thunder roared outside. The lights went out in the unit. Kali didn't care. She kept staring at candle flames.

"I understand how you could turn your back on us, but not on surfing."

Kali looked up. She felt as if she was about to start crying. "When you live in the Sydney suburbs, it's easy to turn your back on everything."

The lights came back on. Zack wondered up and down the length of the room. He came back to the empty fire place and rested his elbows on the mantle. Kali got up. She couldn't sit still anymore. She stood against the window.

She looked at her own reflection. She looked like a girl who was looking for something, but didn't know what she was looking for; like a dreamer without a dream.

"I thought Damien had my board." She said wistfully.

Zack went back to sit on his couch. He finished his drink, then shook his head. "He wanted you to have it."

Kali turned around and walked up to the table. She grabbed the empty glass and then filled it up again. She drunk half the wine and then looked around the room again. "Are you seeing anyone Zack?"

Zack shook his head. "Not at the moment, no."

"Are you sure?"

"I think I'd know."

"Whose sweater is that?" She was looking at a grey girl's jumper, in the corner of the room, near the television. "There are also two cups, on the coffee table." She pointed out. "One of them has lip stick on it."

"Damien's girlfriend came to play the Sony with me this morning." Zack shrugged. "She must have left stuff here."

Kali looked up quickly, surprised. She actually felt stunned "Damien has a girlfriend?"

"Yeah." Zack said surprised by her reaction. "Her name is Danielle."

Kali nodded. She stood rather awkwardly in the middle of the room. She put, the half full glass of wine, back on the table, and grabbed the bottle instead.

She glanced at the surfboard on the lounge, and reached out to touch it. She streaked her finger down the edge of the fin. Then she headed back over to the window, and stared outside, vacantly.

Kali buried her head in her hands. "Zack… Can you move that thing? Please. I don't want to see it."

"What thing?" Zack asked, exasperated.

"My surfboard." She told him. "I don't want to see it."

"Why?" He asked desperately.

"It hurts too much."

Zack got up. He uncertainly walked over, and hesitantly grabbed the surfboard. He walked out of the lounge room, then came back, a moment later, without it.

"Kali are you ok?" He asked, as he came towards her. "I've never seen anyone get drunk this quickly."

Kali looked at the bottle. She went to have another swig, but then stopped herself. She put the bottle on the floor. "I don't usually drink." She whispered. Then she shook her head. "No." She decided to tell him exactly what was on her mind." I'm sick of feeling this pain. I'm sick of it being so strong. Why don't you love me back?"

Zack came over to her. He reached in his pocket, and then he was doing something to her.

He moved her hair around. He pushed it to the side. He had her gold necklace. He was putting it on around her neck, and he secured it. "Who says I don't love you back."

"Do you?"

"I might, if I thought I could trust you."

Kali nodded. "I wouldn't trust me either. Especially if I got pregnant to someone else."

"What?" Zack accidentally stepped back and fell over the wine bottle. He fell on the floor. "Kali be serious."

Kali looked into deep space. "I am."

"Is that why you came back? Cause you're in trouble." Zack asked irritably. He wasn't sure what to make of her confession in her drunken state.

Kali shrugged her shoulders. "I don't want to ruin that friendship. I never did." She said, feeling ever so tipsy.

"What are you talking about? What friendship?"

"I didn't want to be a burden, or make you hate me." Kali knew she was drunk. She couldn't make her words make sense.

Zack didn't understand either.

"I don't know what this is about." He reached out to touch Kali's face, and streaked his finger down her cheek. "I have waited for you" he turned to the window and looked outside at the falling rain "Always."

He watched the drops of water run down the window pane. From the corner of her eye, Kali could see his reflection in the window. She stood silently still, looking at his reflection. Outside the sheets of lightning still lighted up the sky. They were far away now.

"Why don't you go sleep in my room? You look like you need to sleep." He said confused.

"I'm not tired." She pouted.

"Your drunk, and you're not making any sense." Zack snapped at her.

"There is no furniture at my house yet. It is coming tomorrow. I can go home, but I can't go to bed. I don't have one." She swaggered.

"You can stay here Kali." Zack said again.

He suddenly decided for her, that he was going to take her to bed. He reached down and picked her up. Just like he had done so many times before. He picked her up like she was light as a feather. He was still so strong and formidable.

He walked her to his room and dumped her on the bed. He pulled the quilt and sheets down from underneath her, and then carefully laid them back over the top.

He did all this with complete detachment. Kali sensing his resistance refused to look at him.

On his way out he flicked the light switch, and didn't even look back at her.

Zack

Zack didn't even realize he was crying. Not until he was in front of the bathroom mirror, cleaning his teeth. She was a runaway, Kali had left him. It had never really bothered him in the first place. Not until now. Four years later.

At least, he had successfully pretended it didn't.

It hurt him more now that she was back. He had not cried this much since after his mother's funeral. It occurred to him suddenly that everything he had ever done had been for Kali.

He had home, an income, and a place for them to settle down together. Right on schedule, she had walked back into his life. In Manly, there she was, and he wanted her so badly.

Nothing ever lasted. His girl was pregnant to someone else. Nothing could change that. Suddenly he hated her. Everything they had ever been through; came down to this. Everything he had ever done, had been for nothing.

Damien's unit was right next door to Zack's.

Zack would crash their tonight. He didn't want to be in the same house as the girl. Damien was in Victoria anyway. He was at Bells Beach at the moment.

He slammed the door to his own apartment, and ran across the lawn towards Damien's' place. He ran, with no shoes on, in the rain. He stood for a moment on the doorstep. Just getting wet, in the cold air, before he went inside.

As he jiggled the key in the lock, and opened the front door, he was surprised to see the television was on. So was the kitchen light.

There was half eaten take out sitting on the bench. It didn't even occur to him that Danielle would be there. He couldn't see where she was. He just searched every room until he found her. She was in the shower.

Danielle smiled at him after her initial shock had worn off. It didn't occur to mind that she was seeing his best friend.

Chapter 35

Kali:

It wasn't a dream it was a vision, but it came to Kali in her sleep. Or at least she thought it did. She had been fast asleep, and then suddenly she had become aware of things around her. Only things that she could hear, or smell, or touch, because her eyes had stayed securely shut. Her mind was still reeling from her vision that continued on, inside her head.

It was a vision of the breaking wave; a perfect wave so real to her that as she stood on the beach and watched it, she could feel the spray coming off the offshore winds. She could hear the roar of white water, and she could even taste the salt in the air.

No one was around in her dream. She just stood there in some swimmers watching the wave break. It was a perfect peeling motion. The sand was golden, the sky was blue; her brown eyes stayed tightly shut. Kali suddenly realised that she was in bed.

She was cold. The blanket had fallen away. She must have been tossing and turning in her sleep again. She had woken up, so many times last night. Outside it was raining again, the gentle patter of raindrops fell consistently on the roof.

The perfect A-frame sets were still breaking in her mind amongst all the things outside of it. Then the phone rang. Kali opened her eyes. Everything vanished. The room was pitch black. The curtains were open. The night sky was devoid of stars, and of the moonlight. Only dark, rain clouds, filled the sky.

Kali quickly pulled the blankets back in line and resettled herself in the bed. She turned to lie on her back, and stare at the ceiling. The phone had stopped ringing now, Zack must have answered it.

There was no phone in the bedroom. If there had been one there, she might not be able to resist the urge to pick it up. She would see who was calling at such an early hour. The hour was unknown, but it was probably about six thirty, maybe seven. It was hard to tell because it was so cloudy outside and dark.

It was none of her business, but she felt a pang of jealousy. Just to think; maybe, it was one of Zack's old girlfriends on the other end of the line. It could have been a girl that woke up in the middle of the night, and decided that she couldn't live without him. He had that effect on girls

Last night when she was drunk and crying; Zack had dumped her in his bed. He had left the unit last night, and gone somewhere else. Just lying there, she had been able to feel the emptiness all around her. She felt the wind, from the storm, that blew through the vacant house, and echoed into the bedroom. She was staring out the window when he ran past and disappeared.

Then out of nowhere, he came back at about an hour ago. She had no idea where he had been, or why he'd come home at this hour. She just woke up in time to see him walk past the window again. She could hear the front door opening and Zack stagger into the other bedroom. She could hear him as clearly as she could, if she was standing in front of him, watching him do it.

She fell asleep after that, but she was awake again now.

Kali spent the next twenty minutes trying to get back to sleep. It was impossible. She got up and slipped Zack's sweater on. Then she walked out to where Zack was. He was sitting at the breakfast table.

"Good morning." She said to him slowly. She had a slight hangover.

Zack stared at for a long time. "Good morning." He said finally.

"Who was on the phone?" she asked softly. Zack wasn't necessarily in a good mood.

He sat eating a bowl of sultana bran. He was refusing to look at her now. "Damien."

"What does he want?" She asked bluntly.

Kali was kind of mad at Damien for not telling her that he had a girlfriend. Not that it would have stopped her from being with him. Kali could be a bitch when she wanted to be.

Zack smirked to himself. He thought her tone was funny. "He got out, in the semi-final at Bells. He will be home tomorrow."

Kali gulped down a lump in her throat. "Oh, really." She tried to even her voice out. "The semi-finals. That's impressive."

"Why? Why do you ask about my phone calls? Why are you up so early?" He asked her. His voice further indicated he *was* indeed mad at her.

"I couldn't sleep."

"Did the phone wake you?"

"Not really."

"Well, feel free to leave whenever you're ready." He practically snarled at her.

"I'm going to my old house today. The moving van is coming with our furniture." Kali tried to explain to him.

Zack didn't look up, or appear to care. He was putting up walls… To say the least.

"So, you ran away before, and now you're running back." He observed. "Probably skipping out on the guy who knocked you up."

Kali chewed on her lip precariously. "I was kind of drunk last night." She told him. "I wouldn't take anything I said seriously."

"So, you made it up?" He asked, severely irritated.

Kali tip toed around the kitchen trying to find a bowl. "I'm not sure yet."

"What the fuck, Kali?"

"I don't want to talk about it. Not yet. I never would have said anything if you didn't offer me that stupid wine. I told you I don't usually drink, and I don't even know yet."

"Well you're not showing. And I thought you were smart enough to know, that you're not supposed to drink, when you're pregnant."

"I wasn't that smart last night."

"Who is your boyfriend?"

"I don't have one."

"So, it was just some random?"

Kali found the bowl and sat down at the kitchen table with Zack. She folded her hands on the table. She put her head down on top of them. "Please don't say these things to me."

"Yeah, why don't you just wait till you're giving birth, before you think about what comes next?" He grumbled. "To start with: Why don't you take a test?"

Kali was still looking down on the ground with her head on the table. "I don't want to."

"You are so immature." Zack sighed. "Why did you come here yesterday? Just to hurt me?"

Kali looked up. "I just came to tell you that I was coming back." She sulked. "I came to tell you that I loved you. I didn't think you loved me back."

"Well maybe I did, yesterday."

Kali nodded. "I just wanted you to know."

"Seriously Kali, who's the father of your baby?"

Kali tensed up, and she started biting her fingernails. "I'll tell you later."

"Are you going to tell him? Is a better question."

"No." Kali said a little quickly. "I mean, not unless I knew for sure."

"Every time things get scary, you run away. If you slept with someone in Sydney, you'll probably never see him again."

"Not necessarily." Kali said awkwardly.

"Do you even know who it is? Is there more than one candidate?"

Kali was shocked that he would go this far. "I've only ever had sex twice in my entire life" she admitted beguilingly. "And they were years apart."

Zack was caught off guard "Twice?" He repeated softly. "Are you going to keep it?" He asked her.

"Please stop Zack."

"I can't imagine you having a child." He paused. "You are a child."

Kali thought that was funny. "Good, we can play in the same play pen."

Suddenly the phone started ringing. Zack just sat there until the machine picked it up.

"Hi Zack. It's Jennifer. I know I haven't heard from you in a while. I mean I know you're busy with your new job, but I thought, maybe, you might want to go out sometime? I wasn't sure why you haven't called me. I mean I know you're really busy, so I thought I'd call you. Anyway if you want to go out on the weekend or something, that would be great. I programmed my number into your cell phone, so I'd love to hear from you. Well anyway, I'll see you. Buy."

Kali grinned at Zack. He looked away embarrassed.

"She must have loved you." Kali noted.

"She hardly knows me." He said irritably.

"It must be hard keeping track."

"I'm not the player you think I am." He defended himself.

"Try telling her that."

"Why are you mad? You're the one that left. I can see who ever I want. I wasn't going to pine for you for the rest of my life."

"You never pined for me in the first place." Kali yelled at him. "Do you know how hard it was to see you with Miranda, or Caroline, or any of the other girls you brought into your room? I'm surprised you noticed when I left. You certainly had your hands full."

"Well it may have been more than two, but at least I know how to protect myself." He yelled back.

"Yeah, try explaining that to Shelly Andrews."

Zack was startled. "Where did you get that name from?"

"Shawn Ashmore told me."

"Well Shawn Ashmore should keep his mouth shut. You're really trying to hurt me aren't you? Feel free open all my old wounds, Kali."

"And pour salt in them. That's what you do. That's what you've always done to me."

Zack stared at her.

Kali nodded. She stopped. Enough was enough. She tried to change the subject.

"What was the new job that *Jennifer* was talking about?" She asked softly, taking a chance he might answer her.

"I work an engineering firm."

"Doing what."

"Engineering." He said blankly. "Damien said you're a check out chick."

Kali stared at him and nodded. "Part time. I just finished a secretarial course at TAFE."

"You want to be a secretary."

"I don't know." She shrugged, and tried to soften the tone of the conversation. "I'm glad you're doing well. You must have just finished University, and you already have your own place."

Zack shook his head. "You know I inherited money." He said pensively. "Money from my grandparents; that was supposed to go to my mother."

Kali nodded. "I know." She smiled at him, but he looked hurt and sad.

Kali reached back and took her necklace off, for the second time.

He was mad at her. She had to make the gesture. She slowly put it in the middle of the table. Zack stared at it.

"I should go." Kali got up. She grabbed her duffle bag from the foyer on the way out. It was just too painful to stay.

Chapter 36

Kali:

"I fold." Zack looked up at Damien for the twentieth time in an hour. Then he threw his cards down on the table.

Kali watched him, watching Damien. She wondered what was on his mind. He looked pale and uncomfortable. Something was definitely on the tip of his tongue. Kali wondered if it was *her* secret that he wanted to tell, or if he had a secret of his own

"Are you in, Kali?" Damien asked her.

Kali looked at her cards again. She shook her head. "I fold too."

"Come on Kali, show some back bone." Damien was looking around suspiciously. He was obviously trying to bluff Joel for the eight dollars on the table. Joel was too smart.

Damien was a terrible poker player. His facial expressions always gave him away. The look on his face right now indicated he probably had a pair of five's or something.

"I'll raise you fifty cents." Joel said earnestly.

Damien raised an eyebrow. "Are you sure you want to do that?"

Joel rolled his eyes. "Yes. Check or bet Damien, hurry up."

"Kali, didn't we say you could only raise the bet in dollar amounts." Damien said trying to rouse her spirits.

Kali giggled. "No."

"Ok then. I guess I'll see your fifty cents, and raise you this American one dollar note that I have in my wallet."

"Don't you have any money Damien?" Joel asked amused.

Damien threw the American currency in the pot, in the middle of the table. "This is good. Just take it to the bank, and they'll cash it in for you."

Zack was either looking at Damien or down at the floor. He suddenly turned to Kali and spoke with much compassion in his voice. "Do you want a drink Kali?"

He was so attentive now that he thought she was pregnant. He treated her like she was fragile and could break at the first sign of stress. He was so considerate of her, that he would offer a drink, at someone else's house.

They were at Joel's house. Joel couldn't leave his son alone while his wife was at a social engagement. They all went to Joel's house for the big 'reunion'.

"Joel already offered me one, but I'm not thirsty." She said softly.

Joel glanced at Kali. He had been reluctant to talk to her since she got here. He looked kind of sad, and she had a million questions for him. Joel was a father now. He had a wife and a son, and a house in North Clover.

Kali hadn't seen the baby yet because the kid was asleep. Joel didn't want to wake him up. The baby monitor was turned on, however, and Joel looked worried. He was very protective of his new family.

"This is too rich for me." Joel said distracted. He threw the cards down on his own mahogany dining table.

Damien looked around at each of them agitatedly. Then he finally spoke his mind. "Ok what's going on? Why does it feel like a fucking funeral parlour in here?"

Zack almost jumped out of his seat. "What do you mean? Nothing's going on."

"Bullshit." Damien looked annoyed, and he looked right at her. "Kali what is wrong with Joel? And why won't Zack look at you?"

Kali shrugged her shoulders. "I don't know."

"Zack, why won't you look at Kali?" Damien was never afraid to ask the most awkward of questions.

"I don't know what you're talking about." Zack told him.

"I hate this." Damien cried. "Every time I go away, there is weirdness when I come back. Why can't everyone just act normal?"

"Things change when you're away Damien. Some people's lives aren't a continuous party you know." Joel dug his heels in.

"I'm not going to apologize for having fun Joel." Damien retorted. "But I work hard to get where I am."

"Why don't we just play nice?" Zack butted in.

Joel glanced at the baby monitor. "I just didn't get much sleep last night. I'm not acting weird. I'm just tired."

"Fine." Damien grinned, and collected all the money in the middle of the table. "Muchas grassius guys. I only had a pair of sixes."

"So, when can I meet Oliver?" Kali asked enthusiastically. She was trying to lift his spirits because he looked so miserable.

Kali was worried about Joel. She had no right to tell anybody else how to life, but this house was more like a museum than a house. Everything was perfect, and in its place. Joel must have married someone with obsessive compulsive disorder.

Joel would never have been ready for this, nor would he have wanted it.

"When he wakes up. I promise Kali. He's a good baby."

"He looks just like Joel." Zack said carefully. He saw Kali's effort, and tried to cheer up Joel, as well.

"Lucky him." Kali said, but she didn't mean to say it out loud.

"I think I broke up with Danielle." Damien said out of nowhere.

"What." Zack jumped again. "Why."

Damien caught Kali's eye. He held it for a moment.

Kali bit her lip and stared back. Then he looked at Zack. "I played up while I was on the road." He waited for a second to catch everyone's reaction. "And I told her about it."

"You cheated on Danielle?" Joel asked, shocked.

"I thought so." Zack mumbled. "I knew there someone in Manly."

Kali almost dropped her cards all over the floor. "Do you often do that?" She asked softly.

"Do what?" Damien asked her.

"Play around on the road?"

He looked her dead straight in the eye "Only once."

"SHE broke up with you because YOU cheated." Zack said indignantly.

"She was really angry." Damien explained.

"She was angry, what a bitch."

"It was my fault." Damien gave Zack a strange look. "What do you have against her? I thought you guys were friends."

Zack shook his head. "Nothing." He grabbed the cards and started shuffling them. "I'll deal."

"If you have something to say, say it."

Zack opened his mouth but didn't say anything for a moment. "She cheated on you too." He paused. "I know that because I slept with Danielle."

"You slept with Danielle?" Joel shouted.

"I'm sorry I didn't mean to."

"Since when do you need my girls? Don't you have enough of your own?" Damien slammed his fist on the table. "When did this happen?"

"Three days ago. When Kali first got here. We had a fight. I went to sleep over at your place that night. I thought it would be empty, but Danielle was there."

"What, and since she was, you thought you'd give her a quick roll in the hay."

"That's not true. I was upset."

"You don't get upset." Damien thought about it for a moment. "Wait Kali, did you tell him?"

"Does Damien know that you're pregnant?" Zack asked Kali.

"Pregnant?" Joel said.

"Pregnant?" Damien echoed. "Kali's not pregnant, I just…" He stopped in mid-sentence. "Is it mine?"

"What????" Zack screamed at Damien.

Kali watched the three of them arguing. She slowly rose and got up out of her seat. "Damien is the first and only guy I've ever slept with." They went silent. Kali could feel her own embarrassment. "It just happened."

"When did it ever just happen? When did you ever sleep with Kali?" Zack asked. "When did you see her?"

"We all saw her." Damien said simply. "In Manly."

"We all didn't impregnate her though." Zack shook his head. "You had to go off and compete."

"It doesn't matter." Kali spoke up. "Damien, can I see you outside for a second?"

Damien glanced at Zack. "Ok."

Kali walked out the back door, as Damien held it open for her. She walked down the path to the garden and picked a flower out of it. "You're not angry at Zack, are you?"

"For what?"

"Being with Danielle?"

"Did you know?"

"No."

Damien shook his head confused. "I'm angry with him, but that's not my biggest concern right now. Is that what you wanted to talk about?"

Kali nodded her head. "If I was the one who broke up your friendship with Zack, I'd never forgive myself." She walked along the plants and picked a flower from the garden. "I'm so sorry Damien."

"For what?" Damien asked in disbelief.

She brought the flower to her nose and smelled it. "Everything."

"I think we got into this together."

"No, I mean for telling Zack. I don't think I'm pregnant. I just haven't got my period yet."

"It's been over a month Kali."

"A month since I slept with you. Not a month since I was due."

"The math confuses me. It always did." He said scratching his head.

"I never meant to say anything. I'm so sorry Damien."

Damien sighed. "Stop apologizing. Hypothetically, if you were, would you keep it?"

"Would you want me to?"

Damien paused looking at her. "Of course, I would."

"One of Zack's girls had an abortion once, because she didn't know if the baby was his, or my brother's. Did you know about that?"

"Yes." Damien seemed a little shocked that she knew. "He still beats himself up about it."

"He beats himself up about everything." Kali commented.

"I would think you *wouldn't* want to keep it, *because* it's not Zack's."

Kali started at Damien for a long time. "I would want to have your child. I just don't think I am."

"But you can't be sure."

"I think I would know if there was something growing inside of me."

"Do you want me to take you to the doctor?"

"You're leaving for California tomorrow."

"So, what, you'll text me?" He said desperately and sarcastically at the same time.

Kali bowed her head. "I got one of those stupid tests. I'll take it tonight. I'll come and see you tomorrow." She started backing off. "I can't go back in there." She said suddenly. "Damien I can't face them." She put her hand on his shoulder. "I have to go home. You know I love you. I'm so sorry."

She ran out the side gate. She had to get away from everyone. It was all too much.

Chapter 37

Kali:

It was Damien that woke Kali. He put his hand on her shoulder and shook her gently. So gently, in fact, that it felt like her dream was becoming real. The dream had been strange and intense. She was inside the wave at pipeline. She was inside the greenroom and Damien had pulled her out.

Kali had to balance herself so perfectly and just a few feet below; sharp coral and volcanic rock sat jaggedly on the ocean floor. She could have hit it, but then she woke up.

Kali was scared. Her heart was pounding, she was sweating. Damien had to hold to her while she was tossing and turning. When she looked up into his eyes, she felt like she was sixteen years old again.

"No." Kali screamed out, she looked around desperately trying to remember where she was.

She was lying in her old bed, in her old room. This was the room, from when she was a kid. Her room was filled with teddy bears, and stuffed toys, and unpacked boxes.

There were posters on the walls. This was the room she grew up in. The room she left behind when she became a woman.

"Kali are you ok?" Damien asked, worried. He still held on to her wrist, trying to hold her down.

"I can't do it." She screamed disorientated. "I'm not doing it again. I can't go back. I'm not ready."

"Kali." Damien squeezed her hand. "It's just me, you're having a nightmare."

"Damien?"

Damien lifted her arm, and kissed the back of her hand. "It's ok little girl, you're safe."

Kali got her focus back. She looked outside at the pitch-black night. "What time is it?"

Damien looked at his watch. "It's One Twenty-Eight in the morning." He said slurring his words as he spoke to her.

"What are you doing here?"

"Zack told me it was too late to ring you."

"So, you came over?"

"I surely did."

As he spoke he lurched forward. Kali got an unfortunate whiff of his breath. "I take it you came straight from the pub?"

"Maybe I did." Damien admitted. Kali watched him. He was blind drunk.

"How did you get in here?"

"The back door was unlocked." He said casually.

"Really?" Kali could hear footsteps. Someone else was coming.

"Kali is everything alright." Kali saw her dad in the doorway. Damien swung around at the speed of light to see who it was.

Her father didn't look impressed.

"Hi dad"

"What the hell is going on?" Her dad asked her.

"Damien came over to say hello."

"It's kind of late isn't it?"

Kali was going to be elusive. "I don't know. What time is it?"

"It's late Kali."

"Hi Mr Lockhart" Damien butted in.

Kali smiled at her dad. He was a tall man grey hair, and he had broad facial features. He had husky whiskers on his chin, and a concerned look on his face. "Dad I'm fine, you remember Damien, don't you?"

"I remember." Her dad told her. "I expected your friends to come round, now that you're back. I didn't think they would come around at this time of the night." He continued looking at Damien shrewdly.

"Sorry Mr Lockhart" Damien gleamed. "I have to leave for California tomorrow. I couldn't go without seeing your daughter again."

"He won't be long dad." Kali tried to assure him.

"Very well, just don't wake up the neighbours."

Kali smiled. "We won't."

"It's nice to see you again Mr Lockhart." Damien called out, as her dad disappeared.

"You're drunk Damien."

"It's the best place to be right now." He looked her in the eyes and touched her cheek with his fingers. "We have to talk."

"No we don't. Come back when you're sober."

"I told you I'm leaving soon," he shook his head annoyed. "I'm always leaving."

"You're always going places."

"Tell me about your dream."

"I don't remember."

"Yes you do."

"I was surfing the pipeline." She whispered. "I was about to fall. The wave was going to crush me. But then you pulled me out, just in time."

"Did I?"

"You saved me."

"I'm pretty good." He boasted. "We were together there, once. In Hawaii."

"I know."

"I wouldn't have let you get crushed?"

"I know."

"Although, not now." He remarked. "You haven't been surfing in years."

"Yeah. I wouldn't be very good anymore."

He laughed. "Pretty ambitious of your dreams to take you to the pipeline."

"We'll I'm an ambitious girl." She looked down. "Although I've never surfed it for real"

"Are you going to try surfing again?"

"Yes." She nodded. "I have been dreaming about it since I got back. The waves are calling me back. I hope I can do it."

"I'm glad." He told her. "That's where you belong. I surf the pipeline every year. I charge it, for you, and for me."

"I just want to go back to Nikita beach again." She said softly.

"And you'll be scared on the little waves." He teased her. "Because they look bigger from out the back, than they do from out the front." Damien laughed at her.

"Yeah, I know. I used to say that." She nodded humbly. "I'm really scared about going back out."

"So..."Damien looked down and shook his head. "You know I didn't come here to talk about surfing."

"I know. I sent you a text message." She said hopefully. I was going to come see you tomorrow. Before Zack took you to the airport."

"I didn't see the message."

"You were too busy drinking?"

Damien got his phone out of his pocket, and flipped it open. He read the message and then nodded. "Don't play coy with me Kali."

Kali breathed in deeply. She looked out the window at the black sky. "I saw this mini-series on TV last night. It was Joan of Arc. You know, if I was Joan of Arc, I'd be dead by now."

"What?"

"Joan the maid died when she was nineteen. In her life everything got revealed to her over time and you realise that everything happens for a reason."

"What's your point?"

Kali smiled to herself. "Life is so short." Kali shrugged. "But even when she was going to die, she was ok with it. Everything was going to be ok with France."

"I don't know Kali, are you trying to confuse me away from the subject?" Damien accused her.

"Maybe. Just a little bit. I don't know." She meandered. "It was just a really good TV show."

"She's telling you that everything does happen for a reason." Zack said out of nowhere. He looked at Kali.

Kali nearly fell out of bed when she saw Zack enter her room. "How long have you been standing there?"

"Since your dad let me in five minutes ago."

"And you've been standing at the door listening?"

"You didn't notice?"

"I told you at the pub I wanted to talk to her." Damien yelled at him. "Alone."

"And you think I would have let you?" Zack scolded him. "You can't come over and harass her, at this time of night, when you're plastered?"

"I'm not that drunk."

"Try again Damien."

"Are *you* drunk?" Kali asked Zack.

"I'm not fully sober." He told her. "I'm sorry, I would have gotten here earlier to stop him, but Damien tried to drink drive, in MY car. So, I had to fight him for it." He gave Damien a sour look and turned his attention back to Kali. "He ran here, and he's fitter than I am. I didn't want history to repeat itself. I didn't want to kill your brother, AND the father of your child."

"Zack don't do this. My father's asleep in the other room. That was never your fault."

"You screwed her Damien." Zack yelled at Damien. "You screwed her like she was any other girl. You didn't care how it affected anybody. You just did it because you wanted to get laid."

"It wasn't like that." Damien retorted.

"This is Kali, she deserves better."

"Kali the maid, no wonder she talks about Joan of Arc. Everyone thought she was going to stay a virgin forever."

Kali felt painfully uncomfortable. "Stop it guys."

"I didn't know if she was or not, but I didn't care either." Zack said. "I was just glad she came back."

"Well then, you won't care if she has my baby, or if I tell you that this wasn't the first time."

Zack's stare was intense. He waited impatiently for Damien to explain himself.

"She was sixteen when I made love to her... the first time. It felt right for us then, and it felt even better in Manly."

Zack nodded. He looked into space for a moment.

It was as if he just put two and two together. He looked at Kali. "Twice. And years apart." He repeated the words that Kali had told him a few days ago.

Kali nodded. "I wanted it."

"You don't have to explain Kali."

"And what? I do?" Damien yelled. "I can't make love to a girl that I love."

"You love her like she was your little sister."

"Obviously not."

"You shouldn't be doing this to her." Zack yelled. He reached forward and pried the keys to his own car, out of Damien's top pocket. "And you definitely shouldn't be driving."

"I had to do this. She knows the result and she didn't call me."

Kali looked at him desperately. "I'm sorry."

"You're the one who dumped this on me, and now you have nothing to say about it?"

"I was the one who let it slip." Zack told him.

"Yeah, but you didn't know I was the father." Damien jumped in. "That's what's killing me. I don't even know if it's true."

"It's not. It was negative." Kali told him.

"What?" Damien yelled back.

"What?" Zack asked her.

"I was going to tell you tomorrow morning." Kali tried to explain, desperately. "I was going to apologize."

"So, you just left me hanging." Damien asked in disbelief.

"You found out this morning. I was going to tell you *tomorrow* morning. It was 24 hours, Damien."

"Yeah and Jack Bauer could save the world in less time." He argued. "I mean, you couldn't have picked up a phone? After you did the test."

"I wanted to tell you personally. I needed to clear my head."

"What about my head?" He cried. "I had no idea what was going on. You don't know how stressed I get, when I have to go overseas. I always get nervous before I leave. You were going to wait until I was leaving for the airport?"

"I didn't think of it that way." Kali tried to explain. "I keep saying I'm sorry, but you don't want to hear it: It's not a problem anymore."

"You think I consider it a problem?" His voice faltered. "What if I wanted to have a baby?"

"You're twenty-three years old Damien.' She said flatly. "I'm sure it will happen."

"But in the meantime, you're allowed to just mess with my head like that."

"I didn't know Zack was going to announce in front of everyone."

"But he did." Damien yelled. "And you have a responsibility to care about someone other than yourself for once. You should have cared enough to tell me."

"You're right."

"You act as if you're so far out of reach." Damien screamed.

"I know. I'm sorry."

"You act as if nothing can touch you." Damien told her sternly. "And you hide away, like you've been doing for the past four years."

It was a harsh comment, and it was true. Kali felt weak all of a sudden.

"My life was boring in Sydney." She told him solemnly, out of nowhere. "I didn't make many real friends. I hardly ever went out. I didn't even have my surfboard, or a beach close by." She said softly. "I couldn't make a fresh start. I just pined for you guys all the time."

Zack and Damien stared at her.

"I just worked a lot, and went to TAFE." Kali continued. She could feel tears in her eyes. "Sometime my sister would take pity on me and take me to the movies, but mostly I just worked a lot."

"You're not trying to make me feel sorry for you, are you Kali." Damien asked, indignantly.

Kali shook her head. "No."

Damien was unmoved. "You know what Kali." He said frustrated. "I don't care anymore. I'm walking home. I'm going to California tomorrow, and getting the hell away from you."

Kali Nodded. He stormed out of her room. She let him go.

"I deserved that." Kali told Zack, who was still standing there.

"Yes you did." Zack agreed.

"I wish I could have stopped myself from drinking that wine. I was confused too."

"I'm not going to defend you Kali."

"I didn't ask you to." She told him, blankly.

"You just hurt my best friend, and you hurt me. Now you want my sympathy?"

"No I don't. I just want to go back to sleep." She whispered.

"You're not the girl I thought you were."

"You said that in Manly." Kali told him, but he had just walked out the door.

Chapter 38

Zack:

Danielle Hall was a natural red head, but she frequently put fudge dies in her hair, to make it more vibrant, and redder; like the colour of fire. She was maybe a little wilder than most of the girls Zack had ever met.

She had a naturally flirty, and fun, and had a fresh attitude. That was his first impression of her at least. The more he got to know her, the more she gave the impression of being a little *too* extraverted.

He realized now that she was reckless, not free spirited. There was a difference, but Zack didn't want to judge her, and she was still a fun person. So, he did like her a lot.

Danielle liked a glass of wine with every meal, in fact, she liked to drink in general. So it was Danielle that had brought over the wine that Zack gave to Kali. He had it in his pantry because Danielle brought it over. Then he gave it to Kali, and it caused so much trouble.

Zack usually didn't drink much. He didn't know why he served it to Kali that night.

Was he just trying to act more sophisticated? More grown up?

Danielle was here with him now, in his lounge room, because she wanted to talk to him. Basically, their relationship had revolved around the Sony PlayStation, and eating take out together, a few times. Of course, with a glass of wine. So he never really got to know her that well.

He knew she was a hairdresser, and she acted like a hairdresser. She was inclined towards gossiping, which Zack never really liked, very much.

It also meant that she and Kali could never be friends. Kali would shrink like a wallflower in Danielle's presence. The two girls couldn't possibly have been any more different.

Today Danielle was acting weird. She was distracted and apprehensive. Zack kept glancing at her. He too, felt distracted and apprehensive.

Danielle had a tattoo of a dolphin on her lower back. Zack hated tattoos. He never would have told her that, but it never would have mattered. She was his best friend's girlfriend. They were just acquaintances, but now he had slept with her. He didn't know how to act around her.

She came over today to pick up the sweater that she left at his house. She ended up staying for a late breakfast, and playing the Sony PlayStation with him again.

"Why do you keep winning?" Danielle asked frustrated.

Zack grinned at her. She sat next to him on the floor with their back up against the couch. "It's a complicated game."

"It's car racing."

"Well it's a guy thing."

Danielle shook her head annoyed. "I came here to talk to you, about something else." She said blatantly.

"What about?" Zack said. Suddenly. Even more apprehensive.

Danielle got a faraway look in her eye. Her mood changed suddenly. She looked around and then boosted herself up to sit on the couch. "Do you know who Damien cheated on me with?"

Zack had to try and relax the tension in his body. He *really* didn't want to answer that question.

He pushed himself up on the couch opposite her, turning his body diagonally to face her. "He's in different countries." Zack started to explain. "I couldn't possibly know what he does. Or who he does it with. When he's on the road."

"Yeah but it was Australia." She moaned. "You were in Manly. Did you see him hanging round with anyone?"

For a moment the reality of what happened in Manly came rushing back to Zack. He found it hard to speak.

"Did Damien tell you it happened in Manly?" He asked carefully.

"Yeah some slut up in the suburbs. I didn't think he'd do that to me." Danielle blubbered.

Zack was taking a sip of water while she was talking. He almost choked on it. "Yeah, but you cheated on him, too."

She nodded but in such a way that confused Zack. It was as if sleeping with him didn't even count.

"Damien left it up to me, if we were going to break up or not. But I couldn't live with it. So, we did."

"You should just move on." He told her doubtfully.

Zack started to realize something about the whole affair. He had only found out recently that Damien and Danielle had broken up. He didn't know when Damien had confessed to his indiscretion, or how long their relationship had been in turmoil.

Zack started to realize that Danielle could very well have slept with him out of revenge.

The truth was, before today, he was thinking of asking Danielle out. She was fun, and that's what he needed right now. He needed fun. Especially now that Kali had come back. He didn't want to get dragged into Kali's world, if they were just going to keep hurting each other.

"I can't move on." Danielle told him.

"Why not?"

"Because I'm stuck" She said idly.

"Trust me, plenty of girls have moved on from Damien Grisham." Zack said sarcastically.

"No, that's not what I meant."

"What are you talking about then?"

"I'm..." Danielle hesitated.

"It's ok, you can tell me." Zack said, suddenly worried about her.

Danielle shrugged her shoulders. She continued looking at the television. She was starting at the continuously replaying introduction to the car racing game. The television beamed with lights and colours. The sound was on mute. "We never talked about that night."

"I know. That wasn't fair of me." Zack admitted straight away.

"We were both responsible for what happened.

"Yeah, but I was upset, and you were…there" Zack couldn't explain it any better than that. She gave him a bitter look.

"The thing is I'm late."

"For what?"

It took about a minute for the statement to seep in. Then it hit him like a freight train. Zack gasped. "Have you told Damien?"

"No, Damien has nothing to do with it, I'm sure of it."

For some reason Zack instantly thought it would be Damien's. It seemed to be the trend these days.

"How can you be sure?"

"Because I haven't been with Damien for ages."

Zack was doing math in his head. "So…?"

"It didn't say I was pregnant, I said I was late. It could be a false alarm." She sighed "I just wanted you to know."

He felt dizzy and disorientated. "But if it's true? Then it would be mine?"

"You think I sleep around don't you?"

"You slept with me"

"I was lonely" she mumbled. "It would be definitely yours Zack."

Zack was stunned. "I can't believe this is happening again."

"Why, who else did this happen to?" She asked suspiciously.

"Kali." He whispered.

"Kali Lockhart?" Danielle asked shocked. "The girl that you used to hung out with in high school?"

"How did you know that?" Zack asked annoyed. "You didn't even go to our high school!" he cried.

"One of my clients told me." She explained simply.

Zack closed his eyes. He felt sick to his stomach.

"Wait." Danielle asked suddenly. "Is her baby yours as well?"

Zack shook his head, bewildered. "No. She's not pregnant. She just thought she was."

Danielle looked down. "I can't believe this."

"Neither can I." Zack rested his head back on the couch. He stared at the ceiling. He needed oxygen.

"I've made an appointment at the doctor on Tuesday. I don't work on Tuesday mornings. If you can ask your boss for time off. You can meet me at the doctor's surgery." She said decisively.

"Ok." Zack nodded. "I can do that." He said, trying not to hyperventilate.

"Ok, it's at 9:50 at the surgery on Bleaker Street. I don't know Zack. I mean maybe I'm at the right time of my life for this. And, you have this house, so you've kind of settled down, so…"

She kept talking for a while. Zack zoned out. He couldn't concentrate, or hear what she was saying.

He was such an idiot. It was almost predetermined that he would screw up everything, all at once.

He was reckless with women, and this was the result.

He was mad at Kali for leaving. Yet he was the one who drove her away. Damien was still pissed off that he slept with Danielle in the first place. Joel had been avoiding him for years. Everything bad that happened; was his fault.

He was thinking of asking Danielle out anyway, but he suddenly realized, he didn't have any feelings for her.

He never had any feelings for any of the girls he asked out. He kept making the same mistakes, over and over. Now he was paying for them.

This had happened before, and he hadn't learned his lesson. But he at the same time, he was only twenty-three. These problems were for adults. Zack was just a kid.

Zack kept nodding. He kept trying to make supportive comments, but he was as pail as a ghost and he felt like he was going to faint.

A man's character was his destiny. His mum had told him that, a long time ago. Now he was realizing what she meant.

Chapter 39

Zack:

Zack groggily opened his eyes, and saw kali sitting in his room. She was sitting at his desk. She looked quite content. Her 'pregnancy' ordeal was over, she looked as innocent as ever.

She didn't know he was awake yet. She had immersed herself in a book that he had bought a few days ago. He hadn't gotten around to reading it yet.

"Is it any good?"

Kali wasn't facing the desk, but she wasn't facing him either. Her chair had swung around so she was facing toward the window, for the light.

Kali sunk down further in the chair and rested her head back, "I've only read a few pages."

"What are you doing here?" He asked, deflated. "I'm not sure I'm in the mood today."

She swung the chair around to look at him. She closed her eyes, and kept them closed for a moment. "I was hoping you would get me my surf board. I want to go surfing today."

Zack sat up. "Really?"

"Yeah, if the conditions are right." She said softly. "I haven't checked."

"It's about two, to two and a half feet. North-westerly, light winds." Zack said slowly. "I heard it on the radio earlier."

Kali nodded. "Two foot sounds good." She looked at him sadly. "Are you still angry with me?"

"I'm not angry, just disappointed." He mumbled.

Zack sighed, if had a cigarette he could have used it right now. Unfortunately, he didn't have one. He had given them up, a while back.

The truth was, of course he was angry with Kali. If Kali wouldn't have made such an untrue confession. He wouldn't have been so upset. The chain of events wouldn't have caused him to get someone else pregnant.

"I wanted you to know that I was with Damien." She said idly. "But I didn't know how to tell you." She paused. "And I didn't know what was going on with my body. I mean I'm never late, I'm usually early half the time. It's just that everything got mixed up, then it was out of my hands." Kali slowly explained. "I just wanted to apologize one more time. I never should have said anything."

Zack shook his head. "Kali, this whole thing is a little played out, don't you think?"

"What whole thing?" She asked, blankly.

"This thing between you and me."

"You never admitted that there was anything between you and me."

"Yes, I did. You forced me to admit it. You made me tell you that I love you, about a minute before you tell me you're pregnant to someone else."

"When did you ever say you love me?" She asked incredulously.

"My exact words were 'who says I don't love you?' and then you told me that were pregnant. I remember it like it was yesterday." He grumbled.

Kali closed her eyes again.

"I know it will never be the same." She began. "I don't want you to hate me."

"I'm just sick of playing this cat and mouse game" Zack said annoyed.

"I'm pretty sure you instituted that game." Kali shook her head. "Why did you ever bother with me in the first place Zack?"

"Because of your brother. I wanted to see the potential he saw in you. Pity it didn't pan out."

"So that *is* why you took me to Hawaii?"

"I wanted *you* to see the potential in you." He huffed. "I wanted you to have some fun." He paused. "Of course, I didn't know you'd have *that* much fun. I can't take credit for you fucking Dane."

"I didn't fuck Dane."

"Well I didn't think you fucked Damien either, but I was wrong there."

"Why are you saying all these things to me? Why are you being so cruel?"

"I always warned you not to get to close to me Kali. It's gets pretty dark in here." He said morbidly.

Kali stared at him. "Is that why I found this anti-anxiety medication on your desk." She held up a small prescription box of medication.

Zack breathed in sharply. "Are you spying on me? That's none of your business."

"When did it ever get this bad Zack?"

"That has nothing to do with you. I have bigger fish to fry than you."

"Zack. You are the strongest guy I know. You are my rock. What would Tom Cruise think of you? We don't take medication."

"You don't know what I'm up against, besides. I'm so sick of waiting for you."

"Waiting for what?" She replied.

"Waiting for you" He said again

"I'm right here Zack."

"You're sitting right there, but you might as well be a million miles away. I can't get to you Kali. I can't touch your heart."

"You've had my heart ever since the day I met you." Kali cried.

Zack turned to lie on his back and stare at the ceiling. "Excuse me if I don't believe that" He sighed. "You were always the ice queen."

"That's what I hear." Kali sighed. "You know that's not true. It was always you."

"You were too young. My hands were tied. Ryan wouldn't have let me touch you. He didn't want that for you."

"I know, and that's why I came here to talk to you Zack. Can't you just stop being mad at me."

"You invited yourself in. I didn't expect to wake up to the Spanish inquisition."

"I'm here in your room Zack. You can have anything you want from me, including my heart"

Zack shook his head again. "I need to get up and go to work, and you're just sitting there."

"Is Danielle under the covers as well?" kali asked annoyed. "I hear you've been seeing her."

"No." Zack spat at her. "She's not."

"Is she your girlfriend now?"

Zack wanted to break down crying. "I don't know."

Kali nodded. "Fine." She got up. "I'm sorry I'm holding you up." She looked him in the eye. "Is *my* surfboard in *your* garage? I can get it myself."

"No, it's in my spare room…Are you going to Nikita?"

"Yeah."

She was about to exit the room, when Zack called her back. "Kali don't go."

She stopped, turned around, and looked him straight in the eye. "I don't want to go, I just don't know what else to say."

Zack sighed. "I have something to say to you."

Zack got out of bed. He was just wearing his boxer shorts, but he put his bathrobe on.

"Can you wait for me in the kitchen?" He asked her softly.

Zack watched her go. He got his clothes ready and went and had a shower. Afterwards, he put his work clothes on, and boots. He shaved. Combed his hair, and put on his aftershave.

When he caught up with her in the kitchen, she watched him silently. He got out his toaster and put two pieces of bread in it.

"Are you hungry?" He asked her.

Kali shook her head. "I wouldn't mind a glass of water."

Zack got a cup from the sideboard, and filled it with water. He handed it to her.

"Thanks." She looked down into her water like it was a crystal ball. "I love you Zack."

"What?"

She paused, summoning up the strength to say it again, even though he had heard it perfectly well the first time. "I said I love you."

"Don't say it Kali."

"Why not?" She whispered.

"Because you slept with my best friend."

Kali looked sad. Her facial expression was completely lost. She looked off into space for a moment. She must have lost concentration. Zack saw the glass slip from her hands. Then it fell to the ground.

It shattered on the vinyl floor. The water spilt all over the floor. So did the glass.

Kali turned red. "I'm sorry." She wasn't wearing any shoes. Zack picked her up and propped her up on the kitchen bench.

He started to walk over to the broom closet, but she stopped him. "Please don't walk away from me."

Zack stopped and turned around. "I wasn't walking away from you Kali. I was going to get a dustpan, so I can sweep up this glass." He stepped towards her. "I don't want to leave it too long. I don't want you to pick it up, and start hurting you yourself with it."

"What?"

"You know."

"I really don't."

Zack brushed up all the glass and put it in the bin. He walked over to Kali, and grabbed her arm before she could stop him.

"*This* is what I'm talking about." He pulled down her watch and looked at her wrist. "Those scars across your wrist. You used to cut yourself, didn't you?"

Kali went pale. She grew silent and stared at her wrist. "I haven't done that for a long time."

"You hurt yourself Kali. Is this how you handle your problems?"

"My life was so hard. It made me feel better." She glared at him.

"I wanted to see if there are any fresh marks." Zack said slowly. "I was worried."

"Well there are no fresh marks. I grew up Zack. I'm not going to kill myself over you. I was never going to kill myself in the first place. It was just punishment."

"You used to punish yourself?"

"Sounds kinky doesn't it?"

"It sounds awful, there were so many ways I had to worry about you, and you just made it harder on me."

"I never asked you to worry about me."

Zack changed tact. "Was it really this bad Kali? That you have to go and hurt yourself?"

"Yes it was, but it didn't hurt." She sniped, "Why bring it up now? Why not before?"

"I noticed it a few days after I met you." He exhaled deeply. "I always wondered about it."

"My brother was dead. My mother was gone. It just made me feel like I could start again, every time that I screwed up."

"We all screw up."

"You had Damien and Joel to help you, but girls don't act that way. I had no one. No one wanted me."

"Explain to me how this helps?"

"I don't know. It was not about you. When I met you I stopped doing it. There were just a few times in my life that it got this bad."

Kali catapulted herself off the bench, and stood on her feet. She looked confused as if she was deciding if she should leave or not.

"I just don't get it Kali."

"You're not supposed to." She shook her head. "Don't make me relive it."

She turned away because she started to cry.

Zack nodded and walked towards her. He stood just an inch away. Then he took her in his arms. "I want to worry about you. I need to know that you're ok."

She stayed pressed up against him. Zack held her for a long time. His arms nurtured her.

He held on to her, until she stopped crying.

Kali finally stepped back. She turned, and then started to leave. "I love you Zack and now that I'm back I want to be with you. I just wanted you to know that, but I'm not naïve enough to think it's ever going to happen." She closed her eyes again. "I had to go away, but you were all I ever thought about. I just came back to get my surfboard today, so that I can start fresh." She shrugged. "I think we should *both* start fresh. You can have your closure."

Zack felt pain that Kali would start fresh without him. Even that she would go surfing without him.

"I never wanted you to just be one of my girls." He said desperately.

"It wouldn't have been like that." She whispered.

"I wanted you to be my wife." Zack couldn't believe he just admitted that.

Kali looked up in disbelief.

"I was looking for you in Manly. I wanted to see you, so I could ask you to marry me. I had a ring and everything."

"You turned your back on me that day. You didn't want anything to do with me."

"I realized that day, that I have been with a lot of girls, but none of them are you. None of them amaze me, or challenge me like you do. I wanted to marry you."

"And then you changed your mind?" She was in shock.

"I bought a ring that day, I saw it in the jewellery store, and I knew it was for you. I was the one that wanted to give it to you."

"But you didn't."

"I wanted us to be together, but it doesn't matter anymore. Now I know that you were with Damien that night. That's why you were so cagy the next day. That's why you've been hurting me ever since."

Kali stood with her head down again. She nodded to confirm that it was true.

"Now things are different. I can't." No words had ever hurt so much, and Zack was the one saying them.

He wanted Kali right now. More than he had ever wanted anything. He wanted to kiss every inch of her body, and make love to her right there on the floor, but he couldn't.

Zack closed his eyes. "I have other responsibilities now."

Kali stepped back.

Zack continued. "I can't have you. Not like this." He told her.

The tears fell from her eyes again. "You won't have me, you never would."

"And now I can't." Zack said.

Kali nodded. "Ok then. Goodbye Zack."

Chapter 40

Joel:

Joel's son Oliver was a wonderer. He had his own playpen in Joel's lounge room. Kali sat in front of it and watched him play with a toy car. He was pushing it around in his delicate little hands.

"He is really cute, Joel." Kali said softly.

Joel reached over the barrier and gave his son a toy truck. Oliver squealed with delight and started playing with it instead.

"He's got your hazel eyes." Kali told him.

"And Justine's light brown hair." Joel explained.

Joel glanced over at Kali, and stopped to really take a good look at the young girl he was sitting with.

She was just sitting there, with her legs crossed. She had a pair of blue jeans on, and a maroon singlet.

She was slender and tall and pretty. She was just as engaged, and interested, to talk to him as ever, but she was still so evasive. Kali was mysterious. To Joel, it always felt like she was holding on to some secret.

Joel had been shocked to find out that Kali and Damien had slept together. He had never seen that coming. He wondered what other secrets she kept.

Today her hair was up in a loose bun. She still had a few strands of curly, golden brown hair that fell down, over her face.

She looked at him enquiringly, and smiled to reassure him. "So…" She continued carefully, glaring at him intently. "That day we were in Manly." She began cross examining him. "We were alone together, that whole day, and you never said a word about all this."

She nodded, and looked around his house. "You know those little details: Like how you have a wife and a son."

Joel didn't answer for a long time. "I knew you wouldn't approve." He told her solemnly. "Just like Zack, and Damien, don't approve." He shook his head. "You would have been so hard on me Kali."

"Would I?"

"Yes." He smirked. "You always are."

Kali nodded, but she didn't stop. "So, tell me what happened." She asked, intrigued. "How did you end up with Justine again? How did all this happen?"

Joel took a deep breath in. "You sure you want to know?" He asked doubtfully.

"I want you to tell me." She enquired, intently.

"Well… Ok…" Joel sighed, and began explaining honestly. "About two years, after Justine and I broke up, I saw her walking around the university campus." He began to explain, and then elaborated. "She seemed to have changed a lot, and so had I. At the time we had so much to catch up on. I mean I know everything about her. I know all her family, and her friends, and she knows all of mine."

Kali nodded.

Joel continued. "So we started going out again, a few times. We had some family gatherings, and it was fun" He hesitated. "I guess old habits die hard, and I was so busy with everything. I wasn't paying attention to how fast things were moving." Joel looked down. Then as you know…" He looked towards his son. "Oliver was the result. We were married soon after, before he was born."

Kali nodded again. "The rest is history."

"Yeah." Joel smiled at her.

"Are you happy?" She asked, staring at him.

Joel lowered his head and sighed. "We make it work."

Kali looked away for a moment. "But you must still be so busy." She enquired. "With University, and a part time job, and looking after Oliver?"

Joel shook his head. "Justine doesn't have a job. She looks after the baby while I am at work."

"And all you had to do was give up your life?" Kali changed her tone, quickly.

"You've obviously been talking to Zack." Joel sighed. He was right about Kali. She was going to be hard on him.

"It's black and white to me Joel." She said simply. "All I know is loneliness, and my dad doesn't care what I do."

"Pardon."

"Do you think you got back together with Justine, because of your dad?" She asked him. "Then you married her, even though this is not 1957, and you didn't have to do the honourable thing?" She looked at him shrewdly. "So your dad wouldn't be ashamed of you. So you wouldn't embarrass the family. You're still trying to be the good son. Your father never believed in you, and you're still trying to make him happy."

"You have no idea what you're talking about." Joel argued back. "I mean you don't know me anymore. You don't know how hard it's been." He scoffed. "You don't know anything about my life. You just left and never looked back." He swore.

"But it's not hard for you Joel." She challenged him. "You don't take chances unless someone's pushing you to take them."

Oliver stopped playing with his toy, and stood up against the mesh wall of his play pen. "Da Da." He said as he looked up Joel.

"Keep playing with your toy." Joel encouraged him. "Of course, I take chances." He argued. "I went to Hawaii. I was school captain. I'm doing corporate law which is my dream." He informed her. "Why do you say all that stuff? Why do you always bring up my father?" He questioned her. "And who the hell do you think you are?"

Kali ignored that last part. "I can't bear it Joel." She pleaded with him. "I can't bear to watch anymore of your family members treat you like a puppet, and their pulling your strings."

"No one's pulling my strings." He vowed.

"But they are." She sobbed.

Joel shook his head. Kali's reply was so arrogant. It was such a condescending girl. Joel thought she had gone too far this time.

He shook his head. "You are so hurtful Kali." He swore at her. "You were always so difficult. You bite, and you kick, and you scratch, and you kick us while we're down."

Kali looked into space. "I was just trying to be useful."

"Well you're not." He glared at her. "And it pains me that *I* was the one who was glad you were back."

Kali looked at him, surprised. "Well, I can't *just* alienate two of you." She said sadly. "I have to go for the trifecta."

"You know I love Justine. She's been part of my life for such a long time."

Kali rolled her eyes. "Joel, you know I notice everything."

"So?"

"So, just don't tell me you're happy."

Joel wiped away a tear in his eye. "Don't psychoanalyse me." He told her. "I know you can, but I don't want you to. Besides, turn your attention on Zack. He's the one who needs help."

"You both equally need help."

"And you're the one who needs help most of all." He yelled. "You're the one who can't make female friends."

Kali nodded, but she was reading him again. "You don't think I met Justine, but I did." She said flatly. "She was horrible to me in high school, and I also came here last week. When you weren't home. She answered the door."

Joel grimaced "What happened?"

Kali shrugged. "She told me to leave. She told me that I should stay away from you." Kali answered slowly. "She told me that I ruined your relationship once before, and that a little slut like me, should stay on Zack and Damien's side of town."

Joel was taken aback for a moment. "Did she really say that?"

Kali nodded. "Yes."

"I can't believe it."

"I couldn't either, but I really was trying to be nice to her Joel." Kali tried desperately to explain. "I didn't care for her, but I didn't think I was ever rude to her." She paused. "I didn't think she hated me that much."

Joel felt exhausted all of a sudden.

"I don't love her." Joel said numbly, because he felt numb. "I wasn't ready for this."

Kali didn't say anything. She was too busy reading him again. Looking past the words and reading his body language and his facial expression. None of this surprised her.

"I wake up at night, and I'm sweating. All I can think about is…" Joel stopped. He was delving too far, and she was making him do it.

"What." Kali asked without moving.

"Jasmine." Joel said out loud. "I wake up thinking about Jasmine, and you. I think about you sometimes. I missed you."

Kali accidentally let her expression slip. For a moment she even looked surprised, but then her face resettled.

"I love my son, but I don't know what I'm doing Kali."

Joel sighed. He was talking to Kali like she was his shrink, but in truth the girl knew nothing about the real world.

Joel was only two years older than Kali, but Kali was still just a young, childish, little girl.

"Does anyone know what they're doing?" She asked dryly.

"But I have to live with this." He paused. "Every day."

Kali nodded. "You're probably not the only one who's going to do the honourable thing" She sighed. "Zack's probably going to propose to Danielle."

Joel looked over at his son, who was now lying down, and half asleep. He wanted a change of scenery, so he got up, and walked to the kitchen. He sat down on one of the chairs of the Kitchen table, and watched Kali, as she followed him.

Kali sat down on the chair next to him.

"So you came here to talk about Zack?" He asked irritated.

"No."

She continued staring at him, and Joel felt so deflated.

"I don't know Zack as well as I used to." Joel admitted. "I don't know what he's going to do." He told her dryly. "And I don't know what I'm going to do either." He murmured.

Kali looked at him empathetically, then suddenly she flung herself over the side of her chair, and threw her arms around his neck, and put her head on his shoulder. She hugged him warmly, and Joel felt her warm embrace, and she just stayed there, for a long time.

"You know what you should do." She finally whispered in his ear, after some time.

"What?" Joel asked.

"Me."

Joel jolted in his seat. "Did you just offer…."

"Yes." Kali said still holding on to him, tenderly.

"Why?"

"To level the playing field." She told him, cryptically. "Do you want to?" She asked him, sincerely. "Right here. Right now. Right on this table?"

"What are you doing Kali? Why are you messing with me?"

"I'm not." She hugged him tighter, and looked towards him, giving him a look so honest, he could hardly breathe.

"You would be doing it to get back at Zack, and that wouldn't be good for anyone."

"I never would have resisted when I was a kid." She told him softly. "It could have been you or Zack or Damien. I was in love with all of you." She explained idly. "Your wife was right about that."

"She's not right." Damien screamed. "But we both know it was always about Zack."

"Don't you want to make it all about you? It's your choice."

"I can't sleep with you kali."

Kali let go of him and sat back on the chair. She shrugged her shoulders. "You don't think you're a loud to have what you want."

"How do you know what I want?"

"Because I wanted you, and the way you were looking at me before. I know the feeling was mutual."

"We can't do this." Joel said, slightly shaken up. "Not right now. I have to tell you something. I invited Zack over. He's going to be here soon." Joel rubbed at his eyes.

Kali was shocked at the sudden change of subject. "Why would you do that? You know I don't want to see him."

"He wants to talk to you. I don't know why. He said that he upset you yesterday. Now he wants to talk to you."

"I don't care. I just wanted to see *you* today."

"But he's my friend and I do care." Joel took a deep breath in. "If you're going to live in this town, we should all be friends."

"Yeah, tell that to Damien who kicked me to the curb, before he left."

"I think he just wants to explain what's going on. He knows I told you about Danielle."

"Explain what? He slept with Damien's girlfriend. Now, she may or may not be pregnant. Enough said."

"Well, that was *your* problem five minutes ago." Joel exclaimed. "And you know what he's like, Kali. He doesn't want you to hate him."

"And I don't." She yelled. "I don't harbour any ill will for him at all. It's just that I'm not ready to see him. Not now, or any time in the near future."

"If you talk to him now; then you can wait another four years, and I won't say anything. It's just that I told him to be here at eleven, and its eleven now."

"How nice for him." Kali said sarcastically. "We wouldn't want to inconvenience Zack or anything."

"I can't make you stay, but he's walking in the door."

Kali spun around, and looked at the door to the dining room. "Don't you ever knock?" She screamed.

Zack stepped inside the room. He looked nervous, but he stood in a pair of off white cargo pants, and a black Billabong t-shirt. His hair was slicked back and formed a sort of a wave around his face. He looked pensive and worried.

"What do you want Zack? You have my blessing! You can marry Danielle, and have a baby with her. She's probably a lot less complicated than me." Kali threw her hair back over her shoulders. "I'm sure you'll be very happy."

Zack ignored her "Hey Joel."

"Hi." Joel said back.

"How are you going Kali?"

"I couldn't be better"

"Can I talk to you?"

"No."

Zack went around the room and sat on a chair at the other side of the table. "You're twenty-one years old Kali; you have your whole life to live."

"I know that." She grumbled.

She watched him, annoyed, but then composed herself. "I've thought about it, and I really am happy for you. We were never together. I can't know what it feels like to be your girl. So, I can't have anything to be upset about."

"You were never my girlfriend, but you have always been my girl."

"No Zack. I think I was Damien's girl." She said trying to hurt him. From the look on his face she had succeeded.

Joel wasn't sure if he should leave the room, but he was curious, and he didn't.

"I'm not going to be the one to break you, Kali" Zack snapped at her.

"To break me in like I'm a horse?" She asked being deliberately difficult.

"Exactly" Zack declared. "You're spirited. You don't even want to get married. You're not ready for it. I couldn't pull you out of your dream world, if I tried."

"It's the same world." She replied. "Besides this is not about me. I didn't mean to make it about me. You said goodbye yesterday and you meant it. I get it. We can't be together. I got the memo."

"If only you knew how hard this was for me."

"If only" Kali marvelled.

"Yeah it's not like you didn't buckle under the pressure of this situation."

"I know I did." She agreed.

"I just came over to make sure we could be friends." Zack pleaded with her. "No matter what happens, we will be friends."

Kali nodded. "We will always be friends" She mimicked him.

"Good."

"I have to go." Kali turned around and walked out of the front door. Then the front door slammed. Then she was gone.

Chapter 41

Zack:

Zack slowly walked across the lawn. He walked across his own drive way, then Damien's drive way, and then headed to Damien's front door.

Without knocking, he let himself in. He heard the radio going and immediately smelt a whiff of burning toast. Zack headed straight for the Kitchen and found Damien, who was looking into space.

"Hey." He yelled at his friend.

"What's going on brah?" Damien asked.

"You tell me superstar. You just came back from Europe."

Damien stepped forward to give Zack a quick hug.

As Damien stepped back he had a slightly worried expression on his face. He looked out into the hall, looked off into space again, and then looked at Zack.

He grimaced "Europe was Europe."

"Yeah" Zack laughed. "Because why would anybody want to get excited about going to Europe?"

"I was in California before I was in Europe. You know how I left." Damien shook his head. "They always say: Don't go to bed angry. Well don't leave the country angry either."

Zack looked at him. "Yeah, but you did well."

"You could say that. I won the Quicksilver Pro in France." Damien boasted.

"I know you won the Quicksilver Pro!" Zack said exasperated. "I was waiting for the phone call from my best friend to tell me about it, and there was none."

"It didn't feel real." Damien tried to explain.

"Well it seems pretty real from where I sit... Watching you on the podium, with the trophy in your hand."

"I've never been more emotional." Damien began. "I put all of my emotions into my surfing. The whole thing was agony, and then I found myself on the podium. With a bottle of champagne. Spraying it over the crowd. I hardly knew what was going on."

"Well, regardless of how it happened... My point was: Congratulations brah."

"Yeah, thanks. I appreciate that." Damien said earnestly. "I just couldn't wait to get back home."

"And now that you are home." Zack asked. "How do you feel? Do you still hate her?"

Damien shook his head. "No, I could never." He sighed. "But she has a way of making me crazy though."

"Yeah, I know."

"I heard all sorts of reports, about what was going on here, during my absence. What happened Zack? What's going on with Danielle?"

Zack sighed. "Danielle thought she might be pregnant, to me, right after what happened with Kali."

"Yeah, that's what I heard." Damien commented. "That's pretty intense."

"Well we went to the doctor, and somehow, amazingly, the result was negative. I don't know if there is something in the water." Zack remarked. "Which I felt was some sort cosmic sign, since it happened to both of us." He said doubtfully. "So naturally, I've sworn off girls ever since."

"Yeah." Damien shrugged. "Good for you."

Zack felt solemn. "Kali hasn't been around since then." He told Damien. "I know she's surfing again, but I haven't seen her much." Zack shrugged.

"So you haven't talked to her?" Damien asked hesitantly.

"Not really." Zack smiled sadly. "I think she's giving me my space." He shrugged again. "It turns out, a bit of space has been good."

He marveled. "She always knows when to back off. Sometimes I think she can read minds."

"She could always read my mind." Damien mumbled.

"She was more trouble, for you, than I ever realized." Zack contemplated.

"What do you mean?"

Zack bit his lip. "You got that anxiety medication once." He said delicately. "I know you never used it, but you got it, because you were worried about something."

Damien nodded reluctantly.

"You said that it was from the tour. That jetlag was turning into insomnia, and insomnia was turning into anxiety. You said you were worried about going from the qualifying circuit to the actual ASP world tour. You didn't want to screw it up."

Damien nodded again.

"But that was when Kali left." Zack deducted. "You slept with kali back then. You slept with her, and she disappeared. She left you hanging."

Damien took a deep breath in. "I suppose, but it was for all those other reasons too. I got over it."

"Yeah, I know." Zack made a face. "I felt anxious when Danielle told me she might be pregnant. I got the pills from your bathroom cabinet. They were out of date, but I just wanted to read the box. Then of course Kali found it."

Damien smirked. "Yeah, of course she did. She's never happy unless she's crawling around in your head."

"Yeah, well she's gone now. I literally haven't seen her in a month."

Damien shook his head. "Don't worry." He smirked. "When one of us gives her the cold shoulder, she runs to the other one."

"What does that mean?" Zack asked curiously.

"Nothing" Damien looked back into the hall way again. "Nothing you'd want to know about."

"That sounds ominus."

"Don't worry about it." Damien looked off into space for a long time. "So what's going on with you now?" He asked.

"Nothing much." Zack explained. "Trying to work hard, and pay extra money into the mortgage."

Zack suddenly got distracted, because Damien was distracted. He kept starting into the hall.

Zack looked carefully in the direction that Damien was looking in. "Who have you got back there?"

"What." Damien jumped slightly.

"You obviously don't want me to know, who you woke up with this morning."

Damien grinned, and laughed to himself, although it seemed to be a private joke. "Trust me Zack. I didn't wake up with anyone this morning."

"So what's your problem?" Zack shrugged. "What's the distraction?"

"Just ignore it. Things had been weird for a while now." Damien said without thinking.

"Ok." Zack sighed. "I don't know what the hell you're talking about, but I'm just glad you're home. Do you want to go to poker tonight?"

Zack was playing the free Wednesday night poker tournaments at the local club.

"Are you eager to get your arse kicked again?"

"I don't know when you started winning poker." Zack grimaced. "You never used to win."

"People change Zack." Damien said coldly.

Zack wasn't sure what was on Damien's mind. His tone was off. None the less Zack wanted to ask him something since he left.

He spoke carefully. "So I was thinking. It's time to find the right one…If that's possible. Which at this point, I'm not sure it is. I just have to ask: is Kali the right one for you?"

Damien laughed ironically for a moment. He looked out into the hall again. He got out the peanut butter from the pantry and his face twisted into a confused knot. He started spreading the peanut butter over his toast, and didn't say anything for nearly two minutes.

"Kali was right for me, but she doesn't belong to me."

That was another ominous sentence.

"What does that mean." Zack asked.

Damien changed the subject. "Did you know Joel left his wife?"

"Huh? What?" Zack asked stunned. "Joel is doing what?"

"Didn't you know?"

"How would I know?" Zack yelled. "I only see him at poker, and he doesn't even really talk to me. I tried to call him a few times." Zack couldn't believe his ears. "Are you sure?"

"He's already moved out."

"What? He did? Where is he staying?"

Damien looked away, then looked up at the ceiling. He looked at Zack, opened up his mouth to speak, but didn't say anything. He just closed his eyes, and shook his head again.

"Here." He finally muttered.

"So he's here now?" Zack shrieked, happily. "I have to go ask him for myself."

"No Zack, don't."

Zack wasn't sure why Damien was trying to block him.

He was already on his way to Damien's spare room. He started to open the door, but he was thoroughly unprepared for what he was saw.

Joel was still in bed, but he wasn't alone. A girl was in there. Joel didn't have a shirt on. He was lying there on his back. Most of the blanket was wrapped around the girl. The girl was snuggled up next to Joel. The girl's head was lying on Joel's left shoulder. The girl was just wearing a negligee, he could just see the spaghetti straps on her shoulders.

"Kali?" Zack called her name, but he could hardly breathe.

Joel looked him straight in the eye. "She's asleep."

Zack could feel his heart break in half.

He was already half the man he used to be. Now there was nothing left.

"You and Kali?" He asked.

Damien came up behind Zack. He put his hand on Zack's shoulder. Zack just stood there.

"You knew about this Damien?"

"I knew."

"And it was ok with you?" Zack asked stunned.

"They are both adults."

"Joel is married! He's a married man, and you just let him do this to her?"

"I didn't do anything to her, that she didn't ask me to do." Joel spoke up.

"What the hell is that supposed to mean?" Zack yelled. He felt so weak and disorientated.

"I have nothing to prove Zack." Joel told him. "This was just… this was just me and Kali."

"I know you love her Joel." Zack tried to find the words. "I just didn't think you loved her like this. What is this? A rite of passage with you guys."

Kali stirred. She obviously wasn't asleep.

She looked up at Joel and nodded at him. She looked around slowly, and acknowledged Damien in her own silent way. Then she finally looked up at Zack. She looked in his eyes.

Zack couldn't look away.

"Don't blame Joel for this." She told him, with her quiet voice. "Don't blame anyone for this. This was what I wanted. I'm happy."

"You said you loved me, and your making Damien watch this. You're doing this in his house."

Kali closed her eyes. She inhaled a long slow breath, and then opened her eyes again. "Damien's happy that I'm happy." She told him.

Zack looked at Joel. "So *this* is why you're been ignoring me?" He said, bewildered. "How long has it been going on for?"

Joel sat up and shook his head. "Look Zack." He began carefully. "This is not what it looks like. It *hasn't* been going on. Nothing really happened"

"What"

"Nothing untoward is going on here." Joel said again, flatly. "I didn't sleep with her." He said profoundly. "I slept beside her. I was having trouble sleeping, and she was helping me through the night."

Zack nodded. He stared at them for a long time. "How long has she been helping you through the night?"

"The last few nights."

Zack shook his head again. "Why doesn't that make me feel better?" he asked, bewildered.

"I don't know Zack." Joel remarked. "She's my friend and she's helping me through a tough time."

"Ok." Zack nodded. "Ok." He said again.

The truth was he still felt a little dizzy. The intimacy between them was a little tough to take.

"I have to go." Zack said suddenly, immediately needing to get out of this room.

He still couldn't handle it. He turned around and walked out of the house. To his own house. To his own bathroom, where he threw up in the sink.

That anxiety was coming back thick and fast. He didn't know what to do anymore.

Chapter 42

Zack:

Z ack let himself get wet, and go surfing, in the forgiving ocean. He tried to let himself cool down, but his blood was still running hot. He couldn't forgive Damien or Joel but the girl: He sort of understood.

There would be no one else for her. She was so screwed up.

He tried to eat dinner, but he didn't feel hungry. He tried to sleep, but he couldn't stop tossing and turning.

The next day Damien and Joel both came to see him. Both separately, at different times. They both explained that neither of them were dating Kali.

Kali belonged with him. Kali loved him, but there was so many reasons this had to happen.

Zack barely heard either of them out, before he *kicked* them out. He was still so mad.

Joel didn't sleep with Kali, but it didn't seem to matter. He was so mad about at the situation anyway.

For the next week, Zack followed the same routine. He went to work early, and worked hard. After work he went for a quick surf. He would try to cool off, from his hurt and anger, but it wouldn't seem to subside.

After his surf, he would have a long hot bath. Then he would kick back, with a blanket, on the recliner, and read more vampire books. Just like when he was a kid. It was still comforting somehow.

It was about eleven o clock on Friday night, when Mr. Lockhart let Zack in to Kali's house. He let Zack in the door, and then went back to bed. Zack slowly made his way to Kali's room.

Kali was lying peacefully asleep in her bed.

A little girl. With golden brown hair and golden-brown skin. No matter what her age, she never got any older. She lived inside her own fantasy world.

She was so young, and still so immature.

Her room was almost the same as when she was growing up. It was all so innocent.

There was a bunch of teddy bears on the dresser. On her desk was a photo of Kali and Ryan together. They both looked so young.

There was a surfboard in Kali's room. Zack stared at it for a long time, because it didn't belong to her. It had belonged to Ryan.

Kali had been lying when she said she got rid of all her other boards.

Finally he stood over her. She was wearing a pink negligee and she twitched in her sleep every now and then.

"Kali." Zack nudged her.

It took her a minute to wake up and adjust her eyes. "Zack?" She asked groggily.

"Hi." He said, simply.

She seemed nervous for a minute, but then she shrugged. "Hi."

"I came to visit you." Zack told her, modestly.

"Yeah." Kali smiled.

"I haven't been able to sleep after what happened." He said.

"I don't know why." She replied, exasperated. "It really had nothing to do with you."

"My gosh, Kali." Zack looked in her eyes. "Do you have any idea how much it hurt? Seeing you two together."

Kali nodded. "I *do* have an idea."

"But you did it anyway?"

"It wasn't about you." Kali said again, indignantly.

"What was it about then?" He asked.

"It was about Joel."

"That was obvious." Zack swore. "When you two were wrapped around each other." He looked away. "An image that will be burned into my brain for the rest of time."

"I *am* sorry if I hurt you." Kali replied. "But I was helping out my friend."

"This is so fucked up." Zack swore. "I was right the first time. This is so played out." He ran his fingers through his hair. "I wish I could let go of you Kali."

"I know you do."

"I wanted to let you go" He swore again. "And I don't know what to think about *anything*, anymore. But you... No matter what I do, I'll never accomplish anything, unless I've made love to you, at least once."

Kali tried to mask her surprise. Then she just contemplated what he had said. The room was silent for a moment.

"Don't you understand?" He cried desperately. "It was all for you!"

Kali looked at him, confused.

"You're a bitch Kali." He swore. "Didn't you know what that would do to me? That you've been so intimate, with two of my best friends, and not me?"

"It was kind of intimate between us, sometimes, over the years" Kali answered back.

"Not seriously." He said, flustered.

"Imagine how that makes me feel."

"I know Kali." Zack replied softly. "It was just never the right time." He ran his fingers through his hair. "But you slept beside Joel for a few nights???"

"I didn't expect you to walk in. You weren't really supposed to know." She spoke, finally.

"I would have found out eventually."

"Maybe I had to let go of you."

"No" Zack shook his head. "You couldn't."

"But I could try. We could both try." Kali sat up. "The minute you find the next Caroline or Miranda. I'm sure the problem will take care of itself." She explained. "I can't take it Zack. I can't watch you be with another girl."

"Is that why you slept with Damien and Joel?" Zack asked, exasperated. "You wanted to hurt me? The same way that you were hurt?"

"No." Kali said adamantly. "What happened between me and them had nothing to do with you." She nodded. "And I didn't sleep with Joel. I slept beside him."

"Great." Zack shook his head. "Is Joel your boyfriend now?" He asked desperately.

"No."

"So it was just plutonic?"

"I wouldn't go that far."

"What does that mean?"

"We kissed a few times. I guess." She meandered.

"What the fuck Kali?"

"Don't yell at me." Kali retorted. "The only thing that stopped me being with you, is you."

"Don't you think I know that?"

"Well, then what is your problem?" She asked groggily. "I love both of them. But not nearly as much as I love you. You know that. You've always known that. So, have they."

Zack sighed. "So, you offered yourself up to Joel?"

"Seriously Zack, he was so unhappy, I couldn't bear it."

Zack stared at her for a long time. "Yes, I know he was unhappy."

Kali nodded again. "Then don't ask me about it." She said boldly.

"You words torture me." He cried. "They always did." He said annoyed, but at the same time, he reached into his pocket and took the necklace he had bought Kali so long ago. He, held it up, and showed it to her.

Kali looked at it, slightly shocked.

"Can I?"

Kali nodded.

Once again, he leaned over. Moved her hair away, and slowly placed the necklace around her neck. Once again, he did up the clasp, and looked upon her. "I have waited for you… always."

"That' how long it's been." She whispered.

"This time it's forever." He told her softly.

Kali bowed her head, modestly.

"Damien thinks we should all go to South Africa." Zack said idly, out of nowhere. "He wants to start fresh…And I think it would work." He paused. "I want to go."

Kali grinned, shocked again. "Damien told me a long time ago that we should go to South Africa." She shrugged. "I wanted to go so much then." She paused. "And now."

Zack nodded. "Good."

"Ok." Kali said softly.

Zack looked in her eyes. "I love you Kali."

Kali stared at him desperately. Her own eyes full of anguish.

Zack sat down on the side of her bed. "I'm sorry if I never said it before, but I love you. I loved you all along. I'd do anything for you Kali. I'd give my life for yours in a second. I love you."

Kali looked at him longingly, but too stunned to react.

Zack turned to her suddenly. "That necklace is the only thing you should be wearing in front of me."

He grabbed the sides of her negligee and pulled upwards. She raised her arms in the air, so that he could slip it off her.

She blinked twice, as she put her arms down. Still stunned.

Zack stared at her for a long time. The gold necklace complemented her recently tanned skin, and her youthful frame. She had gone back to being athletic and toned. Especially after surfing so much lately.

"You're so beautiful." He whispered to her.

Kali smiled, but blushed as well.

He looked in her eyes for a long time. "You know why I came here."

Kali nodded again.

"I wanted this to be a bed of roses." Zack said patting the bed with his hands.

"It's a bed of teddy bears." She said wistfully.

"I'm serious Kali."

"So am I."

"I have wanted this for so long" He told her.

"So have I."

She said that, but she had a look of vulnerability in eyes.

She sat in bed, so exposed. She was breathing in and out deeply. Her exposed breasts, rose and fell, with every breath. Her lower body was still wrapped up in the blanket.

She really was so beautiful.

Zack took the opportunity to take her in his arms.

He grabbed hold of her body, with all of his might. He held her close; clenched in his grip.

His hands, his mouth, his body, they were finally able to wrap around hers, without all the guilt.

He tore at her body so passionately. He had never felt so much heat and desire. It overcame him, and her too. She responded to everything he did, and every move he made.

With no restraint, no inhibitions, and a lifetime of passion. Zack took her the way he always wanted to.

He wanted this one night to last forever. When it was over, so would go their entire history. He was finally free.

Tomorrow there would be another world of challenges, but...

It was the price you had to pay, because nobody rides for free.

www.ingramcontent.com/pod-product-compliance
Lightning Source LLC
Chambersburg PA
CBHW062118170626
46813CB00002B/500